D1525085

TWENTY-ONE TREES

Linda Cousine

Cover art by Damonza.com

ISBN-13: 978-1530271191
ISBN-10: 1530271193

CHAPTER ONE

Memories, sharp and fragmented, colorful as the pieces of glass in a church picture window, faded in and out of my mind, cutting and broken. I saw Bobby Lee, smiling and laughing, and a wisp of a memory of his anger. Birdy was there, too. Birdy with his sad eyes, dark, behind his glasses—Bobby Lee's best friend. And my best friend, too. The keeper of my secrets … so many dark secrets.

The smell of blood, acrid and harsh, and the scent of something sweet, permeated my nose. Peaches, maybe. Throbbing pain, so blinding I couldn't open my eyes, and a heaviness in my chest, hot and sticky, with hands on me, pulling and tugging to release the pain while fluids ran down my middle, wet, until they dried, turning pasty as gravy. And that smell. That smell of something honeyed.

Happy memories, the flowers, and the crown—of winning. Of laughing, and knowing I'd done it. I'd won the pageant. And Mama and Daddy proud of their baby girl and crying in the crowd, and Bobby Lee smiling, and proud of his girl, too. We'd be married soon, after my year was through, and all our dreams would come true.

More pain, and unspeakable sadness. Waves of it coming at me in accelerated expansion, dense and chaotic, set in motion, far-reaching. And I'm falling down, but pulling in at the same time—all that energy, all that hurt.

Come back to me, Savannah May.

I struggled to pry open my eyes, still caught somewhere deep down below where shadows lived, my body dense and lethargic, weighted down with the heaviness of something I could not place. I opened my eyes and quickly shut them against the blinding light that stabbed at my head, making it pound harder, the harshness streaming through a grimy window I'd never seen. A foreign window with shades raised on a slant and the dirty string long broken, a window that looked out over a parking lot. And beyond, to a highway I couldn't quite recall.

I closed my eyes and surrendered to the nothingness.

Voices, hushed and low. My mama, maybe, and Birdy, and the mournful sound of someone crying. Feeling something wet and seeping, sticky as molasses, running down my side. A pulling at my chest, to relieve the pain and discomfort, and the sounds of a machine hissing and sucking, and feeling a forgotten sorrow, the memory of a white sheet and the shiny glint of metal, on a day not meant for evil.

I surrendered to the call of coming back.

An accident. I had been in some sort of accident. I opened my eyes and gazed around me at the worn hospital room with mottled walls the color of moldy bread, and pictures dusted with age and hanging crookedly. A car crash? A fall? I could not recall a thing. I closed my eyes and tried to remember. But nothing came. No memories of a violent crash, of feeling the pinch and the squeeze of my body trapped in the metal of my car or the sounds of breaking glass, shattering, and ringing in my ears. No crushing of bone, or unbearable pain, except for the one in my head, now tolerable. No worse than that terrible hangover after my high school graduation, a hangover so bad I wished I were dead. I raised a hand to touch the bandages on my head.

At least I remembered who I was.

I am Savannah May Holladay of Atlanta, Georgia. The daughter of Roy and Marylou. And the recent winner of the Miss Georgia Peach beauty pageant. I was head cheerleader at Robert E. Lee High and both junior *and* senior prom queen, along with the king, my longtime boyfriend. Bobby Lee Thomas is my boyfriend, and Birdy Johnson is my best friend.

It took too much to remember, and I closed my eyes.

A different dream, an unusual dream, a dream more daylight than dark. Of Birdy's hands on my breasts, of a pulling and a kneading …

I opened my eyes to the dream.

Birdy knelt on the floor beside me, his knees on the spattered worn linoleum, his head resting on the sheet at my side, his right arm stretched across my middle. Gingerly, so as not to wake him, I touched his hair, lighter than I remembered, brown with russet threads, and then I stroked his stubbled cheek, the hairs neither soft nor coarse. My fingers continued, outlining the unfamiliar strength of a jaw, and a scar I hadn't seen before. Birdy looked tired and old. So old. Almost thirty would be my guess. Why did he look so old?

My head throbbed, weighty, but not nearly as cumbersome as the heaviness in my chest, reminding me of the feeling when Bobby Lee lays on top and crushes me with the length of him, only sometimes getting off when I ask, but mostly crushing me until he's finished with his business.

Bobby Lee … I swallowed a distant memory and felt a pull in my breasts, a hurt. Raising my hand, the tubes of the IV pulling taut with the effort, I lifted the top opening of my hospital gown and saw them—ripe and heavy with blue veins and oozing liquid that dripped down and stained the sheets below. Fear spread through me. Fear, and a sense of despair. *I must be dying.* Breast cancer. The cancer leaked from the pores in my breasts, hot and lumpy with tumors, and dripped onto the sheet below, taking with it my life. Seeping onto the black worn vinyl of the bed in a rundown hospital room in Atlanta.

Not yet twenty-one, and I was dying. Some sort of advanced stage breast cancer that must have spread to my brain.

Birdy woke up and eyed me warily beneath his black eyeglasses, taking them off to rub at a dirty spot before putting them back on. He tentatively stroked my hair, an odd thing for Birdy to do, I thought, as he rarely touched me, unless I touched him first.

I am embarrassed to say, I do not know Birdy's given name. For as long as I can recall, I've called him Birdy, a nickname of his original nickname, Bird Dog Johnson. Birdy got the name Bird Dog because he resembles a sweet, sad chocolate Labrador, only Birdy has a chestnut hue to his dark brown hair. But mostly he got the name Bird Dog because he was the catch-and-fetch-it guy for everyone, from his alcoholic father, "Birdy, go catch me some fish for supper, and fetch me another beer," to his best friend, Bobby Lee, "Birdy, here's five dollars. Go catch a movie, and leave me and my girl alone for an hour," (*although fifteen minutes would have been enough.*) "But first, fetch me a pack of them condoms from Kroger's."

Even I took advantage of Birdy. "Catch me, Birdy," I said, the time I was drunk and I climbed to the top of the lifeguard station wanting to fly away from the knowledge of what I had done that night with Bobby. To leave behind the harsh vision of it, the sound, the smells. The night I made Birdy drive me all the way to the lake to try and run from my shame.

On unsteady legs, I scaled to the top of the tower, standing on top, not caring Birdy was hollering at me to get down, it wasn't safe. I stood on the top of that tower while the wind whipped my hair and dried my tears, dizzy with the tilting of time and space and wanting to fly away, far away. I looked out to the water, dark in the night, spread my wings … and I jumped.

Birdy caught me before I hit the ground, and he stumbled with the impact. We both went down in the sand, crushing Birdy with the length of me, my tears mixing with the sand and the moisture in the air. Crying so hard I could hardly breathe and Birdy holding onto me tight, while my hair covered our faces, and him pushing my hair to the side, searching my eyes, confused, and wanting to know why.

Not, why I jumped, but the bigger why. Something I didn't have an answer for. I remember staring back at Birdy, suddenly overcome with the desire to kiss him. Which I did. I French kissed him deep and long, the taste of the beer strong in our mouths, knowing the whole time it was wrong, I belonged to Bobby, just the same as his car, I belonged to him. And then me pulling away just moments before I threw up all over the front of Birdy's long-sleeved shirt. He froze all the way home

5

that night because the window was broken on his old truck, and he'd given me his coat to wear to keep me warm.

Birdy caught me the time Bobby Lee dared me to jump from the cliff into that cold creek, when I knew there were dangerous rocks hidden just below the surface, dark and deadly. Birdy dove in headfirst, seconds before I jumped, and tread water right below me so he could catch me when I hit. Good thing too, because there was a big black rock less than two feet below, hidden in the murky water, sharp as broken glass, and the force of our bodies twisted Birdy so his back caught the impact of most of it, tearing his skin so badly he later had to get stitches. All the while, with the blood pouring down Birdy's back, red and slick as oil, and holding me in his arms, treading water, kicking his strong legs to keep us from sinking, Bobby Lee was on the other side of the creek, laughing and calling us pussies and saying we were pathetic and deserved each other.

And Birdy, catching me again from freefalling into despair the day my dog, Sugar, died—hit by a truck as she ran out in the road chasing after a squirrel, those big wheels crushing her and leaving her bloodied body in the middle of the street, while I watched, helpless to save her. Watching as she struggled to take her last breath, stroking her silky hair, seeing the life drain from her and feeling some of mine going with it.

Birdy came, soon as I called, to gather Sugar's body from the road, placing her in a box he'd lined with magnolia leaves and covering her with the fragrant flowers. He put the box in the shade for Sugar to rest while he dug her grave beneath the rose bushes that trellised up the side of the house to my bedroom window on the second floor. Birdy said, that way Sugar would always be near when I lay my head down at night to sleep, and that I'd remember her each time the warm air brought the scent of the roses through my bedroom window, carrying with it the smell of sweetness, the smell of Sugar. Birdy listened to me talk, telling him all my memories of my beloved dog, memories he was a part of too, and he stayed with me that night while my parents were out doing whatever it is social parents do. He stroked my hair, wiped the sorrow from my face, and held me late into the night, slipping out after I fell asleep, and leaving Sugar's collar on my nightstand where I'd find it first thing come morning when I opened my eyes.

Birdy Johnson, always the voice on the other end of the phone after a bad day, and the shoulder to cry on.

The slightest whisper of a memory tugged at my subconscious but slipped away before it could take shape. *Catch me, Birdy*, I'd said, time and again.

I closed my eyes to sleep.

"Wake up, darlin'. Wake up, Savannah May."

I opened my eyes to Mama and Daddy, colorful as a carnival, wearing clothes I had never seen before, and daddy with his light brown hair now the color of freshly churned buttermilk, and not the same as I remembered. He leaned his body toward me over the bed, wearing a silly orange sweater, the color of a sunset, tied around his shoulders on top of his white golf shirt, the sleeves of it hanging down the middle and over me on the bed.

Mama stood behind him, her hands over her heart, as if to slow the beating of it, or maybe to make sure it still beat. Her hair was the same as I remembered, the color of wheat in the fall, but her forehead pulled tight, smooth as marble, making her face appear frozen, and her lips were plump and full, swollen, almost, as if she'd fallen and hit them on the sidewalk. Mama bowed her head, in prayer, I suspect, and her sunburnt face rested on the top of her printed green ruffled blouse with pink flamingoes standing on one leg in some grass.

The door to my room quietly opened with a whisper and a whoosh, and a doctor with a nurse following close behind him entered the room. The doctor was young and Korean, although on both accounts I may be wrong. He had black hair and almond eyes that wouldn't keep still, bouncing with impatience. His nametag read Dr. Kim, Neurologist, so I knew he'd come for my head and not my cancer, because then he'd be Dr. Kim, Oncologist.

"How are you feeling?" he asked. Not waiting for an answer, he reached into the pocket of his white lab coat and removed a penlight, flashing the light into my right eye and then the left. He wiggled it back and forth and clicked it off. "Can you tell me your name?" he asked, without raising his head. He took the chart offered by the nurse and made some notes, his pen scratching.

"Savannah," I said softly. "My name is Savannah May Holladay." I struggled to sit upright on the bed. "What happened to me? Am I dying?"

"Do you know us, child?" Mama asked me, her hazel eyes anxious, her spotted hand with skin as thin as crepe reaching out to take mine.

"Of course, Mama, but you look different. And I can't say I like it. No one wears blouses with pink flamingoes. At least not in Atlanta."

Mama and Daddy smiled a weary smile.

My eyes cut to my father. "Daddy, if I didn't know you better, I'd think you were gay. What's with the sweater? And what did you do to your hair? The color makes you look old."

Mama started to cry, and Daddy patted her on the back, swatting at her flamingoes. They inclined their head toward the doctor, waiting for him to speak.

Dr. Kim made some notes in my chart, and then he stared at me hard, maybe not liking what he saw—the privileged daughter of the rich folks from Atlanta. Except that couldn't be true, else why would I be in that rundown county hospital and not the nice one on the other side of town? He lifted the bandage and touched my head, examining it before going to the wall and turning on a light box with pictures of my brain showing through it, cobbled and squiggly, same as a peach pit nestled in the center of the peach.

He came back, sat on my bed, and reluctantly took my hand, only because he thought he should. Dr. Kim squinted at me, and he began to speak, sounding bored, as if it was something he'd memorized, or he was reading off a paper, same way as you'd read someone the weather, if they inquired, or that yellow corn was on sale that weekend, four for a dollar, down at the corner market.

"You fell off a ladder and hit your head, resulting in brain trauma."

"I don't have breast cancer?" I asked, surprised, but relieved. "Then why are my breasts oozing pus and sickness?"

My daddy started to cough and mama started to tear, dabbing her eyes with a lace handkerchief she had hidden up her sleeve. Mama nodded ever so slightly, as if to say it was a question she might answer later.

The doctor ignored my question and continued his reading. "We've had you in a medically induced coma for five days while waiting for the swelling to subside and to reduce the blood pressure to the traumatized area." He dropped my hand and stood up, glancing at the doorway, as if he wanted to escape. "We discontinued the Diprivan, which is why you're now awake." He capped his pen and put it back in his pocket. "I'm confident your memory will return in time, but you'll need to address that with your psychiatrist. My assessment is you should recover. You'll just need to take it easy. I'll see you again before you're discharged." He patted my arm while reading the time on his watch.

"So it will all come back to her?" Mama asked Dr. Kim. "She'll remember everything again?"

Dr. Kim paused at the doorway, briefly checking his cell phone vibrating in his pocket before answering Mama's question. "Every case is different, but the injury isn't as severe as we originally thought. The psychiatrist should be able to help her. You can call my office if you have any further questions." He exited the room, his footsteps fading down the hallway.

A slow dawning crept over me, a sinking despair. Five days, the doctor said, I'd been in a drug-induced coma. Only five days, and yet my parents had aged not by days, or even months, but by years.

My eyes took in that faded room with the walls the color of molded bread, the pictures that hung crooked. Nothing made any sense.

"Mama? What year is it? How much time have I lost?"

Mama and Daddy were silent, their faces drooping with the passage of time. How much time, I do not know.

"Well, sugar, you'll have to be the one to answer that. Can you tell us who the president is?" Daddy asked.

"George Bush?"

Daddy and Mama exchanged a look I couldn't read. "Do you want to tell her, or should I?" Daddy said, a tight smile on his face.

"Oh, never you mind. That's the least of her worries." Mama frowned and shook her head at him.

A heat surged in my chest, foreign and uncomfortable, and I turned on my side, away from Daddy and Mama, to face the wall for what little privacy it offered. I balled up the worn hospital gown, gathering it in my hands, and stared at the white liquid that dripped down the sides of my swollen breasts, pooling under the creases of me. Holding the sheet high to shield me from my parents, I reached down to collect some of it with my fingers. It was lightweight and smelled sweet, not the scent of sickness or pus. I rubbed it together between my fingers and then sniffed it, before taking a lick. It tasted like … *milk?*

Oh, dear God, it must be breast milk! I carefully extended my neck out and bent over my breasts to see the lower half of me, horrified by what I found. I was fat!

How could this have happened? Just how much time had I lost? This was worse than TV, when the character gets in an accident and then wanders around without memory for a season or two, until the storyline grows stale and they have to remember or get killed off so the storyline doesn't drag. I think I'd rather die than be fat and covered in stretch marks. Beauty queens don't have stretch marks. And they don't have kids. Least that I know.

Tears stung my eyes and opened the floodgates to my breasts. Milk, and not cancerous pus, dripped down my middle and onto my fat flabby stomach and into the forks and crosses of the lines resembling the markings of a map. I was going to kill Bobby Lee. If I told him once, I told him a hundred times, he needed to either pull out or wear a condom. My eyes dropped to the ring finger on my left hand. The promise ring Bobby Lee gave me one Christmas, the one with the tiny diamonds, was missing, but at least in its place was a simple gold wedding band, so Bobby Lee must have made things right and married me. But with the damage to my stomach, he made things wrong. So wrong.

Tears continued to well in the corners of my eyes and then fall, until they dripped off the end of my cheek and dropped into my hair. *My brown hair.* I pulled at the length of it stuck behind me on the pillow of the hospital bed. My hair was brown! Why did I have brown hair? I've had blond hair ever since I can remember. Ever since my naturally blond hair started to darken and I got it lightened at the Cut and Curl every other month since the summer of eighth grade. I studied my left hand with the simple gold band. My nails were short and jagged, as if I'd been biting them, and the cuticles were split and covered the moons.

"Mama. Where is Bobby Lee? Is he coming to take me home?"

My mama started to fuss at her clothes, pulling and patting. "Darlin', what a strange question. I'm sure Bobby Lee is over at his daddy's mill, the same as ever. But I don't think you've laid eyes on him now for … how long would you say, Roy?" She turned to my father. "Almost seven years? Not since you got married, and certainly not since the girls were born. Is that right, Roy? Probably around the same time we rented out the big house and retired to Florida …" she droned on.

Married with children? And not to Bobby Lee?

Things started to swirl, same as the churning and the twirl of a carnival ride, where up is down and down is up, twisting shapes that once seemed so clear, now drawn out and misshapen as the reflection in the funhouse glass—undulated and distorted.

The door opened six inches, and a blond-haired nurse poked her head inside.

"Her husband has just arrived. Let me know when you're ready for me to send him in." The door closed.

My heart hammered in my chest, and the pain in my head intensified and threatened to explode. I was married, and not to Bobby Lee! I was married with a child, no—*children*, and to someone I could not remember.

I sat up and reached for my mama's hand. "Mama, please, quick, before he comes in. Who did I marry?" I begged.

"Oh, for heaven's sake, Savannah May, calm down. Don't be so melodramatic. It's not as if we'd let you marry Jack the Ripper. Although, you eloped, so technically, we didn't have much of a say in the matter. You've known this boy almost all of your life, and he adores you and all those kids." She leaned in and kissed me softly on the cheek, nodding at my father it was time for them to go. She smoothed her tailored slacks and then placed her hand on my daddy's arm. They both stepped toward the door. Mama paused and took a deep breath and turned around.

"You married Birdy, Savannah. You married sweet Birdy Johnson, the boy from Tennessee."

CHAPTER TWO

Swoon is a southern word—a corny word—a word from the generation of my mother, and my mother's mother, the same way as *beau* is an old-fashioned word, a word that made me cringe every time my mama would use it to introduce people to Bobby Lee, instead of saying he was my *boyfriend*.

But swoon I did. When I heard my mama say I married Bird Dog "Birdy" Johnson, I fainted dead away. Poor Birdy walked into that hospital room and found all of those people fussin' and clustered around me in a panic, and he thought I'd died. Died and gone to heaven. Or hell. When I came to, he was clutching onto me like a corpse in a coffin and him at a wake, sobbing into my chest, shaking so hard it reverberated through me. Between Birdy's tears and all that sticky milk, I was a wet, hot mess.

My parents left us to go back to their hotel, once the doctor assured them I would be fine, my mama whispering in my ear, *"His given name is James. James Russell,"* somehow feeling it was an important thing for me to know, leaving Birdy and me alone to get to know one another again, they said.

But alone was the last thing I wanted to be.

Well, maybe not the last thing. The fourth, maybe. In order of importance: I wanted to be childless, thin, and blond again. Married to Birdy was still an unknown, unfamiliar and strange, so there was no way to determine if it was something I wanted or not. How do you know if you like Neapolitan ice cream if you've never tasted it?

Mama was right. I had known Birdy almost all of my life, after he moved here from Tennessee, after his mama died when he was six and his daddy moved them both to Atlanta to get away from the bad memories and the debt collectors. I am ashamed to admit it, I did not know Birdy's proper name was James, even the teachers in school called him Birdy, but it makes sense, because people called his daddy Jimmy when they weren't calling him a no-good piece of white trash, which was most of the time.

Birdy untangled himself from me and was not as embarrassed as I was, although I would have expected him to be, since he was always so shy. Quiet and shy.

"I thought I'd lost you," he whispered in his soft Birdy voice, a voice that had deepened with age. Birdy pulled off his black-framed glasses and dried his reddened brown eyes with his fingers.

Without those awful glasses, Birdy was a nice-looking guy. Not heart-stopping handsome, the way Bobby Lee was, who older folks said reminded them of a fair-haired version of Elvis Presley. Bobby was so handsome sometimes I'd watch him after he'd finished with me, after he'd fall asleep, and I'd just stare. Stare at the perfection of him, the way his hair swept over one eye, and his perfect nose, not too big or too small, but just right for him, and the lips that knew all the parts of me. Just stare, feeling lucky that he loved me, when he could have had his pick of any girl.

Bobby Lee, every girl's dream, the catch of our school, the town, even. The star football player, and the rich kid, who drove a fast car and lived life on the edge. The complete opposite of Birdy, who was so quiet most people missed seeing him sitting in the last row of science class, or history, or hugging the side of the building at lunchtime in the quad. Not saying much, just watching, and sometimes eating some boring sandwich he brought from home. Bologna and pickles, maybe. Or just bread, with a swipe of mustard for taste. Birdy had a solid face, Mama said, and he could get lost in a crowd if he wanted, which most times he did. He resembled Matt Damon, I thought, once we became teens and I knew who Matt was, only Birdy's hair was darker than Matt's, and he has those sad eyes.

Birdy leaned in toward me with an intimacy I didn't remember us having, and he kissed me full on the lips. His were warm and soft against mine, and I held still for a quick moment, because I knew I should, before turning my head away and resisting the urge to wipe my mouth.

I used the side rails to pull myself forward on the bed. "I'm sorry, Birdy. I can't. This is all so new to me. I don't know if they told you, but I don't remember us. I mean … I remember us when it was you, me, and Bobby Lee," I corrected, "but I don't remember *us*." I pointed back and forth. "You and me as a couple. I'm sorry." My eyes stung with the effort not to cry, but the sight of Birdy's eyes filling with tears intensified mine, and I felt them drip down my face, warm and salty. "The last thing I remember was winning the pageant. After that …

nothing." I wept softly into my hands, shielding my face to keep from seeing the misery on his.

Questions flooded my mind. How? Why? Questions that did not have answers. At least none I could recall. And not just about the passing of time. But questions about Birdy and me together. *Married!* I didn't love Birdy. I mean, I've always loved Birdy, as one does a friend. But as my husband?

A swirling twist of emotions, a funnel cloud of thoughts, filled with darkness and punctured with bits and pieces of vague memories unrelated, curled and coiled, bringing no answers to my questions.

Birdy let me have my space, as he always did, and didn't touch me, waiting for me to touch him first, stepping back from me, his body tight with tension, his face pallid in the harsh light of the room.

"Birdy, what happened to me? Why am I married to you?"

I know I hurt him with my questions. I saw his eyes darken and sorrow change his expression, the despair covering his face even more than the weeks' worth of his beard. He took another step back, stricken, as if I'd slapped him or doused him with cold water, hearing the desperation in my voice as I asked the question, as if it was such an outlandish one, and taking it to mean I wish he wasn't my husband, that I wished it could all be undone. I reached out to touch him, to pull him back, but struggled with the effort, moaning from the ache of my breasts.

Birdy's gaze dropped to my chest, noticing the source of my discomfort. "You need to pump or the pain is only going to get worse. Do you want me to help you? Or can you do it yourself?" he questioned, his voice flat.

"Screw my breasts, Birdy!" If the situation wasn't so tragic, I might have laughed at the slip. The man was my husband, or so I was told. He might want to take me up on the offer. "Birdy, what's happening? Have I gone crazy? Who am I? We have children together? Biological children?" My voice rose high, and an overwhelming panic spread through me.

"James," Birdy said, his body still, his breathing shallow.

"What?"

"Savannah, my name is James Russell. You've called me James since the first night we got married, seven years ago, when you told me you could never sleep with a guy named Birdy."

"Oh, Birdy." I sighed, and wiped a lone tear from my cheek.

Birdy stood by the side of my bed, his hands jammed in the pockets of his jeans, his blue plaid flannel shirt worn and rumpled, as if he'd slept in it for days, if he'd slept at all. From the dark hollows beneath his eyes and the way his skin pulled tight across his cheeks, my guess was he hadn't done much sleeping, or eating, for the better part of a week.

"Ask me the other question, Savannah. I know you want to." Birdy's voice was low and deep, and his gaze intense.

"Ask you what, Birdy?" A muscle in his jaw twitched when I called him Birdy, the only name I'd ever called him.

Birdy took a step away from the bed, putting physical distance between us. I knew Birdy well enough to know he was suffering, and not just by the hunch of his shoulders, or the way he swallowed, or how he kept touching the back of his neck to rub the base with his hand. I *felt* him. I felt his struggle, radiating outward and filling the space between us, same way as the heaviness of the moist air touches ground, just before the summer storm hits and the sky crackles white with lightening.

"You want to know if you love *me* now, or if you're still in love with Bobby Lee, don't you?" Birdy shuffled over to the window, watching the rain fall soft and light, his posture bent, crooked as a question mark. Beyond him, I could see the sky had turned a dark gray and rain fell in big shapeless drops, hammering on the roof and the tops of the cars parked below.

"Talk to me, Birdy. Tell me what I need to know. Who are our children? And how many do we have? Obviously one of them is a baby. I pulled at the front of my hospital gown and stared again at my huge breasts, filled with enough milk to feed the whole lot of them, it seemed.

Birdy turned back around, and his body straightened with pride. "Yes, we have a baby girl. She's almost eight months old and she's beautiful. She's the spitting image of you. Only she's blond."

"Ha ha," I said, sarcastically. As soon as the bandage was off and my head healed, I would get my hair lightened. Brown hair?

Birdy reached toward his back pocket, where the fabric was lightened in the shape of a square. "Do you want to see pictures? Maybe it will help you to remember." He pulled out a worn brown vinyl billfold.

What kind of wife was I if I let my husband carry a brown vinyl billfold that probably came from the drugstore, or the corner gas station on the shelf next to the work gloves and jumper cables? I grew up wealthy, in a beautiful big house large enough for the annual debutante ball, and I drove a Mustang, a new one each year, painted pink, custom for me, since the year of my sweet sixteen, and yet my husband carries around an old plastic wallet so worn the picture sleeves were yellowed and cracked? But now I have raggedy nails and brown hair, so things must not be so rosy at the Johnson homestead. It must be because of all those kids we have. We must be poor because of all those darn kids.

Birdy handed me a wrinkled but recent picture, according to him, with an adorable baby girl, and me, holding her in my arms. She had blond hair and big blue eyes underneath long eyelashes, and the cutest little pink mouth, and she wore a flowered dress and white shoes on her feet. In the picture, I had long brown hair and some gray eyes I'd never seen before, eyes that stared into the lens of the camera, vacant and hollow. I wore a top without color—tan, perhaps—and some mom-style jeans, shapeless, as if there was something to hide, something besides the fat and the stretch marks. I was holding that baby in my arms and standing in front of a fountain. Or maybe it was a pizzeria; it was hard to tell because of the crease.

"I'm not smiling. I seem sad." It must be the pizzeria. Probably I never learned to cook and now we have to eat at cheap restaurants so we don't starve to death. "What's her name?"

I traced her shape with my finger, with no sense of recollection, no maternal pull at all, as if tracing the lines of a stranger, same as a picture in a magazine. How strange it was going to be to nurse a baby I didn't know, couldn't remember giving birth to, couldn't remember conceiving. Or remember anything of the children who came before her. It would feel completely foreign to me to put her to my breast to nurse. Almost as strange as when that Hispanic actress went to Africa, or whatnot, and put that little black baby to her chest to feed it—with the suck heard 'round the world—winding up in all the news for weeks. At least she'd nursed her own baby girl first, so she knew just what to do, and the black baby seemed to know what to do, too. One breast must be just as good as the next.

"Her name is Dolly Sue."

"Dolly Sue!" I spat, feeling the heat of anger color my face. "Please tell me you're teasing. I let you name our child Dolly Sue? Is it too late for an annulment? Birdy, you know I can't stand those hillbilly names. What were you thinking? I always told you, from the time I first started going out with Bobby Lee, that when he and I got married, I was going to name our children normal names, names such as Amanda or Jessica, or Christopher or Brian if it was a boy, not old-fashioned southern names. Stupid names. I talked about it enough, even wrote them down and showed you, I'd think you'd remember. And you gave me a Dolly?"

Birdy flinched and jerked back. "She's *our* daughter, Savannah May. Yours and mine. Whatever you and Bobby Lee talked about don't make a lick of difference. And for your information, *I* named her Anna Sue, it's *you* who started calling her Dolly." He yanked the picture out of my hands. "And she's not named after Dolly Parton, if that's what you're thinkin'. Who if I recollect, I've heard you sing her songs so many times in my life I could puke. You call her Dolly because she's so pretty you said she looks like a doll." Birdy turned away from me, his expression wounded.

"Don't holler at me, Birdy! I'm doing the best I can here."

The fight went out of Birdy. He sat down on the edge of the bed and stared at me for a moment before putting his hand on the side of my face, his palm warm and callused, except for the spot where his thin gold wedding ring rested, cool, and smooth. I closed my eyes and remembered another time Birdy put his hand on my face. The night he found me sitting on the bumper of my car and he dried my face with the tail of his shirt and then soothed my stinging cheek with the coolness of his hands.

Birdy heaved a deep sigh. "I'm sorry. I know. But Savannah, if you knew what hell I've been going through, worrying about you, and taking care of the kids. They miss you and can't understand why you haven't come home. I didn't know what to tell them. The doctors, they didn't know how long they'd need to keep you asleep. Or what you'd be like when you woke up …" His voice trailed off.

I patted his hand and gently removed it from my cheek. "Kids? We have two?" My tone was hopeful. Two didn't seem too many. One for each of us to care for.

"Darlin', we have four."

"Four!" I sat up so fast I set off the alarm. Machines beeped and buzzed and the nurse's voice came over the intercom. *Not four!* Dear Lord, I was the mother of four children. Four loud and annoying children. I assumed they were loud and annoying, having never met a child who wasn't at least one of the two.

"Coming," a voice warbled from the intercom.

"No, it's okay," Birdy spoke into the microphone. "Savannah just found out we have four children. But she's fine. I think she's fine. Or at least as fine as someone who's just been told they have four kids would be," he ended.

The nurse chuckled and clicked off the intercom, and Birdy got up to pace the room, his shoulders stooped, his steps uneven. "I know it's a whole heap of stuff to grasp. I don't understand much of it myself. Savannah, there's so many things going on here. So many things … I can't say I'm smart enough to weed through it all." He stopped and leaned against the counter with the small metal sink where the nurses and doctors washed their hands, where a mirror hung above it pitted with age, the silver backing missing at the bottom.

Birdy ruffled his hands in his hair, his head down, his mind processing the words he wanted to say before coming back up, his eyes reaching mine. "There's a psychiatrist they made me talk to." I widened my eyes in surprise. "Not for me. I'm fine, believe it or not," Birdy said, but I don't believe he was. I don't believe he was fine at all.

He came forward and pulled up the bedside chair, straddling it to face me, his arms resting on top. "To explain things …" Birdy collected his thoughts before continuing. "You see, Savannah, after each baby comes, you get sad. Real sad for a while. So blue it's like when the sun goes back behind the clouds right before it rains and things get dark. It breaks my heart to watch it, and the kid's hearts, too. You do your best. Best as you can, but they can feel it—your depression—making you pull away from us. It makes them quieter, and frightened I think, while they wait for you to come back to them, and to me, too." He paused, his head down, and pulled a loose thread from the worn blanket.

"Oh, Birdy." I reached out to touch his hand.

"Then when you get pregnant, you're happy again. For a time, at least. Filling our home with the best parts of you, the light and the smiles. But after the baby is born, a while later, you go back to being down, to some dark place you escape to, and we all wait until you find your way back home to us." Birdy turned from me, trying to gather his thoughts. "The doctors, and you've seen a few, they tell us it's something called postpartum depression, and that a lot of women go through it, some more so than others. Your mama said she got it after having you. But then your daddy threw her a big party and bought her a new necklace, and she said she felt better." He shook his head in disbelief.

Birdy paused, and I sensed there was more to tell.

"Go on, Birdy. I need to know."

Birdy tilted his chin down, frowning. He picked at the rust on the chrome of the chair with his fingernail. "The memory loss is something different. It's not from the concussion, the doctor says. There's even a name for it. But I can't say I can recollect it."

I felt Birdy's sadness seep into me. Like a sponge, I sucked it inside, the thick and the thin of it, until it consumed me and made it hard to catch my breath. Poor Birdy. We'd spent a lifetime sharing grief and both of us not yet thirty. At least I think we were still in our twenties. Nothing else made sense. But Mama and Daddy were still holding up pretty well, so we couldn't be much older than that.

Birdy reached out to trace the bruises on the inside of my arm and struggled for composure before continuing. "I love you, Savannah," he softly said. "I'm sure you know that. I don't know if you love me the same way. I hope you do. I've been in love with you ever since we were kids, when I taught you to swim, and we climbed those trees in your neighbor's yard. And even when you were with that prick, Bobby Lee."

I started to speak, but Birdy held up his hand to stop me. "Don't! Don't you dare defend him. He may have been my friend once, but he was a bastard and a mean drunk. And I should know. I lived with one until the day my daddy died."

My relationship with Birdy was always so one-sided. I would pour out my burdens to him and he would listen, always without judgment, mostly without comment. Just listen. In return, what did I give him? Companionship of sorts, I guess, someone to share time with, both me and Bobby Lee. I gave Birdy friendship on my terms. I'd have listened if Birdy ever wanted to share, which he seldom did, holding everything inside him like bees in a bottle. From time to time, I could hear the hum of them, of the things he wanted to say, hear the nervous buzzing of it, trapped deep inside, flying around in circles, but never settling. They never came out, those bees in the bottle, and sometimes I'd wonder, what would happen if they ever got loose?

"I wasn't going to defend Bobby Lee," I said, shyly. "I was going to give you a compliment." I twirled my brown hair around my finger nervously. At least I still had long hair, even if it was the dullest shade of brown.

"Sorry. You go. I'll shut up." He removed his glasses and pinched the bridge of his nose.

"I was going to say if we have four kids, then there's one thing I must love about you." I blushed and held the sheet up with both my hands to cover my face, peeking over the top to see Birdy's reaction.

An odd expression, doubt, or disbelief, maybe, crossed Birdy's face, before it smoothed out and Birdy threw his head back and laughed. For a moment time stood still and he was the old *young* Birdy Johnson, my best friend and confidant, the sweet shy boy who was never far from my side. *Savannah and her sidekick*, they would say.

Birdy pulled down the sheet. "Are you wondering if you love me, Savannah May?" He stared at me, searching for the answer. "I hope you do. No," he said, shaking his head, "I pray you do. But I can tell you one thing, sure as I'm sitting here with you right now. As much as I wish that were true, if you love me, I suspect it's for something other than *that*."

CHAPTER THREE

A shiver ran through me thinking about having sex with Birdy—not a memory, but an emotion—and I felt my breasts tighten, the muscles pulling, and the oddest sensations inside them, a pulsating of sorts. I pulled the top of my hospital gown open about four inches, as far as it would go, staring at my breasts. The breasts of someone else. Someone older, someone capable of being a mother—not mine.

"I think I've sprung a leak," I said, surprised at what I'd found. "Are they supposed to do this?" Thin watery liquid sprayed straight up from several pinpoint openings, and I stared in wonder. I'd never seen such a thing. In all of my life, I'd never seen such a thing.

"Yeah. I reckon."

Birdy started to assemble the pump components the nurse had left on the side table: some long plastic tubing and a pair of megaphone-looking things attached to plastic bottles. When he was finished, he handed me one and pressed the machine's on button. A buzzing filled the air, and I blushed, embarrassed at what was to come. I didn't rightly know, but I'd seen cows get milked once, over at the fairgrounds the one summer, while

Bobby, Birdy, and I stumbled around the pens tipsy from the beer we'd drank while hiding behind the twirl-a-whirl drinking a six-pack Bobby had stolen from the store.

"I can help you get started, if you want."

I stared at the machine, with its tubes and its noises. "Do I have to do this? Will it make me sick if it stays inside?" Maybe it gets old and sours, the same way real milk gets when it's left out on the counter all night when you forget to put it away. Maybe the milk inside your breasts gets poisonous, same as rattlesnake venom, and makes you blind and crazy before it kills you. And the baby, too. It might even kill the baby.

My eyes pulled back to the machine and the noise of sucking air, my eyes tearing.

"I can't, Birdy." I shook my head no. "I can't do this." I reached and pushed the power off. "Can't she have cow's milk or formula? Isn't there some kind of pill or shot to dry me up so I don't have milk? This is *disgusting.*" I hugged my arms to my chest while the fluid seeped out, and my breast ached. "I don't know anything about breast-feeding a baby. How does it all even work?" Apparently, the birthing part I had down to a science, but I was foggy on the feeding part. "Isn't she old enough to drink cow's milk out of a cup?" Tears ran down my face and into the corner of my lips. I used my top sheet to wipe them, the IV tubes still in my arms, tugging. "Birdy, I can't even change a diaper. I don't *want* to change a diaper. You know I never liked kids, and I've never babysat a day in my life. There is nothing I like about children."

Birdy sighed, loud and heavy, removing his glasses, rubbing his temple with the fingers of his left hand, his eyes closed. He opened them and slowly put back on his glasses, pushing them tight against the bridge.

"Is that what you want, Savannah? You want Dolly to go on formula? One way or the other, you need to tell me quick, because I only have three bottles left at home, and that baby's going to be hungry." His cell phone made some strange chirp noise, and he reached inside his shirt pocket. Instead of flipping up the cover of the black thick phone I remembered, he slid his finger across the face of some new thin slick phone to read the message. "We're down to two bottles, so tell me now what you want to do."

I needed to get a grip. This was Birdy Johnson. And even if it was strange he was now my husband, Birdy had seen my chest when it was flat as the two-by-fours at Bobby Lee's daddy's lumberyard back in those years when we were kids, when we'd go swimming in the creek wearing nothing but bottoms, and then again when we were full grown, and in that same water, when I had something worth showing. But those times, mostly I tried to keep below water from the neck down, so Bobby Lee wouldn't get mad someone other than him got to see his girls, as he called them.

There was only one time Birdy saw me full naked. It was the weekend my parents were away and I threw that big party with all our friends from school, and half the county, too. Somebody had spiked the punch. Twice. Not knowing the other did it. And with two different kinds of liquors. Whiskey and gin. By night's end, I could barely walk and was seeing double, bumping into the walls and falling down, my blouse hanging off my shoulder and my bra strap showing. Birdy took me by the hand and upstairs to my bathroom, stripping me down, every last bit, and putting me in the shower to sober me up. He even got inside the shower with me at one point, still dressed in his clothes, to hold me up and keep me from falling and cracking my sorry head open. He held my naked body, his arms around me with my backside against him, and let that cold water run down the two of us, until I couldn't stand it any longer and begged him to turn it off. And the whole time, Bobby Lee sleeping downstairs on the sofa, passed out from all the liquor he drank. When I woke up in the morning, Birdy was asleep on the bed next to me on the outside of the covers, his clothes still wet from the shower, and I was on the inside, snug and warm and wearing my pajamas that Birdy must have put me in, although I don't remember that part. Bobby Lee found us and was madder than hell, but he was too hung over and sick to go on much about it.

I blew out a breath and pushed the on button and then untied the tie at the side of my gown, letting it fall. Birdy's eyes widened, but he remained quiet. With four kids, I'm sure it wasn't the first time he'd laid eyes on them, so it's not as if he was going to make much of a fuss, the way I seemed to be doing.

"All right. I'll do it. I'm trusting you, Birdy, to know enough for the both of us." My cheeks flushed with embarrassment. "Show me what to do."

Wordlessly, Birdy placed the suction cup around my swollen nipple, holding it tight against my fevered skin, while his other hand supported the weight of my breast from underneath. His touch wasn't exactly familiar, but it wasn't foreign, either, and I watched in silent horror and amazement as the machine started to suck and pull all the milk right out of my breast and fill up that bottle, and then the second one on the other side.

"This one is for Dolly," Birdy said, tightening the plastic yellow lid on the bottle and holding it up to read the ounce level on the side markings. He set it down on the table and wiped the bottle off with a tissue from the box on the table beside the bed. "And this one I'm saving, to go with my coffee," he joked, straight faced, fitting the lid on the second.

"Birdy Johnson! You made a joke. Maybe being married to you won't be so bad after all. Tolerable, even," I teased. Instead of smiling, Birdy frowned and his face darkened. I'd hurt his feelings. "I'm teasing, Birdy. Goodness. I'm kidding. You don't have to be so serious."

"Well, don't."

"Don't, what?"

"Don't tease."

I glanced at Birdy, confused.

Birdy walked over to the sink and rinsed out some of the pieces of the pump, thoroughly and much longer than necessary, trying to gather his thoughts, I'd imagine.

"Savannah, let me tell it to you straight, that way you have time to get used to it before you come home." He pushed his fingers through his hair again, making it stand up straight, reminding me of a dog that's been riled and is ready to fight. Only Birdy wasn't much of a fighter. With all those damn kids, he must be more of a lover. "You married poor Birdy Johnson. And we ain't poor the way I was growing up, but it's not the life you had before, either. I'm a truck driver, but the truck is mine—*ours*," he corrected. "And in three more payments it will be paid off. We live in a three-bedroom house on the other side of the city, not in a big old mansion like your parents' house. We don't have a cook, or a housekeeper. We only have me and you, and four kids: twin girls, six years old, a son who is four, and the baby. And if I had my way, we'd keep having them, but you needed a hysterectomy when Dolly was born because you wouldn't stop bleeding, so you'll get your way, and there won't be any more."

Thank heavens. Was Birdy insane? Four kids and he wanted to have more? I took some time to digest the information. One minute I was Savannah May Holladay, a twenty-year-old debutante and Miss Georgia Peach Queen, engaged to Bobby Lee Thomas, heir to Thomas and Son Lumber, and now I was Mrs. Birdy Johnson and lived in a three-bedroom house with a truck driver husband and four kids. And probably some hunting dogs, too. It would be so "Birdy" to fill our house with kids and some mangy dogs.

I touched Birdy on the forearm, resting my hand and feeling the strength and muscles underneath his shirtsleeve. Birdy, the boy, had become a man. "Are we happy as a couple, Birdy?" I resisted the urge to hug him, to make him smile. "I know you said I was sad, but are we happy as a couple?"

"I am, Savannah. You're not." He wouldn't return my gaze and instead turned his head away to stare out the window.

I could guess why. Birdy was sweet and kind, and I'm sure he was a wonderful husband and father, but the life he described wasn't the life of my dreams, the life I set for myself from as far back as I could remember. The one that included parties and travel and dinners at the country club. And Bobby Lee. Maybe, just maybe, one child, far off in the future, when I was closer to thirty and before my body shut down completely.

Birdy pushed his hands deep down inside his jean pockets. "The doctor says you can be released soon. Do you want to come home?"

Did I have a choice? I wanted to go *home*. Back to my big, beautiful house on Scarlet Oak Road. The big old historic house built generations ago in English Tudor-style, not one of those white-columned *Gone With the Wind* houses most people think are on every street corner in the entire state of Georgia. I wanted to go back to the house on five acres with the six bedrooms and eight bathrooms, and the guesthouse out back, the rose garden, and the pool.

Birdy stood, intently watching my face. As connected as we'd been all of our lives, I'm sure he knew exactly where my thoughts were taking me. His eyes were shiny and his face melancholy.

"Please say you'll come home with me, Savannah May."

———— ● ● ● ————

I remembered them, these silly pajamas. I might not recall my adult life with Birdy, but I remembered these. As I stared at them, I clearly recalled the story behind these goofy things. The month—June. The day—a Saturday. The weather, even—a sunny day with an afternoon thunderstorm in the early evening, when Bobby Lee came over for Mama's fried chicken supper and made fun of me for buying "*those stupid things*," when I showed him what I bought at the mall.

I drew a complete blank about marriage … or children … or anything important—but Paul Frank monkey pajamas? *That*, I remembered.

"You're kidding me, right?" I stood beside my hospital bed, not knowing whether to laugh or cry, holding the ridiculous pajamas Mama brought me to wear.

I was tired of having my fat fanny and thick thighs hanging out of my hospital gown for everyone to see, and after asking the doctor if it was okay, I called Birdy and asked him to bring me some real nightclothes to wear for my last two nights. I had to. I told the doctor it was imperative for my mental health, because after showering and catching sight of my back end in the bathroom mirror, I almost wanted to kill myself. Honestly. The nurse had to give me a sedative to calm me down. My newfound theory is this; the world would be closer to obtaining zero population growth if girls knew how lumpy their bodies would become after having a baby. Or in my case, three or four.

"Mama, is this a joke? *This* is what you brought me to wear?"

Mama blinked her eyes with dark eyelashes that had to be artificial, and seemed genuinely clueless. "Why, whatever do you mean?" She glanced over at Daddy who stood next to the window and gave him some silent signal to speak up. "You kept them in a box at the house; I assumed you must have liked them."

Since my head injury, and the strong possibility I'm crazy, my parents give each other sly looks and sideways glances every time I say something they don't like or understand. And they're tentative around me, as if any second they expect me to start speaking in tongues, or rip off my clothes and run stark raving mad through the hospital after smearing myself with my own poo. They also maintain a safety zone of two feet from me at all times. Just in case it's finally proven that crazy is contagious.

Daddy fiddled with the collar of his baby blue golf shirt, pulling the back of it up but turning down the collared points on the front before speaking. "Darlin', James Russell had to take the baby for her wellness checkup," he began, giving me a recap of things I'd already heard from Birdy, "so he called and asked us to bring you a robe and some pajamas—"

"And don't forget about the mementos," Mama cut in, fingering the diamond and gold cross on her necklace.

"Oh, yes. And some mementos," Daddy added.

I held the junior-sized, Paul Frank brand, pink and black heart fleece bottoms with the sock puppet monkey faces to my hips, the elastic leg ending at my calf, and tugged on the waistband, checking the stretch on them. Heaving a sigh, I threw them on the hospital bed.

"Mementos? He told you to bring me mementos?" I began to sift through the black carry-on bag, withdrawing a white T-shirt with the monkey's face emblazoned on the front. Checking for size, I read the inside label: *small*. Except for a pink fleece robe that now ended (or maybe it always ended) at my knees, there were no other clothing options. There was, however, my jewelry box, and I remembered it, along with those silly pajamas I got the last year I was in *middle school*, for goodness' sake, with a clarity as if it were yesterday.

"*Don't open that!*" Both Daddy and Mama cried out at the same time as I lifted my jewelry box out of the bag.

Mama reached over and snatched it from my hands, quickly passing it off to Daddy with the speed of a quarterback in the fourth quarter and the game tied with just seconds left on the clock.

"It's for your therapy session this afternoon with James and the doctor," Daddy said, tucking the cherry wood box under his arm.

"My what?"

Mama tentatively touched my bare arm, and then withdrew it, glancing at the table next to my bed. I think she was searching for the hand sanitizer. Or maybe she just needed a tissue and I was becoming paranoid.

"Your session with the psychiatrist, honey. Birdy will bring something more recent, but the doctor asked if we could provide anything from an earlier time. He's trying to see just how far back the memory loss is."

"I think it's safe to assume, it's post middle school," I said, trying on the pink fuzzy robe and patting at my hips. Feeling something inside, I reached in the left pocket and pulled out a thin piece of printed paper, folded in half and faded with the passing of time. I opened it up to read it. "And high school, too. Here's a parking ticket for illegally parking in the red zone in front of school."

"Good girl!" Daddy said, clearly impressed I remembered something as insignificant as a parking ticket from what must seem a hundred years ago in aging-parent time.

"Well I can't say I recall getting this exact one. But I know I liked to park in the red zone the days I was late for class." Which was most times, according to my memory.

I smiled at Daddy and he smiled back and gave me the slightest bit of a nod. I never paid the tickets myself, so I assumed Daddy must have paid them and never told Mama.

"See, Roy. I told you it was just a matter of time." Mama patted her over-sprayed hair. "Our girl will be over this nonsense soon enough." She walked over to take her carry-on bag from me. "Won't you, Savannah May?" She stared into my eyes, as if her command would bring my life all back to me. "Your memory will return, and hopefully you'll finally quit tormenting that poor husband of yours."

Sparks shot to the wound in my head, and immediately it pulsed and throbbed beneath the dressings.

"*Tormenting!*" I exploded at my mother, pushing the bag at her before taking a step back, horrified. Tears stung at my eyes. "Mama, is that what you think I do to Birdy? I torment him? Daddy?" I turned to question my father, blinking back my tears.

"Sugar, calm down." Daddy advanced on me, his hands outstretched, his expression apologetic. He needn't be sorry. Mama said it. "Well, now … no. Not intentionally. It's just that he loves you so much, Savannah May, and it hurts him when you're hurting." At least Daddy was kind enough to be diplomatic in his presentation.

"Go! Just leave me be." I climbed back into the hospital bed and held my bandaged head in my hands, my eyes closed against them and Mama's harsh words.

"I'll hand this to the nurse to give to James." I heard Daddy tap the side of my jewelry box. Bye, darlin'." Daddy gently patted my arm. "She'll be fine, Marylou. Come on, now. Leave her be."

CHAPTER FOUR

If I thought the pajamas silly earlier, it was nothing compared to my opinion once I saw them on me.

The shirt was far too tight and bordered on the obscene. No monkey's face should look that way, with that wide split red mouth and those hugely distorted ears bulging forward with my milk-engorged breasts. Luckily, the robe almost covered the shirt. The pants, however, were another story. They ended at my calves and were so tight around the waist I had to remove the elastic and rely solely on the drawstring.

As bad as I looked, it was still better than walking the corridor and over to the next wing of the hospital wearing a tattered hospital gown, with my back end exposed, to meet with Birdy and the doctor. I stuck my feet into some hospital-issued slippers and stared at myself from the chest down, shaking my head.

The psychiatrist's office was nothing the way they appear in the movies or on television. In the movies there's a big wood carved desk in the center of the room, with floor-to-ceiling bookcases behind it, and all the shelves are filled with leather-bound books, neat and orderly. There's always somewhere to lie down, too, a couch, or an oversized chair, a place to get comfortable while you share all those stories and secrets. Also a plant, or a tree, in the corner. Real, or artificial. But a nice silk one, and not those cheap plastic kind. And all those certificates and diplomas on the walls, proof it was a doctor who actually went to school and graduated, I imagine.

The only thing this room had in common with the one in the movies was the diplomas.

The doctor's "office" was just another hospital room, only without the beds and the monitors, or the small bathroom with a shower the size you'd find in a motor home. The walls were the same dingy green, the windows just as covered with dirt, the floor the same worn linoleum. The doctor's chair, (he was currently absent from it), was black vinyl and on rollers, the arms worn and rubbed raw. But those diplomas were impressive. There were many of them, and they covered the walls in haphazard formation, the letters now faded with the passing of years spent trying to help the crazed and the confused.

"Hey, Savannah," Birdy said, unfurling himself from one of the two small torn vinyl chair on one side of the doctor's gray laminate desk. He hugged me and gently kissed me on top of my bandaged head before releasing me. He gave my clothes a once-over, but said nothing, although he started to smile.

"Hey, yourself, Birdy. Nice shirt." I said it sweetly, but I was being sarcastic. It was a faded gray T-shirt and said *All-American Reject*. The full name was in smaller letters at the top and bottom, and in the middle of it were the initials in yellow. AAR, it said.

"Thanks. You bought it for me." Birdy's eyes regarded me behind his glasses, and he stuck his hands deep in the pockets of his jeans, the movement pulling his shoulders forward.

"There's a story behind it, I'm willing to bet."

"There is."

"Was I *tormenting* you at the time? I'm sure the shirt is symbolic."

Birdy shook his head in confusion. "Tormenting me? Are you okay? Why don't you sit down for a spell while we wait for the doctor?" Birdy removed my jewelry box from the chair seat, placing it on top of the desk, and pulled the chair out for me. I sat down, and Birdy sat beside me.

I continued to eyeball Birdy's clothing choice. "Why would I buy you a shirt that says All-American Reject? That doesn't seem very nice. Am I evil now, Birdy? Am I mean and evil?" I tried to keep my voice even, but without much success.

Birdy regarded me, his head tipped slightly to the side. "No, Savannah, you're not evil," he said slowly, but not as if he had to consider the question, that's just the way he talks. "Most that can be said is you get crabby. And depressed," he added. "But you're quiet when you're depressed."

I pulled my robe tighter across my chest and retied the sash.

"Not the pajamas you had in mind when you called me, I reckon." Birdy smiled and his cheek dimpled, but it wasn't a smile where his teeth showed.

"Not exactly."

"Do you remember them?"

"How could I not? Honestly, Birdy, as silly as these things are, I have to wonder why I ever bought them at all, not to mention why I'd keep them."

41

"And yet, you don't remember buying me this shirt?" Birdy pulled at the front of it, all signs of his smile gone from his face.

"No. I'm sorry. I don't. Was I trying to be insulting? Or was it just the unintended result?"

"It's the name of a band. An alternative rock group. You had me take you to one of their concerts when they were at the Lakewood Amphitheater. You said you liked their songs. One in particular."

The way Birdy was staring at me, I knew it was some sort of test. But alternative rock? That didn't sound like me at all. I'm more mainstream pop, with classic country thrown in.

"And that song would be ...?"

Birdy sat silently in that chair and I saw emotions battle across his face, if such a thing is possible: sadness, confusion, disappointment maybe. He remained silent, but his breathing became deep, and I saw the rise and the fall of his chest beneath his shirt. That insulting shirt I bought him at some concert we attended.

"I'm serious, Birdy. What's the name of the song?"

Birdy didn't move a muscle, if you don't count the one in his jaw that twitched. It was obvious he didn't want to tell me. I think the memento Birdy brought to the session to trigger my memory was the one covering his chest.

"'Dirty Little Secret,'" he finally said, his voice low and soft. "The song you said you like is called 'Dirty Little Secret.'" He repeated the title, only louder this time.

"*Oh my God.*" I covered my face with my hands and an unspeakable sadness washed over me. A cloud of *something*. A nameless shame and vague memories of past deeds. And regret.

No wonder Mama said I tormented Birdy. My adult anthem was the song "Dirty Little Secret." I pulled some tissue from the box on the desk and cried into the wad.

"Don't!" I said, when Birdy tried to put his arm around me to comfort me.

"Excuse me." A nurse rapped on the doorframe, her arms full of charts, her glasses pushed up on top of her head. "The doctor had an emergency, and he'll need to reschedule your appointment. Sorry for the inconvenience."

"So, my wife can be released without meeting with him first?" Birdy asked, using the word "wife" easily, but the word jarring at me and making the hairs on the back of my neck prickle.

"I imagine he thinks your wife is fit to be released. We can schedule the follow-up appointment after she's home. I'm sure she wants to get home to those babies."

If that's what she thought, she needed to think again. The squeaky sounds of her rubber-soled shoes faded down the hallway. I reached out to grab another tissue and blew my nose, tossing the tissue in the metal trashcan next to the desk where they landed on top of a crumpled empty package of Marlboro cigarettes. Figures a shrink would feel the need to smoke.

"You okay?" Birdy asked.

I blew out a deep breath. "I've been better. Oh, Birdy," I sighed and hugged my arms to my chest, knowing soon it would be time to pump again. The thought deepened my depression. "What now?"

Birdy glanced down at his watch. "I still have a few minutes before I need to get the kids from school. Do you want to talk?"

He reached over and pulled my jewelry box from the desk. "Or, there's this." He handed it to me.

"*Pandora's box …*"

"Who?" Birdy asked.

I held the dark wood box in my hands not knowing what I'd find. "Pandora. Remember? We learned about her in school. She's from Greek mythology. Pandora was the first woman made out of clay. Zeus, her father, sent her to Earth to marry—"

"Can't say as I recall the story."

Well I did. And as I couldn't recall much, I felt it important to share what little I could. That way, I didn't feel nearly so stupid about forgetting so much else.

"Pandora's father gave her a box, with strict instructions not to open it. But her curiosity got the best of her, and she did, and by doing so released into the world every kind of sickness, and hate and envy. All the bad things that people had never experienced before."

"That's a terrible story."

"It has a happy ending," I said, my voice soft. I outlined the inlay on the top of the box with my raggedy-nailed finger. This wasn't Greek mythology, this was my life, but it was quickly becoming a Greek tragedy in the making.

"Go on, then."

"At first Pandora thought the box was empty, but there was one thing left inside the bottom of that box, one small bug that hadn't yet been set free." I traced the mother-of-pearl leaves and the vines, the swirls, and the curlicues. "Do you know what that was?" I raised my head and faced Birdy.

"No, but I believe you're about to tell me."

"It was hope, Birdy. The one thing left inside that box waiting to be set free, was hope." With trembling hands, I opened the lid, and immediately the sounds of what I recognized as the music from *The Nutcracker*—Tchaikovsky, I think it was—filled the room.

Birdy leaned forward to get a closer look.

The top tier held jewelry: rings and necklaces, some earrings, and even a small stone, smooth and with rounded edges, in the shape of a tiny heart.

"I gave that to you." Birdy pointed to the stone.

"Yes, I recall that. What were we? About nine at the time?"

"Ten. I think we were ten. I found it down by the creek where we used to go fishin'."

I tried on some of the rings, though most were too small to fit, except on my pinky finger. One ring I especially remembered, and as I put it on my finger, memories came flooding back. It was my promise ring from Bobby Lee. I extended my hand, the light reflecting in the tiny diamonds.

"You recognize that one."

"I do." I removed it and gently placed it back in the box.

Birdy slumped back in his chair and blew out a deep breath, closing his eyes for a moment. This couldn't have been easy for him, forcing him to walk down my memory lane, as broken and sketchy as it was.

I removed the first tiered tray and set it on the desk, revealing the contents below. Pictures. Dozens of them. Mostly of Bobby and me, although Birdy was in two or three, and not looking happy to be in them, the way he scowled at the camera while Bobby's arm draped across my shoulder or I sat on Bobby's lap.

Birdy opened his eyes, just in time to see me open a silver locket with a small picture inside, a picture of Bobby Lee. And on the right side of the locket, nestled inside the recess of it, a tiny lock of his hair.

Birdy bolted from his chair, knocking it over in the process.

"I can't do this. I just can't," he choked, his expression anguished. "I have to go. I need to pick up the kids. I'm sorry, Savannah." Birdy righted the chair and turned to leave.

"Stop, Birdy!" I grabbed at his arm. "Don't you dare run out on me, Birdy Johnson. Don't you dare make me go through this on my own! One of us running from the past is enough. This box has been in the back of the closet in my old room for years. You can't take this personally, Birdy. This isn't about you." I didn't know that for sure. But odds were it was more about me and less about him.

Birdy's face had gone pale, and his eyes were shiny behind the lenses of his glasses.

"I'm not supposed to take this *personally*? You don't remember a damn thing about our life together, or our children, and yet you remember the lock of Bobby Lee's hair you've had for, what? twelve years?" he sneered. He went to the stack of pictures and rifled through them until he found the one he wanted. "Look at this picture!" he commanded. "Savannah May, look at this picture!" He shook it and held it up in front of my eyes. "What do you see?"

"Me and Bobby sitting at a picnic table?"

"What else?" he demanded. "What's that on your wrist?"

I looked closer at the picture. "A bandage?"

"*Christ.*" Birdy ripped the picture in two and threw it in the trash, and then he grabbed the rest and threw them on top, turning towards the door.

"*Birdy, don't go!* Please don't run away from me. I'm scared."

Birdy hesitated in the doorway for a moment, and then he turned around, taking in the short pink robe, the crazy pajamas, and the slippers on my feet, then back to the top of me, and the swathes of bandages covering my head. His face softened and his voice became gentle.

"You think I'm running from you, Savannah May?" He took a step towards me, shaking his head, his stare pained. "I'm not running away from you. I'm running *towards* you. To you, and our children. For most of my life, over twenty years now, I've been running towards you."

CHAPTER FIVE

I watched from the window, the cars pulling into the parking spaces of the lot down below, and wondered which one was ours. Probably some old rusted truck or loser-cruiser mom van. With four kids under the age of seven, it had to be something big enough to seat the whole lot of us, and the car seats and all the baby paraphernalia crap that goes with kids: strollers and diaper bags and stuff.

Maybe it was a good thing I couldn't remember any of it. Not if what my mama said was true, that I spent years *tormenting* Birdy. No matter how hard I tried, and I did try, all night long and most of the morning, I couldn't remember anything that had happened since the night of the pageant.

I left the window and started to change into the clothes Birdy had brought for me last night after he came back from dropping off the bottles for Anna. I was not calling that baby Dolly, no matter how much I admire her songs. The other Savannah may have named her Dolly, but the new Savannah was renaming her. I'm sure that baby was too young to have grown much of an attachment to it anyway.

I untied my hospital gown, the monkey pajamas long since tossed, letting it fall to the floor and opened the brown paper sack that held the clothes Birdy brought for me. *A brown paper sack!* I think from Birdy's parts, they used to call it a "poke." This one was from Kroger's market and still had a piece of old lettuce still stuck to the inside bottom of it. Birdy caught hell from me when he handed it to me. Do we not own a suitcase? Or a gym bag? I know I used to have a pink gym bag at my house on Scarlet Oak Road. I never used it much, at least not for the gym. But I used it a few times when I spent the night over at Sara Jane's and twice when Bobby Lee and I snuck off and slept outside under the stars last summer. I guess it was now *many* summers ago. I didn't want to think about Bobby Lee. I was Birdy's wife. Thinking about Bobby Lee made my head hurt.

I pulled off my panties and searched inside the bag for a clean pair. I didn't find any. Did Birdy forget, or didn't I wear panties anymore? I took out the rest of the clothes and put them on the bed. I put the bra on first. It was some ugly nursing bra with plastic tabs that held the fabric closed until you pressed the tab, and then the front folded down and your breast jut forward the same as they did in those old advertisements for bras that gave women those pointed rocket ship kind.

The shirt wasn't much better. It didn't have a collapsible front, but it was brown and made out of some cheap fake silk fabric. I checked the label. Well that explained it. The label said Jaclyn Smith for Kmart. I don't know what was worse—the fact the shirt was meant for old ladies—or that it came from a place you could also purchase feminine douche and toilet paper. It hung shapeless on me, which may have been better than the alternative. But for the life of me, I couldn't figure out what to do with the long ties at the neck. A bow was silly, all limp and droopy, so I just let them hang straight down the front. At least that way it covered the lumpiness from that darn bra. The bra had all the smoothness of a bag of fire kindling. I shrugged on the jacket. It was too tight to close, so I left it open. It was from that same "collection," and was fake leopard with some of its spots rubbed off and a stain on the left elbow. Maybe the kids used it as a blanket and that's why it was all worn and faded, but that didn't explain why it was ugly.

Birdy bought me jeans to wear, and at least they fit. But they were maternity jeans with the elastic front panel, and the shirt and jacket weren't long enough to hide the seam. The shoes were brown cowboy boots, and from the newness of them, I wasn't much of a cowgirl.

At the very bottom of the bag was a red scrunchie hair band that even years ago was outdated. I threw it inside the trashcan next to the sink, along with the other things in the bag, a tube of dried-out mascara and a frosted pink lipstick that was either melted or eaten and chewed down to the plastic. God bless him, at least Birdy tried. I took out the hairbrush and went to the mirror above the sink to brush my hair.

What have you become, Savannah May?

A person I didn't recognize stared back at me in the mirror, forlorn and pitiful. This wasn't someone who got lost in a crowd; this was someone who couldn't even be found in a crowd. It was as if I had tried to make myself invisible.

My hair was longer than I remembered, almost midway down my back, but it hung limp as nylon stockings and without any style. The drab color made my blue eyes more gray than blue, and without makeup they were just plain ordinary eyes. Not the big cornflower blue ones people noticed, even those judges in the Miss Georgia Peach contest, where I heard one say they were my best attribute.

My body was thick, and yes, I had had a baby, but that baby was four months shy of a year, and there was no excuse not to be back in shape by now if I wanted. My cousin Lindsay Jo spit out five kids by the time she was twenty-seven, and she was thin and trim just as soon as those kids cut their first teeth. I pushed my shoulders back and stood up straight, the way I'd been taught back in cotillion classes and the way we practiced for the Miss Georgia Peach Queen pageant. Standing up tall, imagining a string pulling us up from the top of our heads, shoulders back and eyes straight ahead, so we'd look like real-life mannequins, but mostly so our tiaras wouldn't slip and ruin our big hair. Even standing tall, I was as far removed from beauty queen as a girl could get, but at least I didn't seem nearly so fat.

I leaned in closer to the mirror. Birdy was right. I suffered from sadness. There were dark circles under my eyes and small lines in the corners where the lashes ended. My face was drawn and tense, reminding me of Mama and the expression she got when I'd come home late, the few times she was home before me, and knowing something must have happened with me and Bobby because I was upset. Mama saying she'd never seen a couple fight nearly so much as we did, and asking what I did to make Bobby so mad at me all the time. I didn't feel sad right now. I felt tired and scared, and my head still hurt. But I wasn't sad. I lifted the brush and slowly began to brush my hair, mindful of the stitches and the shaved part covered by a bandage and the size of one of Zula's biscuits. By changing my

51

part to the other side and brushing it over, I was almost able to hide the bandage. I colored my cheeks pink by pinching them and lightly bit my lower lip to do the same, wetting them with the tip of my tongue to make them shiny.

I didn't hear the door open, but I sensed Birdy in the room, before he came to me, his arms closing around me with the comfort and warmth of a winter coat, and I saw his reflection in the mirror, standing behind me. He leaned his head down toward mine and kissed me on the neck, like it was natural and something he was used to doing, right below my ear, and so close I could feel his breath, hot and moist, and hear the catch to it in the back of his throat. He felt my body stiffen and immediately he broke free, stepping back and pushing his hands deep inside his pockets, as if he didn't trust himself not to touch me.

"I'm sorry, Birdy," I whispered, knowing I'd hurt him again. "You caught me by surprise, that's all. It's okay to touch me if you want," I spoke to his reflection in the mirror, nervously playing with the hairbrush, turning it over and over in my hand. "And I like your sunglasses," I added, trying to lessen the tension. They were a current trend and not those glasses with the black frames he'd worn since we were children.

"They're prescription," he said, his voice hoarse, and I could tell he was trying to hold his emotions together, bringing them back inside to bottle up, the way you'd bottle back up the honey by turning it the other way before replacing the cap. All this had to be hard for Birdy, who had four kids depending on him now that I was a nutcase of a mother. Or maybe I was always a nutcase, and now I was just a nutcase who couldn't remember crap.

I knew Birdy would keep back and make me go to him first. That's always been the Birdy way. In all our days together, and for those few times we kissed as teens, and then again that one time when he touched my breasts, it was me who started things. The time he felt my breasts it was because I made him. I took his hand and put it underneath my shirt and on top of my first bra, to prove to him I'd finally grown me a set. He touched the first side because *I* wanted him to, resting it there so still and long I felt the heat of his hand through the fabric of that new bra. But touching the second one was all Birdy's idea.

That was the only time I remember Birdy touching me in any way sexual, and even then, it wasn't so much sexual as it was educational. Either the man was made of stone, or he had the strongest willpower of any man I'd ever met. Not that I can say I've many to compare with. With the exception of Bobby Lee, who doesn't have much restraint to speak of, I've never been with another.

I turned around and crossed the distance between us, hugging Birdy tight, my arms going around the inside of his jacket, and resting my head against his heart, hearing its strong beat. Hugging Birdy was familiar and comforting, bringing with it a flash of a recent memory that quickly extinguished.

Birdy folded his body around mine, and he moaned a sound deep inside, his heart hammering between us. "Oh, baby, I've missed you." His hands worked their way inside the back of my shirt and he touched my bare skin, before moving them lower and cupping my backside, bringing me in closer to his thighs, his leg coming in between mine.

"Birdy—"

His mouth found mine, silencing me, and he kissed me hard, his tongue seeking mine.

"Birdy! No." I used both my hands to push him away.

"Savannah, but I thought …" His voice trailed off and he broke free, taking two steps back, his brows together in confusion.

"I wanted to hug you, Birdy. You know? Same way I always did. You need to take this slow. I need to have time to get used to us. In my mind, the last tongue kiss I had was with Bobby Lee."

Immediately I knew I'd made a terrible mistake.

Birdy twisted his body sharp to the right, his face rigid with anger, and he barreled his tight fist into the wall, denting the sheetrock and making such a noise a nurse busted through the door to see what happened, throwing her charts aside on the unmade bed.

"What in Lord's name is going on in here?" She went over to Birdy, who held his fist in his other hand, his body heaving. "Boy, let me see your hand." Birdy shook his hand, scattering blood all over the floor and the wall in crimson drops. "Here," she demanded, wetting a towel before pulling Birdy's hand and wrapping it around it to stop the bleeding. "Mr. Johnson, I don't know what's eating you, son, but you're going to have to pay for the repair of that wall, and the bill to have your hand x-rayed."

"I'm fine." Birdy pulled his hand away, but one balled fist and one bloodied one proved he wasn't fine. The nurse left the room, shaking her head and mumbling under her breath that she needed a new job.

I struggled, trying to catch my breath. Something about what Birdy had done gave shape to the shadows. A feeling as strong as a river undercurrent pulled me to a dark place. Sounds, loud as a cacophony assaulted my ears, and I covered them to stop the noise. I sank to the floor, choking on a sob.

"No! Savannah. I'm sorry." Birdy got down on the floor beside me, crouching down next to me, uncertain whether to touch me or not. "Don't cry. I'm sorry I lost my temper. Savannah, don't cry."

I felt dizzy and sick to my stomach, faint, as if I was free falling from the light and back into the darkness from which I had emerged. I leaned over and emptied my stomach all over that dirty floor, heaving and retching until there was nothing left. With tears filling my eyes, I whispered, "Catch me, Birdy." I fell into Birdy's arms, not in a faint, but in surrender.

Birdy stretched out on the floor beside me and pulled me onto his lap. He smelled clean, of soap and the outdoors, trees and the air, and maybe a little of the dirt. Not the dirty dirt, the way those nasty Ellory kids smelled, because the family was too poor or too stupid to use soap to wash with, but earth dirt, the same way the lane up to my house smelled in the summer when the sun shined down and before it got so hot you'd be sweaty and sticky and in need of a shower.

"I'm here for you, Savannah May," he whispered, pulling me close. "We're in this thing together. We'll take it as slow as you want. I waited over twenty years for you to be mine, and I reckon I can wait some more, if that's what it takes to keep you." He held me until I relaxed against him, resting his head on the unhurt side of mine, breathing in my smell, from the sound of it. Once I was calm, he moved me to the bed and cleaned my mess as best as he could, coming back to gather me in his arms again, holding me as if he couldn't get enough, rocking me like a child. I have to imagine he'd had some practice from holding all those kids.

We didn't know the doctor came into the room until he cleared his throat, standing behind us. "Mrs. Johnson, you're free to go." Birdy lifted me up in his arms and stood. "You can set her down, Mr. Johnson. The nurse will wheel her out to the curb while you get the car. It's hospital policy." He flipped through pages of my chart, making notes.

Birdy set me down, but held my hand tight. I asked Birdy to catch me, and he wasn't letting me go, taking my request literally.

"You have an appointment in three days with the psychiatrist," the doctor said, handing some forms to Birdy to sign for my release. Birdy took the papers and quickly scanned them, a half-smile playing on his lips when he read something he found funny, before signing them and handing them back the doctor. "My opinion is your memory should return, but you're in Dr. Stanley's care now. He seems to feel your past bouts of postpartum depression may be somewhat to blame. But that's his area of expertise, not mine." He pulled off his copies of the forms and gave the rest to Birdy. "Good luck, Mrs. Johnson. Mr. Johnson," he said, nodding at Birdy.

"Thank you, doctor. I'd shake your hand, but I had a run-in with the wall." Birdy's hand was cut and starting to swell, but the bleeding was less, and so far it didn't seem broken.

"I see that. Well, good luck to you both." He turned and left the room.

I let go of Birdy's hand and took the papers from him, adding them to my growing pile of things to take home— flowers from Mama and Daddy, and some pictures done by Birdy's kids. *My kids*. Pictures of flowers and the sun and some raggedy scarecrows. It was us, Birdy said, and there was a hog standing next to us in the drawing, but Birdy said it was supposed to be our dog, Moonshine. We didn't own a hog. Our development wasn't zoned for farm animals, he told me.

"Are you ready?" Birdy said, offering me his hand.

"As ready as I'll ever be, Mr. Johnson."

CHAPTER SIX

"A school bus!" I shouted at Birdy as he pulled up to the side of the hospital loading zone in a yellow bus, complete with all the markings, just as I was ready to wheel myself right back inside that hospital until Birdy could come get me a vehicle that wouldn't make me the laughingstock of Atlanta and the entire state of Georgia. "You came to pick me up in a school bus?" And it wasn't even one complete bus; instead, it was one of the short yellow ones the special education kids rode on, the kids who wore helmets and such.

The air brakes hissed, and Birdy put the bus in park, opening the door with some manual lever, before stepping down the few steps and coming to stand in front of me.

"I am not getting into that bus, Birdy Johnson! What on earth are you thinking? Do we not own a car?" I glared at him, hoping this wasn't a sign of things to come.

The nurse navigated the wheelchair to the curb. "Here you go, darlin'. Don't forget your things." She handed me my flowers in a glass vase, and my brown sack.

I refused to get up.

"Savannah, get up," Birdy demanded.

"No! I am going to sit right here until you call me a cab or send Mama and Daddy to come get me in their car. I am not going to ride through the streets of Atlanta on a short bus." I folded my arms across my chest while the nurse waited, not knowing what to do. She couldn't very well pitch me out of the wheelchair and onto the sidewalk.

"Savannah, get in the bus. I'll explain it to you on the way home." Birdy sighed and took the bag and the flowers out of my hands, and he went inside the bus to put them on one of the green vinyl seats in the front row.

"Mrs. Johnson, I really need to get back inside now. If you'll please get up—"

"No!"

"*Savannah* …" Birdy's voice was so low I knew it meant he was hot mad. When Birdy was mad, his voice got softer, so soft sometimes it was a struggle to hear him.

"Oh, all right then!" I got up and climbed the steps of the Magnolia Montessori school bus, stomping my way to the back row and down the middle as far away from Birdy as I could get without walking my way back home. Which would have been tough because I had no clue where we lived.

Birdy closed the door and released the brakes. "We'll be stopping at all railroad crossings," he joked, trying to make me smile.

I ignored his attempt at humor. "You wonder why I'm sad, Birdy?" I yelled out to him, my eyes scanning the interior of that vehicle, the torn seats and the peeling paint with the scribbling and the who-knows-what smeared beside it. "Well, this bus might be a clue!" Birdy suddenly slammed on the brake, and I pitched forward, almost falling out into the middle of the aisle.

I think he did it on purpose. I righted myself and yelled up, "Where is my Mustang?"

"Sorry," he called back. "It's safer if you sit on the sides. That way, the seat in front of you will protect you from impact if we get in a wreck."

I didn't answer, but moved over a bit in case he was right. "What have you done with my car?"

"Savannah, come sit up here closer to me. I can hardly hear you from back there." Birdy shifted gears.

"Fine," I muttered under my breath and held onto the seats while I walked back up to the front of the bus. I sat down in the seat behind Birdy and on top of some sticky stuff, probably kid snot or gum, and unstuck myself, moving over a few inches.

"I can tell you're mad—"

"No shit."

"Your Mustang is in our garage, safe under a car cover." Birdy spoke to me in tones you'd use with a small child, or a helmet-wearing older one. "We don't use it much because it's too small for the family." He watched me in the rearview mirror in between his glances at the road. "I still have the old Chevy truck, which also won't fit all of us, and right now it's in the shop getting the engine overhauled. And we have the rig," he added. "I didn't think you'd be too happy to see me pull up in that." Birdy came to a railroad crossing and actually did stop the bus just short of the tracks, opening the door and looking both ways before continuing. "And the reason we have this bus," he paused, regarding me in the mirror and holding my gaze for a second, "is because I drive it part-time for Magnolia Montessori, so our kids can attend school there for free."

I threw back my head in defeat, hitting it on the seat bar behind me and making my eyes sting. Something didn't make any sense. I think I recall I had a trust fund set aside for me. In fact, I was fairly certain I was rich. Not celebrity rich. Not famous-for-doing-nothing rich, but rich enough to afford a car and a decent house. I could even recall the fight my parents had with my Granny Ellie about my trust, the year it was set up, when I turned eighteen. Granny Ellie wanted me to have my money when I turned twenty-one, but Mama said I was too irresponsible and I needed to wait until I was thirty and had some sense in me.

"I'm twenty-seven now, is that right, Birdy?" I spoke to Birdy's reflection in the mirror above him. It was so long it ran almost the length of the window and reflected all the seats behind him to the last row.

Birdy seemed startled by the question. It's not every day a person has to be reminded of their age, and my question threw him off guard. Then his expression smoothed, and he replied, "Yep. You're twenty-seven. Same as me."

"Is my Granny Ellie still alive?"

"Yes, she is. She's old." He hit the blinker and changed lanes, merging onto the interstate. "But she's still sassy. Your mama put her in Shady Oaks about five years back. She likes it just fine there. She has friends. Although most weeks one of them dies."

That was the answer. I'd go to my Granny Ellie and tell her I needed to have access to my trust. I'm sure Granny Ellie would agree Birdy and I needed my money now, assuming Granny wasn't senile and demented, which she may well be. A lot can happen in seven years. A husband and four kids—*a lot*.

I could see why my daddy and mama wouldn't give me the money. Daddy, he was poor when he was growing up, and believes a man needs to make his own way. He's probably tickled pink I married poor Birdy Johnson and not rich Bobby Lee Thomas. Besides, Daddy never did much care for Bobby Lee, not that it mattered, because my mama thought Bobby was handsome, and she admired his family, and that was enough. Daddy thought Bobby Lee was spoiled rotten and couldn't hold his liquor. Although he told that to Mama and not to me. It just so happened I was on the other side of the door and overheard the conversation when he said it. We were all underage and not supposed to be drinking anyway, so our parents pretended not to know we drank. Or if they knew, they never said anything about it. Just the same way Mama never talked to me about birth control. It was like that military saying about gays: "Don't Ask, Don't Tell." Mama didn't ask, and I didn't tell. Some things you just have to figure out on your own.

We had money ever since I can remember, and I know Mama's family had lots of it, because Granny's house was even bigger than ours, and it sat on ten-plus acres surrounded on all sides by water, some crazy canal thing that resembled a moat. Although Granny says that's plain stupid talking, it's just decorative water, and I need to stop reading so many of those old stories about knights and castles. It's Yankee money that got Granny her house, according to Daddy. And I'm pretty sure he says it as a joke.

These days, people my age could not care less who lives north or south of the Mason-Dixon Line. If we'd have our way, we'd all live out West, in California, near Hollywood or Beverly Hills, or East, in New York City. Or if you're into country music and have a decent voice and a shot at success, out in Nashville, waiting to be discovered. The kids I know who went there are still waiting—on tables mostly, at the Golden Buffet Corral and Grill, serving up the fried chicken and pot roast, except on Mexican food night, when it's tacos and enchiladas.

My daddy, he put himself through college and got a business degree and started investing in commodities: corn and cotton shares, and even though it's now a world of synthetics, same as this ugly shirt I was wearing, there was plenty of money to be made in cotton years ago. Now, Daddy says, not so much. This might explain why Daddy took the money and ran, and now is retired and living in Florida and wears clothes you see in advertisements for J. Crew, and not on real people. Or not on the real people we know at the country club.

Birdy pulled that old bus onto the interstate, taking the lane heading toward the direction of the airport. The bus sped up to keep with the flow of traffic best as it could, and the wind blew inside my window, catching my hair and those ties on my blouse, covering my face so I couldn't see a thing.

"Roll up the window!" I shouted to Birdy, gathering my hair and holding it in my hand.

"They don't roll. You'll need to stand and pull them up."

"Ugh!" I struggled to pull up the window. After I figured out how to lock it shut, I sat back down, folding my hands across my chest, feeling it begin to tighten—full and warm with milk—and tried to calm myself. In just a bit, I'd be nursing some strange baby and see the three other children who were mine—that I could not recall to save my life.

Part of me thought this was some sort of terrible joke and wanted to leap out of the emergency door exit of that bus the first full stop it came to and run off and find my way to Bobby Lee and the life I remembered, and then kick his butt for playing this joke on me. The other part of me, the part with the brown hair covered in stitches and bandages and a body ruined from babies, considered what Birdy said was true, that I was his wife and the mother of four children, and living in a three-bedroom house not far from the Atlanta airport, if the signs were any indication.

How could this happen? *Why did it happen?*

I stayed quiet for the rest of the ride, and Birdy did the same. Not that I expected much different. Birdy says what needs to be said and he doesn't bother much with the non-essential stuff. Not that I ever minded. Bobby Lee always said I talked enough for the three of us and would tell me to shut up when he'd had enough. Not Birdy, though. Birdy always told me he liked the sound of my voice, and sometimes he'd call me up on the phone just to hear me say hi. But he'd have to do it in secret, when his daddy was away at work or out at the bar, which was often enough, because his daddy wouldn't let him use the house phone, and Birdy never owned a cell phone the way the rest of us did. After his daddy died, he got to call more often, because his aunt who came to stay with him, she didn't care if he talked all night on the phone or not.

I stared out the window, watching the cars drive by, but not seeing, and tried to imagine what my children looked like. I knew the baby resembled me, but I had no idea who the twins or our boy took after. And come to think of it, with so much going on, I'd forgotten to ask their names. What a terrible person I'd become. First, some sad bust-out beauty queen who let go of her good looks and kept spitting out all those babies, and now, a girl who couldn't remember the past seven years of her life.

Birdy turned off the road at the exit. We passed an old hardware store, a newly built pharmacy, and a truck stop complete with restaurant and showers and diesel fuel at $2.35 a gallon, according to the big neon sign. It was probably the one my truck driver husband frequented, and might even have showered at if he weren't married to me and living in a terrific three-bedroom home with indoor plumbing in some old subdivision I'd never heard of.

Deep Creek, read the sign on the first street where Birdy turned right.

I read the sign aloud. "So far, that sign pretty much sums things up." I wasn't smiling, and neither was Birdy.

Birdy made a right at Hillcrest and then another at Rocky Road, where that sign, on the opposite side of the street read "Dead End." I almost laughed. We had arrived. I lived at 1313 Rocky Road, less than ten minutes from the Atlanta airport and miles away and another world from where I used to live. Instead of living in a beautiful home belonging to my granny's family for generations, I now lived on a dead-end street near some dangerous deep creek, where there were few trees in front, mostly rock—if the sign was correct—and row after row of houses that were alike, some more tired than others. If you came home drunk, there was a good chance you'd find yourself in your neighbor's bed sleeping next to your neighbor's wife, until the sun came up and you got a second glance.

Gone was the town of my birth, with long lanes of leafy trees covered in Spanish moss that hung and dripped like cotton candy and wispy as lace, or acres of sloping hills and white fences that held horses running free and separated the big houses and mansions with their stone and brick facades.

The bus pulled into the driveway of a low-mortgage house and behind a Kenworth tractor-trailer parked on the cement part of the driveway with half of the wheels, nine of them I suppose, on dirt that ran alongside the house to the left where the property ended and a field began. And not a pretty field of wildflowers, but a gnarly field of weeds and scramblers.

The house wasn't going to win any awards, but in fairness to Birdy, neither was it immediately in need of a bulldozer to level it, the way those rotting dumps needed on that home makeover show on TV. The show with that obnoxious guy yelling into a megaphone for the people to wake up, and where the family always had those children with the mysterious lung diseases or husbands in a wheelchair that couldn't fit through the door of the trailer.

"You okay? You still mad?" Birdy asked, watching me in the mirror. "Or are you madder now that you're home and you've seen it?"

I tried to be objective. The house wasn't hillbilly poor. At least that was good. It was a single-story with a small front porch complete with a wooden rocking chair and a wreath on the front door that said "Welcome." The front of it was white vinyl siding with some brick at the bottom—real or fake, I couldn't tell from where I sat on the bus—and it had a black asphalt shingle roof that was newer than the house, so I could assume the roof wasn't ready to fall in. And the reason I'm so smart about building materials is from all the time I spent hanging around the lumberyard with Bobby Lee at his daddy's place.

Mr. Thomas would take me up and down all the aisles, pointing out all of the different types of materials, even going so far as to quiz me on some things. He'd say, "Savannah, someday this will all belong to you and Bobby Lee, and one of you needs to know which end is up or this business will never survive." Mr. Thomas never thought Bobby Lee was the sharpest tool in the shed, and that's exactly what he'd said. He said, "Savannah May, I love my son, but that boy is not the sharpest tool in the shed." And then he told me it was going to be up to me to keep the business going after he died, and we needed to have sons so we wouldn't have to change out the sign.

Birdy cut the engine and pocketed the keys, standing up and waiting for me to do the same. He held out his hand, his palm trembling just a bit, waiting for me to take it.

I couldn't accept his hand. I sat there, my eyes filling with tears, and shook my head no. I wasn't ready for this. You can't suddenly go from nothing to something. You can't go from being a girl to being a woman with children, in a day. Even a pregnant girl has nine months to get used to the idea before that idea becomes form. Nine months to adjust to the thought there would soon be a tiny living person she was responsible for. To love and to keep safe from harm. Not days—not hours—in which to wrap your broken mind around the fact you have not one life depending on you, but four. Assuming Birdy could take care of himself, or it would be five. Five lives depending on me.

I felt sick to my stomach, my insides rolled and twisted. There was no way I could do this. I shook my head no. "No! Birdy, I can't! I can't do this. How can I act as if I know them when I don't?" I held onto the metal bar in front of my seat for support, my fingers wrapped tight around the metal, gripping it so tight my knuckles whitened. "I don't know them!" I cried, breathing air in gulps, trying to calm myself, wanting to stay inside that bus, or better yet, drive far away from that house that was supposed to be my home, the home I shared with Birdy and my children. Children I had no memory of giving birth to. "What kind of mother doesn't remember her own children?" I moaned into my hands, my shoulders heaving. "I'm not capable of being a wife and a mother." I raised my head. "I can't cook or clean or sew. According to Bobby Lee, I'm not even a decent girlfriend," I said, blurring my present with my past.

Birdy struggled for composure at the mention of Bobby Lee. His breathing grew ragged, and he tightened his fists, breaking open the cut on his right hand, the blood trickling down over the knuckles. Birdy went still, and then his shoulders relaxed, his face adjusting itself. He knelt down on his knees in front of me, brushing the hair back from my face and pushing my tears aside.

"Breathe, Savannah. Just breathe," he said, doing the same. "Look at me," he softly commanded. "It's me, Savannah. It's still me. Older than you remember, but still same as ever. The same as when we were kids. You know me, right?" I nodded. "We're still the same people. It's still us, Savannah and Birdy— best friends forever. Remember? That's what you said. Best friends forever. Just breathe." I felt him taking the air deep in his lungs, and I matched him breath for breath for sixty seconds or so until I felt some of the tension slip away. "Better?" he asked, tucking a lock of hair behind my ear, compassion etched in the lines at the corner of his tired eyes.

"Yes."

"You can do this," Birdy said, I think trying to convince himself it was true. "Whether you remember them or not, they are your children and they love you. They love you so much, Savannah. And you are going to need to pretend you love them, too. At least until you feel it again. Do you understand me? You need to pretend that you love them." He took my hands in his. "You can do this, Savannah. I know you can. You can do this."

I took another deep breath and straightened my shoulders. Birdy was right. They were my children, and a part of me. It was easy enough to love my dog and my horses, and I didn't give birth to them. Surely, this would be the same.

The door to the house opened and an attractive teenage girl with blond hair and holding a baby waved from the doorway. Behind her, I saw two young girls hovering close to her side, but they were too far away for me to see clearly.

"That's Becky Lou. She lives on the corner," Birdy said, answering before I could ask, and standing back up. "She's been staying here while you've been in the hospital, and she helps out with the kids when you have your spells." Birdy put his hands in his pockets and nervously glanced at me, and then at the house, and the pretty girl with our kids.

"My spells?"

"Your sad spells. The times you take to bed and don't come out. For days, sometimes. But since Anna, things have been mostly good."

"Oh, Birdy," I sighed, and put my head down again on the railing within the circle of my arms. "What kind of miserable life have I given you?" I shut my eyes.

I heard the baby start to cry from the front porch, a sound not much louder than the mew of a kitten or the coo of a dove, and immediately my milk let down. Big wet circles radiated out, and milk coursed down the front of my shirt. My chest suddenly ached for release, throbbing, it hurt so much. I dipped my head in despair.

"It's time, Savannah. I believe it's time." He reached out his right hand and took it firmly in his, knotting our fingers together. "I'm here," he softly said, facing me, his expression kind. "I know enough for the two of us. I promise."

"And I'm holding you to that promise." I wiped my eyes with my free hand.

Birdy took the first step down, and I followed behind.

We exited the bus and walked the length of the driveway, beyond the one-car garage where Birdy said my car—my only link to my past—was safe inside, and over the brown front lawn and up the steps of the porch, to the front door where Becky Lou stood holding my baby.

I may not have recognized my child, but my child recognized me. That pretty baby in the lilac print dress and pink socks smiled and started fussing, her body leaning toward me, her arms outstretched, and her sweet mouth opening and closing, making baby noises. Not words, just sounds. Birdy reached for her, giving her a quick kiss, and then he handed her to me, where she started to nuzzle the front of my brown shirt, rooting for my breasts, her little mouth searching to find me.

"She's hungry, Mrs. Johnson. I gave her some strained pears about an hour ago, but she's hungry again." Becky Lou smiled at me. "And welcome home. I'm glad you're better. Aren't we girls?" The girls hovered behind her, and she pulled them forward with an arm around each of them.

"Come say hello to your mama. She's better now. Come on," Birdy encouraged, "she won't bite."

I hugged Anna close to me, same way as I would a load of laundry, and maybe a bit too close, because she started to fuss and wiggle, and make gaspy sounds, so it could be I was suffocating the child. Birdy leaned toward me and took her out of my arms, trying to soothe her, as the twins stepped forward.

My breath caught, and feelings I am too ashamed to admit to flooded through me. Mean, hurtful things one would never say aloud, and certainly not things one should think about their own children. If indeed, these children were mine.

They were identical girls, with red hair and freckles jumping out all over their faces, reminding me of chocolate sprinkles on a vanilla cone. They looked nothing like me, or Birdy. In fact, they were the spitting image of that Wendy girl in the hamburger advertisements. Only their orange-red hair was in braids, and not pigtails. And oh, dear Lord, they were missing some teeth.

My worst nightmare had come true.

It was all Birdy's fault! His, and that trashy daddy from the hills of Tennessee who never went to school past the ninth grade and probably was the result of intermarriage with a sibling. Those girls must take after someone from the Johnson side. The only thing that resembled me were their blue eyes, but only the color of the eyeballs, and not the whole eyes themselves, because my eyelashes are dark, not missing, the way they were on these girls. Or maybe they had eyelashes and they were blond and just hard to see.

"Hi," I said, struggling to regain my composure, trying to play this terrible charade. I forced a smiled and bent down so

I'd be more on their level and noticed their clothes seemed homemade, and poorly made, at that. "Mama's been in the hospital and hurt her head, so it's hard for her to remember things. You're going to have to help her, okay?" I said, speaking in the third person for no real reason that makes any sense.

"Okay," one of the two said, while the other shook her head up and down, her expression dimwitted. Could be she was scared, and my shock was overriding my intellect, giving me a prejudicial inclination.

I straightened up and whispered at Birdy, "*You never told me their names.*"

"Girls, tell your mama your names," he instructed, bouncing Anna in his arms, quieting her cries with the practiced ease that come with years of repetition.

"I'm Minnie Ray," said one.

"And I'm Minnie May," said the other.

I wanted to shoot myself. The hillbilly horror was never ending.

The babysitter watched, her smile fading, sensing my discomfort, and she turned and spoke to my son who must have been standing behind her and the twins. "It's all right, Cody. You can come out now. Your daddy's home. Your mama, too. Come on out and say hi."

Cody. At least his was a normal sounding name, but I was still going to light into Birdy just as soon as I was inside and out of earshot of those kids.

A little boy, the spitting image of Birdy, with dark hair, brown eyes, and wearing black glasses, same as Birdy's, only smaller, came out from behind his sisters. He had his head down in that same shy way I remember Birdy doing all of those years back, and he wouldn't tilt his head up at me until I leaned down and put my finger under his chin to raise it.

"Cody, darlin', it's your mama." I gently lifted his head.

Poor little Cody stared at me, his one good eye, and the lazy one too, filling with tears.

The baby started to wail, Cody began to cry, the girls joined in, and I totally lost it. The only people not crying were Birdy and the babysitter, but pushing my way past her and heading inside the house, it seemed to me Becky Lou was tearing up too, so I guess that only left Birdy not crying and carrying on with all of the Johnson family and the neighbor girl.

I stumbled across the living room and down the hallway, throwing open the first door I came to. It held a crib painted yellow and a plywood youth bed in the shape of a racecar. I left the door open and yanked on the next. That room held only a white bunk bed and a dresser, with a rickety chair in the corner missing a spindle, and the entire room was smaller than my bedroom closet on Scarlet Oak Road. I ran to the end of the hallway, a distance the length of that small bus.

"Savannah!" Birdy called, as I tore into what must have been our master bedroom, with a queen-sized bed covered in a quilt my Granny Ellie made for me for my tenth birthday, and a double dresser against the wall. I collapsed onto the bed, tears falling, mixing with the milk, sobbing and rocking, and wishing I were back home, back in my big house with my mama and daddy. "Savannah," Birdy said, sitting down on the bed beside me and putting his hand on my knee.

"Don't you touch me! Don't you dare touch me."

"What? I … I don't understand." Birdy got off the bed and stood in front of me, his face tight with emotion, glancing back over his shoulder at the closed door, hearing Anna wail. "You're scaring those kids, Savannah. They've been through enough. They don't need any more. You hear me?"

"How *could* you name those girls Minnie!" I shrieked at him, "That hick name after that old *Hee Haw* woman from Tennessee? And those girls have no teeth! Have you no shame? Are we so poor we can't afford dental insurance? And that poor boy, Cody. Is there nothing to be done to fix his eye? Surgery or something? Are you so proud you won't let me work or go to my family for some help?" I pulled up the comforter and held it to my face, remembering better times. A better place.

Birdy turned to leave the room. "I'm going to get Dolly. She needs to be fed," Birdy said, his voice low and deep. "*By you,*" he said, deeper still, and just as angry with me as I was with him. He slammed the door, and I heard his feet walk down the laminate fake-grained wood flooring of the short hallway and into the front room to fetch Anna from the sitter.

"Unbutton your shirt," Birdy commanded when he was back in the room with Anna, who reached for me, her face as wet with tears as mine, and hiccupping only slightly less.

"Birdy … I …" I stared up at him, helplessly.

"Dammit, Savannah. If a blind hog can do this, you can, too. Now do right by this baby and feed her." He handed me Anna and then started to unbutton my blouse to get things moving quicker.

I may have been clueless, but Anna knew just what to do. She went at my breast, clamping her little mouth around my swollen nipple and pulling hard with a sucking motion, the milk filling her mouth and some spilling just a bit around the sides. After the initial shock, it didn't feel so bad. Truth told, it felt good. Not sexual good. But good as in releasing the pain and emptying them, so they didn't hurt nearly so much. After she drank her fill of the one, Birdy told me to switch to the other, and then he taught me how to burp her by sitting her on my lap and rubbing her back until she burped. Which she did, and made me laugh, and then she laughed too, looking just like a little doll. A dolly.

"You ready to listen to me?" Birdy asked, now that I wasn't crying and in so much pain.

"Yes." Anna fell asleep in my arms. I rocked while Birdy talked.

He sat next to me on our bed, stoking Anna's face with a finger while she slept. "Our daughters are not named after Minnie Pearl. Their names are Melissa Ray, who was born first, and Emma May, who was born four minutes later. *You* were the one who nicknamed them Mini, because they were so little when they were born. And you spell it: M-i-n-i, same as Mini Cooper, the car, not Minnie with an e, like Pearl or the mouse." Birdy moved his finger to touch Anna's little hand, and she stirred and opened her fist, holding on tight to Birdy's finger before falling back asleep. He watched her for a moment, his face flooding with emotion—love, I think—and let her hold his finger while he continued.

"We have dental insurance, and those girls' teeth are just fine. They're better than fine. The minis have never had a cavity in their life. They're six years old, Savannah, and that's what happens when kids turn six. They lose their baby teeth. I'm sure their new teeth will be just as nice as yours or mine when they come in."

Birdy may have been poor, and only to the dentist a few times in his entire life, but he had perfect teeth, white and straight, and never once had a cavity. Unlike me, with nice straight teeth, but whose parents spent a fortune on bleaching and fillings that were white and expensive, instead of having the more affordable silver ones.

"But Birdy, those girls don't resemble either of us. Red hair? Freckles? Are you sure they came out of me?" Anna moved, and I gently rocked her from side to side. I still didn't feel that rush of love I'd heard so much about and that thing called "maternal bonding," but holding her in my arms gave me a nice feeling. I bent my head and kissed her on the forehead, inhaling her baby scent, the same way you bend your head down to smell the bouquet of flowers someone hands you.

"I'm sure. I was there the whole time. Holding your hand and helping you through it. You did fine, if you were wondering."

I wasn't, but it was nice that he said it.

"And Cody? Isn't there anything that can be done for him? That eye. And does he talk? Is there something else wrong with him?"

"Cody, he's just got weak eyes, that's all. Got 'em from me, I guess. The doctor had him wear a patch on the one for a year, hoping to strengthen the bad one. Poor boy got teased something terrible. That might be why he don't say much. He talks some. I'm sure he'll talk plenty when he has something important to say." Birdy continued to sit, staring at our daughter while she slept, watching her with adoring eyes.

"What about surgery? I know there's surgery to help correct things like this. I have a cousin who had the surgery. And his eye came out as straight as could be and people quit callin' him crab eye."

"Yes, but it's expensive, and that's insurance we don't have. The doctor said to try the glasses first, and if it don't work, we can do the surgery. I've been taking some shifts over at the feed store between driving loads with the rig, to help save up, but with you being sick and me needing to be home for the kids, and now the accident, well, we don't have too much left over each month." Birdy let go of Anna's hand and touched my hair, his hand trailing down its length, and then took off his glasses and rubbed his eyes, moist with emotion. "I'm sorry, Savannah. I said it once, and I reckon' I'll be saying it again. You married poor Birdy Johnson, and I know you deserved more."

Birdy got up and left the room without a backward glance.

CHAPTER SEVEN

I can do this. If an eighteen-year-old recent high school grad can do it, so can I. And if I said it to myself enough times, maybe I'd start to believe it.

Birdy sent Becky Lou home after she helped fix supper, washed and dried the dishes, and then gave the kids a bath and got them ready for bed. He handed her some money and offered to walk her home. I don't know why. The walk part, not the money, the money was well deserved. She only lives four doors down and across the street, but maybe this subdivision is in a dangerous part of town. It may not be safe to cross the street after dark. I didn't want to consider there might be another reason Birdy wanted to walk her home. She didn't wear makeup, and her clothes were probably from a discount store, not that I could talk, but she had a nice slim figure, much nicer than mine, and green eyes with gold flecks, and thick naturally blond hair that fell below her shoulders, with some wave to it, not limp and straight the way mine was.

I watched Becky Lou and Birdy before Becky left to go home, and the way they acted together. I sat in the cheaply paneled front room on a navy blue sofa with toss pillows with boats and oars on them, and I watched. I watched the two of them cooking supper together, stirring side by side, and handing each other the spices, like an old married couple. Only difference is, she called him Mister Johnson, and he called her Becky Lou. Except for the one time when he called her "darlin'," and then caught himself and saw me staring and he flushed red. Becky Lou and Birdy moved about the kitchen together in a manner that proved it was something they'd done many times before.

Becky Lou knew where the pots and pans were, the salt, the cheese, and all of Anna's baby food. She showed Birdy her surprise for him, that she had arranged the food alphabetically in our cupboard so he could find them easier. Apples, bananas, carrots, corn … with all the labels pointing out. I wouldn't even know what to buy for a baby much less think to alphabetize the cans. When Becky Lou showed Birdy what she'd done, he smiled wide, the first time I'd seen him smile that way in forever, maybe even counting when we were kids, and he thanked her, and then, accidentally or not, he touched her on the bare arm. I say accidentally because Birdy kept stirring the pot, and his color didn't change, but Becky Lou, she flushed pink and then got the casserole out of the oven, her hands shaking so much she almost dropped the dish, peering up at Birdy from beneath her long eyelashes every chance she got, and subconsciously licking her lips in anticipation of the meal. Or something more.

It was strange to be sitting there on that sofa, in a room I didn't remember, watching Birdy and the babysitter, and all our children clustering around her, calling out her name and begging for her attention. And Becky Lou, still a child herself, handling them all as if she'd been doing it all her life. Birdy told me she had, since she has five younger brothers and sisters she helps with because she has no daddy. Just a mama, who works most days. That's the only thing that took away some of the sting of watching them together—cooking and cleaning and being a family—was knowing Becky Lou had plenty of practice. I couldn't quite tell if it was jealousy I was feeling or not, since I only remembered Birdy as my friend and not my husband, but I felt flushed, and my heart started to beat quicker, trying to tell me something. My children clustered around her like chicks to a hen, and they might as well have belonged to her and Birdy, and I just came by to visit, same way as some annoying Jehovah Witness they let inside the house, just to be nice.

I didn't eat dinner with them. I wasn't hungry, and no one seemed to miss me, although Birdy did try to get me to come join them, but I told him my head hurt and I needed to rest, and he didn't press me. He kissed me on the cheek and then went to sit at his place at the supper table with Becky Lou next to him, in my place, I'd guess, and next to her the baby in her highchair, and across from them, the minis, and Cody, who still hadn't said a word.

"She's pretty. Don't you think so, Birdy?" I said, after Birdy came home from walking Becky home. I sat on the sofa, fidgety and nervous, and dying for a beer, but was told earlier by the eighteen-year-old *babysitter* nursing mothers were not supposed to drink because the alcohol gets mixed in with the milk, and it's bad for the baby. Something I would never stop to consider.

All our children, and my, did we seem to have many—so many our little house was spilling with them—were in their beds. Not asleep, except for the baby, because I'd fed her and then handed her off to Becky Lou before she left so she could do the rest, but reading or talking or doing whatever it is children do at night when they have parents too poor to afford a television set for their bedrooms.

Birdy kicked off his work boots and neatly arranged them in the row by the front door, next to the kids' shoes. I don't know if there was a rule shoes were not allowed to be worn in the house, or that Birdy was just proud to show off we were a family who owned a whole mess of them, since where he came from in Tennessee, shoes were hard to come by, and you only got one or two new pairs a year. Unless a family member died and you wore the same size, then you got your pick of the lot, according to Birdy. Bobby Lee said I was an ass to believe Birdy, and that Birdy was pulling my leg. Walmart is everywhere, Bobby said, and even poor folks can buy themselves some shoes.

"Birdy, I asked you a question. Do you think Becky is pretty?"

"Don't start, Savannah," Birdy said, sighing with exhaustion. There were dark hollows under his eyes, and he needed a shave. "That girl is eighteen, and she's been helping us out since the year she turned twelve. You were at her high school graduation less than four months ago, and it was you who gave her a sweet-sixteen birthday party." Birdy sat down next to me on the sofa and put his feet up on the coffee table, a wicker basket of sorts, with a lid. "You cold?" He opened the lid and handed me a fleece blanket with a picture of a lighthouse on it. I wasn't especially cold, but I felt a coldness coming off Birdy. I think he was mad at me for something.

Birdy collapsed back on the sofa and unbuttoned the first few buttons on his flannel shirt. From what I could see, he had some hair on his chest with muscles beneath them. He took off his glasses and tossed them on top of the basket.

I gathered the blanket around me. The ugly shirt I'd been wearing had since been discarded, and I still wore the maternity jeans, but with an old T-shirt of Birdy's I'd found in a drawer that read *Built Ford Tough*. I wasn't wearing a bra and still had on my boots. No one thought to tell me yet that shoes weren't allowed in my house. That's probably because you always let the door-to-door salesmen, the evangelist, and the repair people keep on their shoes, the total strangers who come into your home.

"Birdy, that girl is sweet on you. Trust me. I know these things."

Birdy opened his eyes and sat up straighter, leaning toward me about half a foot from my face, a spark of something in his eyes I couldn't quite read. "And how is it," he began, "you know that in the short time you've been home? In the time that you found it, too …" Birdy searched for the right word, "*inconvenient*," he stressed, "to be a part of your family?"

Some ugly cuckoo clock on the wall behind me chimed the hour.

Anger born of my fear and frustration unleashed. All of the anxiousness and the apprehension of the afternoon forced down deep inside me bubbled up and exploded.

"*Inconvenient?*" I shouted at Birdy, throwing off the blanket and getting up from the sofa, standing in front of him, pushing his chest with my hands. "Birdy Johnson, you think I find it inconvenient to be here? You have no goddamn clue!" Tears sprang in my eyes, and I wanted to break something, to crack the bottle where I stored my memory. "I wake up in the hospital thinking I'm still Savannah May Holladay, Miss Georgia Peach, engaged to Bobby Lee Thomas, and instead, I find out I'm married to you and the mother of your four children. And you think I find it *inconvenient*?"

I wanted to throw something, or hit something. But more importantly, I wanted to *feel* something. Something good. Something familiar. Something that would let me know I was *home*. I thought about grabbing the keys and leaving the house, but I had no idea how to drive that stupid bus.

"Daddy? Mama?" The minis came out into the hallway, and Cody stood behind them in his Ninja Turtle pajamas, his glasses off, and his hands caught tight in his sister's pink nightgown. Which sister, I had no idea.

"Are you fightin' again?" said mini one.

"And why is Mama calling you Birdy, Daddy, when your name is James?" said the other.

"Are you a blue jay or a sparrow, Daddy?" I thought I heard Cody whisper.

Birdy broke free of my gaze and turned toward the children. "We ain't fightin'. Y'all go back to bed, now. Daddy and Mama will be there in a bit to tuck you in. You go now."

My patience had hit its end, and I knew I'd gone from pissed off to full-scale bitch. "*Really*, Birdy? Really? *Ain't*? We '*ain't*' fightin'? We drive a freakin' school bus so our kids can go to Montessori and get a decent education, and that's the best you can do? You graduated high school, same as me, and yet you talk to our children that way? Like some hillbilly from the holler?" It took less than ten seconds for my mind to register I'd just massacred the English language, in much the same way as Birdy. "The same as I did!" I shouted in correction. "You graduated from high school, the same as I did!"

Birdy flinched and his shoulders dropped, surrendering to my assault. A flush crept across his cheek, and his eyes touched on our children standing scared in the doorway, almost as if he were offering them a silent apology for his lack of education or affluence.

I felt terrible. I'd hurt Birdy. I'd hurt him bad. *Damn*—I mean "badly."

See, that's what happens when you don't go to college and you have a whole mess of kids by the time you're twenty-six or twenty-seven or whatever the heck I was and you live in the South. You get lazy and start talking as if you're the first cousin of Loretta Lynn. If I'd have used the scholarship from Miss Georgia Peach, become Miss America, and earned another one along with the title, I can guarantee you, I'd be much better educated and not be speaking the way I was. Or be so classless that I was browbeating my poor husband from Tennessee with the dead parents who practically raised himself and then watched after me for the better part of twenty years.

I clapped my hands to my mouth, my eyes wide in horror. "Oh, Birdy! I'm sorry. I'm so sorry. I didn't mean it. Birdy, I didn't mean it."

The kids stood stock still, too frightened to move, and I reached for Birdy, trying to put my arms around him. Birdy glanced back over at our children, their eyes wide and wet, and trying not to cry. Jesus, their mother was a lunatic. I had no business being back in this house and scaring these poor kids to death. I needed to get out and let them be. Birdy let me hug him, but he was ramrod stiff, and he only let me because he didn't want to frighten the children any further.

"Mama's sorry. It's okay, we're not fighting. Mama loves Daddy, and she's sorry." I hugged Birdy. He didn't hug me back, but he did let me take his hand and followed me down the hallway. "Come on. Let's get you all to bed. Mama will sing to you."

"But Mama, you don't sing," said one of the minis. "Only Daddy sings, and he plays the guitar, too!"

"You do?" I turned around to stare at Birdy. I'd never known Birdy to sing or to play the guitar. "You play the guitar?"

"What, you thought it would be the *banjo*?" he said, sarcastically.

"*I said, I'm sorry,*" I whispered, pulling him into the minis' bedroom. "Cody, darlin', hop up on the bed of Mini …" I looked to Birdy for help, but he was still too mad to offer assistance.

"May, Mama. I'm Emma May," she said, smiling a toothless smile. As if it were everyday a child had to tell her idiot mother her name. What made it worse was I had half a mind to correct her and tell her she was wrong and that *my* name was Savannah, not Mama. But I didn't think Birdy would go for it.

Cody ignored my instruction to get up on the bed, and instead ran out of the room. I glanced at Birdy, and he shrugged, still too pissed to speak to me, but with that expression I'd seen on his face more than once. Mostly back in the days when Bobby would complain to Birdy about me, and I'd complain to Birdy about Bobby, both holding an arm and tugging him two ways at once. Birdy would have that same bitter expression for the better part of a week, not saying much. When he finally spoke, he'd say he didn't want to hear about it from either of us, and that we both were fools, and he didn't know why he bothered with such friends. That he needed to find some new ones. It must have been hard for Birdy to be my best friend and Bobby Lee's at the same time, with each of us telling him our sides. But I'm happy to say, most times Birdy was on my side. Least that's what he'd say.

Less than a minute later, Cody came back inside the room, lugging a guitar bigger than he was.

"Here, Mama," he whispered. "Sing to us."

My eyes misted and my heart opened to his innocence. "*Oh, Cody,*" I whispered, accepting the guitar and setting it beside me, my eyes filling, and gathering that little boy with the same shy smile of his daddy in my arms, and hugging him, both of us hanging on tight. That little boy held on as if I was a life preserver and he was drowning and never letting go. I rubbed his back until he quit his crying and I quit mine. God, I was a mess. But the kids were beginning to grow on me a bit now that the shock of them was wearing off. They still didn't feel like mine, but a little more like family, a second cousin maybe, once removed.

"All right. Let Mama go. Get in the bed with Emma, and I'll sing."

"Mama, is Daddy a blue jay or a sparrow?" Cody said, a bit louder than before, but still so soft I needed to lean toward him to hear.

I turned my head toward Birdy, who stood leaning against the doorjamb, leaving me to sink or swim without his help, his hands in his pockets and still mad, but not steaming mad.

All five of us, if you counted Birdy, half in and half out of the room from his position at the door, were jammed in that little room with the white bunk beds, the ruffled pink comforters, and the skimpy valances at the window, while I stood in the middle of my family, and for a lack of a better word—"winged" it.

"Your daddy's name is James Russell Johnson," I began, glancing up at Birdy to see how I was doing. He said nothing, but he didn't seem nearly so angry. His face softened, and he took his hands out of his pockets, letting them fall. "But most of my life … at least until we got married … back in … um …" I hesitated, having no clear idea of when that was. "Well, a year before the minis were born," I felt it safe to say, "I called him Birdy."

"Why, Mama?" said Mini Ray, Melissa, I guess, since the voice came from the top bunk, and the bottom held Emma.

"Because your daddy has such a sweet face, he reminded everyone of a hunting dog. A bird dog, to be exact. A Labrador, I think. The one with the big brown eyes and the brown coat. The kind that is loyal, trustworthy, friendly, kind, obedient, brave …"

"Good one, Savannah. Add clean and reverent, and you've recited the Boy Scout creed," Birdy mumbled.

I ignored Birdy because he'd been hurt by me.

"See?" I said to the children. "Not only is your daddy similar to a bird dog, he has all of the qualities of a Boy Scout." I twisted to glare at Birdy and resisted the urge to give him the finger. I turned back to the children. "And instead of calling him Bird Dog, I changed his name to Birdy."

"Why didn't you name him Doggy?" asked Mini May.

I smiled and glanced at Birdy, who chuckled. The question seemed valid. My voice softened with the memory, and I spoke the answer to Birdy. "Because one day, when I wasn't much older than you are, I came home from school and there he was, standing in the middle of my bedroom, with the curtains still fluttering behind him, as if he'd flown inside the second story window with the breeze. Just like a bird. A birdy."

"Why did you change it back to James, Mama?"

"Yes, *Mama*," Birdy said, staring at me, his expression unreadable, but clearly issuing me a challenge. "By all means, tell our children why you decided to call me James." He folded his arms across his chest and tilted his head at an angle.

The children all watched me, their faces open with expectation, enjoying the conversation. It must have been the sad Savannah didn't share or talk much. It must have been what Birdy had said—I stayed in my room, sad and crying most days, the days when we weren't fighting. What a loser.

"I ... uh ..." I studied my children and their eager faces that hung on my every word, blooming under the slightest notice from me—a word or a touch—desperate to find a mother they'd obviously been missing for some time. I would love to say that I stared into the faces of my children and all the memoires came flooding back. The joy of their birth, bringing forth the life Birdy and I created out of the love we must have shared. The joy of holding them in my arms and staring with wonderment, feeling the desire to snuggle them against my chest, and the all-consuming love a parent should have for her child. But nothing came. No waves of knowledge, no flashes of the memory of their first steps or their first birthdays, their

Christmases, or their Easters. To me, theirs were just the open faces of children. Sweet children, just as any other.

I walked to the bunk bed and held onto the post for support. "I called him James," my eyes touched upon each innocent face, starting at the top bunk and working my way down, "because we were no longer children, and I wanted to be Daddy's wife, and your mama," I finished, not knowing what else to say, or if it were even true.

"*Mama*," one or two of them said and started to cry. And I cried too, feeling like a complete fraud. A stranger in the midst of a nice family. A family with a loving father and his great kids. And me, a misfit. A woman out of sorts, who didn't know who she was or where she belonged. A complete stranger to all.

I untangled myself from all of them, Cody, and both the minis, as the top bunk mini had climbed down and was hugging me, too.

"All right then. Settle back in your beds, and I'll sing. I know your daddy is sick to death of me singing Dolly Parton songs, but he'll have to hear one more." I tipped my head towards Birdy, and he smiled, coming inside the room and sitting on the bottom bunk with the mini and Cody, and then the second mini too, who climbed back up, but then climbed back down and into his lap, along with her siblings. He put his arms around all three of our children and watched me.

Sink or swim, Savannah. It's time to sink or swim.

I pulled out the small chair from the corner of the room and sat down, tuning the guitar, as best as I could remember. It didn't need much, so what the kids said was true. Birdy played the guitar.

"Like I said, this is a song of Dolly Parton's."

"Same as our Dolly, Mama?" a mini asked.

I glanced up at Birdy. "Well … uh … I suppose." Birdy tried not to smile, but I knew he wanted to. "And it's called 'But You Know I Love You.' I think it fits the situation. Y'all ready?" Everyone nodded, including Birdy, who gaped, downright shocked.

Birdy knew I could sing. Hadn't he heard me sing the "Star Spangled Banner," practicing for my pageant while hurling two fire-burning batons high into the air for the Miss Georgia Peach Queen contest? My voice couldn't have been all that terrible, or I wouldn't have won, especially not with that wonderful rendition Carol Lynn Hopkins did singing "Amazing Grace" while balancing all of those dishes spinning like tops, about a hundred of them in all. And hadn't he heard me years before, when I first learned to play the guitar and he'd cover his ears from the horrible sounds of it? The guitar sounds, not my voice. My voice has always been nice.

I started strumming and singing, feeling the words of the song. Feelings running so deep they went straight to my core, breaking my heart in half. Feeling the pain of all of those faces staring at me, wanting something from me I wasn't capable of giving. Wanting my love. They all just wanted my love.

I sang about waking up, and the sun streaking across the room, of broken dreams, of sad hearts, and dollar signs keeping us apart, and of finding my way back to another time …

My eyes touched on Birdy, and his were shiny with unshed tears.

"I love you," I sang to him, "… Oh, how I love you," meaning every word, maybe not in the romantic sexual way Birdy wanted, but in the way of a childhood friendship that went far deeper than most. Birdy was there for me almost all of my life. Knew things about me no one else knew. Bobby Lee may have known my body better than anyone else, but Birdy knew my soul.

I searched deep in the faces of those babies, watching me with adoring eyes, blue or brown, the eyes of their mama and their daddy, and then to Birdy, wearing an expression much the same, holding my eyes, begging for me to come back to him. And I couldn't go on.

I dropped the guitar and ran from the room, down the laminate floor hallway, out the front door with the "Welcome" wreath, past the rig and the school bus and down Rocky Road to the dead end. I collapsed at the end of the street, the part where the identical houses stopped and there was nothing but trees. Trees that headed out to some deep creek. A deep creek I had a mind to drown myself in. I pulled my knees to my chest and cried. Cried so hard I thought I'd never stop.

How do you start over? Where did my life end, or where did it begin? I was a girl who had become a woman, but who still felt she was a girl. I went to sleep with thoughts of tiaras and pageants and woke up to children and poverty. I could not play this charade.

"Baby girl, don't cry." Birdy sat beside me and gathered me in his strong arms. "I'm here. Savannah, don't cry." Birdy took me on his lap and rocked me, just the same way I'd done with Anna. He held me in his arms and let me cry myself out.

"Who … who's watching the kids?" I hiccuped, wiping my nose on the back of my hand.

"They'll be fine. The minis will take care of Cody and Dolly, if need be. The doors are locked, and they know to call Becky if they have to."

"Why? Why don't I remember?" I moaned and held my face to my hands, but suddenly an idea entered my mind and I raised my head. "Kiss me, Birdy! Quick, kiss me. Maybe if you do, I'll remember."

And he did. He brought his head down to meet mine, and he kissed me. Long and deep, his tongue seeking mine. A flicker of a memory stirred, and it was enough to make my breasts release, the milk wet and sticky, down the front of Birdy's trucker tee. It was nice, I'm not sayin' it wasn't, but it felt like the kiss of a first date, or maybe a second. A date with someone you didn't know well, but you'd want to see again, knowing you'd need to take it slow and not let your body overrun your senses, or you'd be labeled a slut, one of the loose girls in town everyone talked about.

Birdy moaned and brought his hand up inside my shirt. And I let him. He'd helped me pump and feed the baby, it's not as if there was much to be embarrassed by now. He caressed them, kneading, the milk wet and slick in his hands, and then he leaned against me, his body covering mine as we both went down to the grass.

"Birdy!" I pushed him off me and rolled. "Stop!" I sat up, wrapping my arms around me for protection, the sounds of crickets and bullfrogs in the distance, hidden in the marsh.

"Oh, shit. Savannah, I'm sorry." Birdy scooted away from me, rubbing his hands in his hair and then adjusting his pants. "I know you want to take it slow. But it's been so long,

Savannah. So long." He leaned forward and buried his face in his hands, his breathing ragged.

I gazed at my husband, and my heart went out to him. Birdy never had an easy life. He'd lost his mother when he was a child not much older than Cody, right before he moved to Atlanta. He'd never said how, and I didn't press. And he had that white trash abusive father, who eventually wrapped his car around a telephone pole while drunk, killing himself, but only after running a family of four off the road, where, luckily, they survived. He might have killed Birdy too, if it wasn't for me, because Birdy was supposed to be in the car with him that night, driving across town to hunt down some money his daddy said was owed to him. I showed up at their house, just as Birdy was getting in the car, begging Birdy to take me to the Sadie Hawkins dance because Bobby Lee was sick. Mr. Johnson didn't want to let him go, but I told him my parents would sure appreciate it, and even though he was already piss drunk, he knew better than to say no. Less than an hour later, he was dead. And I know it's awful of me to say, but I'm glad he died, because Birdy suffered enough at his hands.

"How long has it been, Birdy? How many weeks since I'd made love to you?"

Birdy's laugh was hollow. "Weeks, Savannah? Try *months*. We haven't made love in months."

"But, I thought … I mean, I just assumed …"

"You're a good wife, Savannah May." Birdy pulled his head up and seemed embarrassed. "You can't cook worth a darn, you've had a tough time with the kids, and you don't like to clean, but you've been a good wife to me." He pulled at a piece of grass and then threw it to the side.

"Birdy, I haven't a clue what you're really trying to say." I studied his face but got no closer to the answer.

"I'll say this as best as I can." Birdy regarded my face, watching, to see how I'd react. "For some reason, Savannah, you don't care for it much when I touch you, but you don't mind touching me."

"I *what?*" I was totally confused. I shook my head, hurting it, where it throbbed underneath the bandages. I pondered for a second, trying to digest what Birdy was saying.

Well, now, that was an oddity. I'd never known myself to be so selfless. Maybe that was a good thing. Although why I didn't want Birdy to touch me seemed strange, especially since he said I could no longer get pregnant.

"Let's go home. The kids must be scared out of their wits by now." Birdy extended his hand.

We walked in silence for a moment.

"Birdy?"

"Yes?"

"I'm sorry about yelling at you for saying 'ain't.' You can say ain't if you want."

"Thanks for your permission." Birdy may have been trying to be sarcastic, but it didn't come off that way.

"You're welcome."

We came through the door, hand in hand, calming our children's fears about any potential breakup, but solidifying the ones about their mother needing to be locked up and the key thrown away. We listened to their prayers and then tucked them into their beds. Birdy carried Cody into the room he shared with Anna and pulled the *Cars*-themed sheet around him, and I trailed behind to kiss my son goodnight.

"You sing pretty, Mama," Cody whispered.

I kissed him on the forehead because I got the sense it was expected of me. "Thank you, Cody. Good night."

"Good night, Mama. And Mama?"

"Yes?"

"I'm glad you're home."

"I'm glad I'm home, too," I lied.

I left the door to the room open about six inches, so I'd be able to hear Anna when she cried. Birdy stood on the other side, watching me the entire time.

"What's Cody's middle name?"

"It's Earl. His name is Cody Earl."

I sighed audibly, shaking my head. "Of course it is. I have one kid with a decent name, and you have to screw it up with Earl." I headed down the hallway to our bedroom.

"It was your idea!" Birdy called out to me. "I wanted to name him Cody Russell. Earl was all your idea!"

CHAPTER EIGHT

I sat on the corner of the bed on top of my quilt. It was the only thing in that old tract house that was familiar, not counting Birdy, who appeared older than I remembered him last, more a man than a teenage boy, but recognizable at least.

There was an opened closet door filled with clothes I'd never seen before. Or not that I remembered seeing. And thank goodness, as they were all ugly as sin, in dark colors: browns, drab greens, and black. My colors before were pink and white. And I had lots of purple too, I remember. Not that I'd wear all those colors at once. Some is fine, but too much of those colors and it comes off as if you've just shopped at Baby Gap, in the little girl's section, or you were taking fashion advice from Britney Spears, way back when.

I left the bed and went digging deeper inside the closet. Deeper, as in eight more inches, because the closet wasn't much bigger than the two-door refrigerator-freezer in my parent's house. I moved the clothes to the side hoping something would trigger a memory. Anything to help me remember. And there it was, something I did recognize. It was a dress bag, long and plastic, with a zipper running down the front, and it said the words *Faye's Formals* in script on the top left side. I took the hanger down off the pole and brought it to the bed, unzipping the bag. Carefully and almost afraid to touch it, I removed the white dress with the gold beads, from the bag, and spread it out full length on the bed.

I remember this.

I took the dress and walked to the bathroom, holding it in front of me, staring at my reflection in the mirror. I remembered.

I remembered the night of the pageant, how nervous I was. Sick even. So sick with nerves, I was throwing up in the bathroom just hours before, and I remembered that Birdy came by the house with Bobby Lee. And how Birdy came into my bathroom and held my hair back while I emptied my supper in the toilet. Bobby Lee was disgusted by it, and he stomped downstairs, still angry I made him wear a suit and tie and was dragging him to attend the pageant. Then Mama yelled up I wasn't supposed to be entertaining boys in my room. As if that's what I was doing, *entertaining* Birdy, doing the dance of the seven veils or juggling for the entertainment of Birdy and the troops, the soldiers of Afghanistan or wherever, instead of puking into the toilet so nervous I couldn't hold down my food.

And I won. I hit all those high notes. I didn't drop my baton, either of them, or set the stage or the audience on fire. I looked good in my bathing suit, too, with the help of those silicone inserts you rest inside the cup at the bottom so they lift your breasts, and I didn't trip or stumble in my dress. I even managed to sound intelligent and made Mama and Daddy proud when I got my question and answered what it meant to me to be an American. I gazed straight out at the crowd at the C.W. Pettigrew Center at Fort Valley State University, and my voice never wavered once. I answered that, to me, to be an American meant committing oneself to abstract ideals of liberty and equality, and accepting all religions, ethnicities, and personal morals in order to come together as one people for the betterment of our country and the world in general. Of course I don't know half of what that all means, because the contestants get a list before the pageant of what might be asked, and I'd gone on the Internet and found the answer. The answer to that and to how feminism has progressed during the twenty-first century.

I changed my answer up some from what I'd found on the Internet. I didn't want to be accused of plagiarism. Thank goodness the emcee didn't ask me to elaborate on what "abstract ideals" I meant, because I haven't a clue what an abstract ideal is.

I won. And when they called out my name I cried. Mama and Daddy cried, too. Bobby Lee, he didn't cry, but I could tell he was proud by the way he smiled and then yelled out, "That's my girl!" Birdy, he missed seeing me win. He was invited to come. I even paid for his ticket, but he said he didn't own a suit, and he refused to let me buy him one to wear, no matter how many times I offered.

I held the gown tight to me, a gown that wouldn't fit me ever again, now that I've had kids, and I saw Birdy's reflection in the mirror behind me. He'd taken off his shirt, and seeing him naked from the waist up, which was all I could see because that darn bathroom didn't have a single full-length mirror, only the kind on top of the counter, came as a shock.

"Wow, Birdy. You have muscles!"

And he did. Lots of them. Not the bulky wrestler kind, puffed as balloons, but the long and lean ones that corded and stretched and gave a six-pack stomach, same as the guys in those underwear ads.

He'd taken off his glasses and squinted at me in the mirror.

"You're remembering, *aren't* you," he said, stressing the word "aren't" so he could prove he did learn correct English back with me in high school.

I turned around to face him, still holding the dress in front of me. "That's the thing, Birdy. I remember every detail of that night. And all of the nights before it. The years, too."

I stepped past him and began to put the dress away, my hand lingering on the beaded neckline, before smoothing it down and pulling up the zipper and hanging it in the back of the closet where I'd found it. "But that's it. That's the last thing I remember before waking up in the hospital." I sat on the bed. "Come sit with me." I patted the space next to me.

Birdy took off his belt, his jeans slipping lower, and showing a line of hair leading to …

He caught me staring, and I turned my head, embarrassed.

"It's all right to look, Savannah. I'm your husband." He sat beside me.

"Birdy, why? Why are you my husband? Did I ever make it to the Georgia Peach Festival?"

Birdy got off the bed and faced me. He didn't tell me if I'd made it to the festival, the festival I was supposed to preside over, the one with the world's largest peach cobbler, with all the people who come from miles away and across state lines to attend and see the queen and her court.

"Is it that terrible, Savannah May? Is it so repulsive for you to think you've spent the last seven years of your life as my wife? That you had my *hillbilly* children, as you call them?"

"You take that back! I never said we had hillbilly children." *Not aloud, I didn't.*

Birdy started to unbutton his pants to undress and stopped when he saw my panicked expression. "Oh, hell," he said. He didn't button them back up, but instead left them unbuttoned and sat down on the floor beside the bed.

"And in answer to your question ..." I thought a moment, not knowing how to respond. How did I know if I found it terrible or repulsive, if I couldn't remember it? I fell back on the bed, my arm over my eyes. "I don't know what I mean," I moaned, while Birdy waited, still sitting on the floor, and from the front room came the sound of that stupid clock. "God, I hate that clock. We need to get rid of that clock."

"That clock belonged to my mama."

"Sorry. Then I guess it stays." I sat up and sat crossed-legged on the bed, pulling off my boots and throwing them into the corner. "I'm not going to drag this story out of you one word at a time, Birdy Johnson, or James Russell, or whatever the heck it is I call you. I won't spend one night in this house without getting some answers. Am I so frail, Birdy? So fragile and unbalanced there are things I won't be able to stand hearing? I need to know. And you tell me now, or I'll pull that cover off my car and hightail it out of here."

I watched Birdy's face flush dark, his eyes going almost black, and a muscle twitching in his jaw so I knew he was clenching his teeth.

"I'll take the baby. I'll take Anna," I threatened.

"*Like hell you will,*" he shot back.

"Then you tell me right now!" I got off the bed and crouched on all fours, facing him, my eyes glaring into his, my long brown hair falling and touching the floor and that awful carpeting.

"No, Savannah. You never made it to the festival. Me neither," Birdy said, his voice tight and angry. "We ran off and got married that same weekend in June, while everyone was out at the festival. You and me got married at the city hall in Savannah, where you wanted, and had our honeymoon at the Howard Johnson, four blocks from the ocean." His eyes never left mine, and I noticed how tired they seemed, and how sad.

"But *why*? Did Bobby Lee and I have a fight? I'm sorry, Birdy, but I find it hard to believe that after knowing you ... for what?" I counted on my fingers. "*Fourteen years*? That I was suddenly so madly in love with you, I'd run off and marry you the weekend of my festival."

Birdy sighed, the sound deep and heavy, and stood up, buttoning his jeans. "You really don't remember, do you? You don't remember a thing."

I stood up and faced him. "Dammit, Birdy, no! You think I'm playing, here? No! I don't remember!" My head ached, with some vague memory of hurt and fear swirling around, but nothing stuck.

"You're right!" Birdy barked at me. You and Bobby Lee got in a terrible fight. When were the two of you *not* fightin'? But I won't tell you why. Too much time has passed, and now it don't matter. That's something you'll need to remember on your own. And if you don't ... all the better." Birdy grabbed a pillow from the bed, and my quilt, heading for the door. "You asked *me* to marry *you*, Savannah May. *You* asked *me!* Birdy Johnson, the hick kid from Tennessee, the one who drove a truck for a living, married rich Savannah May Holladay, the cotillion queen, Miss Georgia Peach. *You married me*, instead of that prick, Bobby Lee Thomas." He slammed the door.

I stomped over and threw open the door, then stopped my pounding because I didn't want to wake the kids. I tiptoed past their bedroom doors and down the short hallway with the plain white walls and the stupid red, white, and blue wallpaper border of the lighthouses. What was with the lighthouse fetish? I stopped to examine the pictures of the family: me with the twins as babies, Cody, and adorable Anna, and some pictures of Birdy and me. Some, where we appeared happy together and some where he seemed happy holding this or that child, and I seemed depressed. Then a few more recent ones, from the looks of the darker color of my hair, where we both are miserable.

There was one small poorly taken picture I found high up on the wall that must have been taken the weekend of our wedding because we were standing in front of a—what else? A lighthouse. Real or fake, who knows? That explained it at least. My obsession with the ocean, lighthouses, seashells, and such. It must have been a nice time, or I don't imagine I'd decorate every last inch of that small house with the silly things one should only see on the inside of a snow globe.

"You could have said no, Birdy," I whispered, sitting down next to him on the sofa, on the end cushion. "You could have told me no."

Birdy took my left hand and kissed the palm, right above my wedding ring, showing me he wasn't able to stay mad at me and making me remember the old days. The days when he would get so mad at me for going back to Bobby Lee after Bobby and I would get in a fight and break up, time and again. Birdy wouldn't speak to me for days, weeks even, sometimes, so angry, and telling me if that what's love is he didn't want any part of it. Until one day I'd come home and find him in my bedroom, having climbed up in my window on the second floor and asking me was I okay, and saying he was sorry for being away for so long.

"I loved you, Savannah. How could I say no?" He raised his head and held tight my hand. "After all the years we spent together. How could I ever say no? Who else would take care of you the way I do?"

"So, that's it, then? I'm you're life's purpose, Birdy? The sad screwed-up mother with postpartum depression who fell off a ladder and hit her head and now can't remember anything but her glory days? Is that what I am? Your good deed for the day? Your cross to bear—because if you don't take care of me, who will?"

I felt my chest begin to fill and tingle and knew soon Anna would wake and need to be fed. It was high time that baby was weaned. Any child old enough to sit in a highchair and eat food with a few of her teeth was too old to be breast-fed both day and night. "I read the papers the doctor sent home. I'm not stupid, and I researched some of those words it said on that old dinosaur of a computer we own, while you and your girlfriend were giving the kids a bath." Birdy tried to pull his hand from mine, but I held firm. "Oh, stop. I'm teasing." He relaxed his hand slightly. "You read them too, right?"

"I read them."

"What do you think they mean? *Dissociative amnesia*, I think it said." I let go of Birdy's hands and lifted mine to place them on the sides of his cheeks, searching his face for the answers. "I'm not crazy, Birdy. Am I? Is that why you take care of me? Because I'm crazy? Were there some cousin marriages in my family I am not aware of?"

Birdy put his palms on the outside of mine, so both sets were holding his face still. "You're not crazy, Savannah May. The doctor said they're finding it more now, since the soldiers are returning from the war. The mind just shuts down and forgets things that are stressful or traumatic. Your memory might come back. I pray it comes back."

What kind of a weak and silly person was I? Someone who loses her mind over marriage and motherhood. Those poor soldiers, I could see. Who knows what horrors they experienced while fighting over there. But what was up with me? A dirty diaper and an eighteen-wheeler in the front yard of a small rundown house in a subdivision was on par with bodies blown to bits and witnessing your friends die in front of you? Sure, driving that yellow school bus was bad. Terrible even. But I hadn't just come home from fighting a war.

I pulled the quilt off Birdy, letting it drag, and started down the hallway away from Johnson's Landing, and Fisherman's Village. "Come to bed. No sense you freezing out here on the sofa. We've slept together before, and I somehow managed to keep my hands off of you," I joked, referring to our years as teenagers, but still confused about our earlier conversation, the one where Birdy said I was a "good wife," and could only guess that meant I was a wife who was at least good at something. Birdy took his pillow with him and followed behind. "Why on earth did you let me decorate the house this way?" I asked when we were back in our room, where the theme continued with a throw pillow on the bed that said Let Your Light Shine, embroidered above a lighthouse sewn in colored thread.

"You didn't decorate it. I did. To remind us of our wedding."

What a pair. I come up with the stupid kid names and Birdy decorates the house modeled after the inside of a fish-and-chips restaurant. The only things missing were the fake plastic lobsters attached to nets on the wall. But my house exploration wasn't complete, so who knew what tomorrow would bring?

I wasn't wearing a bra or underwear, and didn't know what I usually slept in. I stood, confused on what to do next.

"Do we wear clothes to sleep? ... *Pajamas*," I clarified. "Are we naked, or do we sleep in something?"

"We do both."

"That's not much help. Who does what?"

"I'm *naked*," he stressed, probably dying to say "nekkid," and you wear sweatpants and a shirt because you get up in the night to feed Dolly." He rummaged around in the dresser drawer until he found some tattered and stained clothes, handing them to me.

How the mighty had fallen. When I slept with Bobby Lee, I'd make sure I wore some sexy Victoria's Secret thing I'd bought from the mall. Although, most times, he'd only see it for about ten seconds before he'd rip those things off me. And it wasn't often we'd ever have the chance to sleep together all the way through the night, because his parents would come home from the country club, or mine would, and we'd be racing through the house to get our clothes all back on and straightened and downstairs before they knew what was going on.

Zula, our housekeeper, she always knew the times we did it at my place, even though her room was downstairs and at the back of the house. She must have heard us barreling down the stairs and into the family room, where we'd quickly turn on the TV and pretend to be watching some show. She'd have that sour look to her for hours, shaking her head, and giving me the stink eye. Sometimes Birdy would be there, too. Not in the bedroom with us, of course, but waiting for us downstairs, watching TV. Come to think of it, his expression wasn't much different from Zula's.

I went into the bathroom to change, and when I came out Birdy was inside the bed with the covers over him.

"I've got on my drawers. It's okay to get in."

I climbed in beside him. "I think I sleep on the other side. The side you're on."

"Oh, you do? And why is that?"

"Because it makes more sense. If I'm getting up in the middle of the night, it makes more sense for me to be next to the door."

Birdy smiled and climbed over my body, his mostly naked limbs and his middle part touching the covered parts of mine. "You're right, Savannah. That is the side you sleep on. See? Maybe your memory is coming back already." He reached over and turned off the lighthouse light, the kind with some little plastic man with white hair and a blue coat and a sailor-type hat glued to the wooden base, and kissed me on the forehead. "Good night."

"Good night." I rolled on my side, facing the door, and then rolled back. "Birdy?" I wanted to touch him, to reach out and stroke his arm or touch his bare chest, but something held me back. Fear, I guess. "Do we say we love each other when we kiss good night?"

"We do."

"I love you, Birdy. If I haven't told you enough, I love you."

"I love you, too, Savannah."

CHAPTER NINE

A sharp pain, starting down at my wrist and working its way up my arm, burning like sparks off a bonfire when you sit too close, hot and sizzling when they hit your skin. The shattering of breaking glass, and the squeal of car tires.

I woke up in the middle of the night after having a bad dream. Bobby Lee was in it, and so was Birdy. We were all arguing, except I couldn't remember who was arguing with who. I think I was calling out Bobby Lee's name. I'm almost certain I was. And maybe in real life, too, because Birdy was on the floor on his knees, his forearms on the bed, and it seemed he was praying. He was on his knees praying. And he was crying, too.

"Birdy, what's wrong? What have I done? Tell me. What is it?" I crawled out of the bed and got down on my knees on the floor behind him in the cold of that room, where we were too cheap or poor to keep on the heat, putting my arms around his back and holding him close, feeling my heart pound into his bare back.

He didn't raise his head, but instead spoke into his clasped fingers, still on his knees in that cold room and wearing nothing but his shorts. Although I did notice they were black Calvin Klein boxer briefs with the body-defining fit, so at least we weren't total losers.

"You're still calling out his name, Savannah. Even in your sleep, after all of these years, you're still calling out his name."

I didn't know what to say. Heck, I didn't even know what to *feel*. Did I still love Bobby Lee? It had been seven years, if what everyone tells me was true. Surely, that was time enough to get over someone. If Bobby Lee still loved me, I suspect he'd have come get me by now.

"I'm sorry, Birdy. I can't help what I say when I'm sleeping." I hugged him tight. He didn't push me away, but he didn't hug me back, either. "Don't cry now."

Jesus, what a sad sack family we were. Those kids, who were more quiet than any kids I'd ever met, hardly talking or meeting my eyes, teary and crying since I'd walked in the door. And now their daddy, praying and maybe crying, too, over what, I don't know. And me, not much better. The sorriest excuse for a mother there ever was. Sad and mopey, all the time, if the pictures were any indication. Well tomorrow, things would be different. The old Savannah—no, the *young* Savannah, the debutante beauty queen one, the one that was fun and playful and pretty, was back. Or would be back just as soon as she got her hair cut and colored, and her nails done, and some decent new clothes. And the sad crybaby one was going out with the trash. Along with that cute babysitter, once I knew what end was up and got the hang of raising a child.

"I ain't cryin'," Birdy said, getting up from his knees, "I'm prayin'." He went into the bathroom and I heard the shower start.

I've prayed tons since I was a little girl. (Of course, more so after Bobby Lee and I started having sex and using the pullout or the rhythm method.) And I know the difference between praying and crying. Even though I admit there are times when the two go hand in hand.

This must have been one of those times.

The cuckoo clock announced the hour, and I heard Anna start to fuss. I went inside the room and got her from the crib, changing her diaper the way Becky Lou showed me and then putting her to my breast to feed.

"Where are you going?" Birdy was dressed, and he grabbed the bus keys from a wall hanger of a painted lifesaver, the white kind you throw in the water when someone is drowning. I needed a real one of those things for me right about now.

"I've got children to get to school. Ours can stay home for the day. I'll let their teachers know." Birdy shrugged on a coat hanging in the small closet next to the front door. It was a camouflage hunting jacket, but I'd never known Birdy to hunt. I don't believe he does. He says it's unfair, the sides aren't equal and the hunter has the unfair advantage. He enjoys fishing, but only because he says if fish are too stupid not to bite on something as dangerous looking as a hook, they deserve to die.

"Don't I make you coffee or breakfast?" Anna drank her fill of the right, so I switched her to the left.

"Not really. I make it most days, or I get it on the road. But you make the kids' lunches, if that makes you feel any better." Birdy avoided my eyes, and his mouth was downturned. He zipped up his jacket harder than seemed necessary.

"You're mad."

"I ain't mad."

"Then why won't you look at me?"

He raised his head, his fingers playing with the bus keys. "Savannah, I'm not mad. Go back to bed. Let the minis and Cody sleep, and put Dolly back to bed. You need your rest." He glanced at his mama's clock. "I'll be back in two hours. If you have a problem, call Becky Lou; her number's on the counter in the kitchen."

"Wake up, Mama. Mini May is sick."

I opened my eyes and stared into wide blue ones. It was one of the minis. I threw off the covers, disoriented. *Crap!* I glanced down at what I was wearing, a milk-stained shirt and tattered sweats, and then around at the room with the fake wood-paneled walls and cheap furniture. I really did live in this dumpy house. It wasn't a dream sequence—one where I ended up back in my room, in my own bed, after visiting the powerful wizard and all those little people. Instead, my own little person stood next to me, her eyes rounded and scared.

I took the mini's hand and shuffled out of the room. "I'm coming! Mama's coming!" I called out to Mini May, still feeling silly saying "Mama." The surplus mini followed me, having little choice in the matter.

Vomit! And it was everywhere. On the floor, on the bed, and all over that poor child, who looked at me for help. The smell and the sight of it overwhelmed me, and I started to gag, my shoulders heaving forward, my throat burning with an acrid taste.

"Mama," she said, her face pale, the freckles jumping out like splatters of blood dried on white paper, "I don't feel good," she moaned. Her thin body curled up in a ball, and her flushed face was red with a fever, her pink pajamas covered in lumpy slime. I gagged again, and the mini started to cry.

I put my hand to her forehead. The child was burning with fever. "It's okay, I'm here. Your mama is here to help." *Shit!* And Birdy was at work. I turned to Mini Ray. "What do we do?" I asked her, ignorant of how to help a sick child. In my home, there was always someone there to care for *me* when I was sick.

"I don't know. Clean her up, I guess," she said, her face damp with perspiration, while her twin started to whimper.

I put my hand on Mini Ray's forehead, or maybe it was May's. I was so rattled, my mind was confused. She was hot, too. Oh dear Lord, not two kids with the flu.

Anna woke up and started to cry from the other room, the sounds of her hunger constricting my breasts. Anna would just have to wait.

Okay, okay, I can do this. I can do this. I patted the standing mini on the head. "I'll clean her up. You hop back up on the top bunk, and I'll get her washed."

I hurried into the bathroom and got some towels and some disinfectant from under the sink, or maybe it was clothes bleach. It smelled the same as something I remember Zula using as a cleaning agent the time I was sick. I wet a washrag and swiped some soap on it to clean the mini.

Cody caught me in the hallway, standing still as a statue, his face pulled tight with pain. "My tummy hurts," he said so softly I made him repeat it. I felt his forehead. Was it hot? Or was that the way it was supposed to feel? It was clammy, maybe. I didn't know what I was feeling for. Was cold good, or was warm better? I told him to get back into bed, and I'd be there in a minute to help him.

"Mini!" I cried out, finding the healthier mini on her knees on the floor, retching onto the carpet, where thick pools of bile and her vomit absorbed into the nylon shag.

Food poisoning. Did they all have food poisoning?

Anna screamed—shrill and demanding—needing to be fed, the noise of her setting my teeth on edge and making me angry, the anger as tart as the taste of bile sharp in my mouth. She'd just have to wait. It's not as if she'd starve to death. Pulling open the dresser drawers, I started yanking out clothes, trying to find some new pajamas for the minis to wear, my arms shaking with anger.

Both girls were crying now, whimpering their discomfort. I wiped my own tears away with the back of my hand. *Goddamn Birdy!* This is exactly why I didn't want kids in the first place. Who needs this shit? Their sickness and their discomfort? I didn't know what I was doing. He should've been here taking care of them himself, not leaving me here alone when these kids needed someone capable enough to help. I wiped off one of the minis with the washrag and picked her up off the bed, where she clung to me, wrapping her arms and legs around me and making me gag with the smell of her. I carried her to my bedroom and put on the new pajamas, throwing the dirty ones in the bathtub. The poor thing curled up tight, holding her stomach in pain, and crying for her daddy. Anna's screams continued, now harder than ever, and milk dripped from my heavy breasts and down the front of my shirt, a mixture of sweetness and pestilence. I pushed the hair from my face, spreading the mess on my hands through it.

I could not do this. I did not *want* to do this.

"Don't leave me, Mama," the mini whimpered, her plea tearing at my heart.

"I'll come back. It's okay. I'll be right back."

But I didn't want to go back. To that room, or any of the others, where there were sick children who needed me. I wanted to run. Fast and far, back to my own home, the home I remembered. Back to the place where there were people to take care of me, to put their hands to my fevered brow, to clean me up and to tuck me tight into my bed. I wanted my parents, and Zula, as ornery as an ox, but capable, her gnarled hands scrubbing at the stains in my life ever since I can remember. And maybe I even wanted Bobby Lee. At least the good times with him. Although most of the good times included Birdy.

With heavy feet, I walked back to the twins' room and cleaned up the other one, wiping her down with the same towel I used to wipe her sister, but using a clean one to dry her. Who was who, I didn't know, or care. I pulled off her clothes and put her in new ones, and carried her back to my room so I could change the sheets on their bed.

"Oh, darlin', no! No, no, no!" The mini in my bed hunched over, her body wracking with heaves and making horrible sounds, and she vomited again on my sheets, crying, and trying to catch her breath from the force of it. "Move over a bit," I gently instructed. "Let me set your sister down and I'll help you." The mini moved toward the edge of the bed, her cries silent, but the tears falling.

I pulled up my granny's quilt, covering up the vomit, mostly bile I noted, with that harsh smell, as sharp as acid must be, and I put her on top, placing her sister beside her. The two little girls clung together each whimpering and crying for Birdy. My shirt was filthy, and I couldn't stand it any longer. Pulling it off me, I flung it in the corner, grabbing a heavy black bathrobe from a hook in the closet and shrugging it on, where it trailed behind me, dragging me down with the weight of my new life.

Where were our clean sheets? I started opening cupboards, pulling out tattered towels and worn blankets until I found some sheets that seemed the right size for bunk beds and hurried back into their room.

"Anna, I'm coming!" I yelled out, yanking the soiled sheets off and putting the new sheets on, as best as I could, never having changed one of my own. It didn't fit on the first way, so I turned it around, not messing much with the elastic, and just threw a second one on top of it without tucking it in. I got on my knees to clean the floor and too late realized bleach isn't meant for cleaning carpet, as the scab-colored carpet turned a brownish white, the harsh smell of it burning my eyes and the caustic solution heating my hands.

The sound of a sniffle made me raise my head. "Mama, I don't feel good," Cody whined from the doorway, his big eyes wet, holding his little belly.

"I know, Cody. I know, baby. I'm sorry. I'll be with you in a minute, just as soon as I feed your sister." I reached for him and carried him back to his bed. Finally, I removed Anna from her crib, her screams raising the hairs on the back of my neck, while I reminded myself she was only a baby that needed feeding and not another insult to my injured life. Tears from yet another child of mine ran down her face, and her nose ran with clear snot. And more smells. Another gross and disgusting odor assaulted my nose. A full diaper on a baby. I quickly changed her, having to re-tape the sides twice to get it right. I cleaned my hands with a wipey and opened my bathrobe to feed her, carrying her down the hallway tucked inside the robe while I rushed to check on the minis.

There wasn't any new vomit, but the smell of what I'd covered hit me and I gagged again. The minis clutched one another and wept, the sickness damp and sticky in their red hair and both in need of a bath.

"It's okay," I said, stroking their hair back from their faces as Anna had her fill of me, "you'll be okay. You just rest now. I'll go in the kitchen and see if we have something to help your tummy."

Why did Birdy think it was safe to leave me alone with these children? *Goddamn him!* I put Anna to my shoulder to burp her, and when she finally did burp, she spit up all over my shoulder. I stared at the mess on my shoulder and sobbed.

I needed Birdy. I needed him home to care for these children. There wasn't even any way to call him. I didn't have any idea what his cell number was. Did Birdy forget I lost seven years of my life? Seven years of any knowledge I may have had? If I knew the number before, I certainly didn't know it now. Yes, I had the babysitter's phone number, but there was no way I was waking up an eighteen-year-old at 6:45 in the morning to tell her I couldn't handle my sick children.

I dragged down the hallway to Cody's and Anna's room. "Oh, Cody, not you, too?" That sweet little boy lay quietly crying while he colored his sheets with swampy stains of diarrhea, covering the reds and the yellows of the cartoon graphics.

I gently placed Anna in her crib, knowing she'd have to cry herself to sleep.

"Oh, Cody, sugar, don't cry." I sighed, heavy and deep, not wanting to breathe at all because of the foulness of the odor permeating the small room. "I'll get you cleaned up in a minute."

"I want my daddy," he whimpered, lying in his filth.

"I want your daddy, too." I used my sleeve to wipe my eyes, willing myself not to be sick. *I will not be sick.* These are children, and they need my help. I can do this. *I will not be sick.*

"Don't cry, now. I'll go run you a bath and get you cleaned up. Don't cry."

I stroked Cody's head and was transported back to another time when I used to stroke his father's hair in the same way, when he couldn't have been more than eight or nine, a day when I found Birdy down at the side of the creek where he first taught me to swim.

Birdy had been crying, sitting on a boulder near the water's edge, his legs huddled close to his chest, his head bent within the circle of his arms and crying because his daddy had beat him again. I came up behind him, my young heart breaking at the sight of his despair, and I stroked his head while he cried. Saying nothing, just stroking his head while he cried. I must have stood there for half an hour, gently touching him, feeling his hair, soft as a bunny and warm from the afternoon sun. I touched him to help ease his suffering. I was just a child, eight or nine, and I stroked his dark hair while he cried by the water that one summer afternoon.

"Don't cry, now. I'll go run you a bath." With slow steps, I went down that short hallway and into the bathroom, turning on the harsh light overhead and turning on the water in that chipped bathtub. I stood, hypnotized almost, mesmerized by

117

the water, watching it fill the tub, hearing voices in my head, the words of the preacher on Sunday mornings.

Water. To wash away all the nasty vileness. Water to wash away the sins of the past.

I let my hands trail in the water, leisurely almost, as if I didn't have a care in the world. Just trailing it through my fingers, watching the ripples radiate out. My fingers twirled the water in circles. Coming back to the present, I turned off the water and went to get Cody.

The bathrobe trailed behind me, dirty with the children's sickness, the hem gritty from gathering all the sand and crumbs from the floor, dragging heavy behind me. I checked on the minis. They were asleep, both spent, their arms wrapped around each other for security, two tiny peas nestled safe and close within their casing. Two little girls forced to take comfort in one another because I was too stupid to help them.

I gathered Cody in my arms and carried him to the bathroom, pulling off his pajamas and throwing them into the small plastic trashcan next to the toilet. I lifted his naked body, noticing we'd had him circumcised, and placed him in the water, asking if the temperature was okay.

"Are you old enough to be in the bath alone for a minute while I find you some clean pajamas?" I questioned, not knowing what age it was safe to leave a child alone in a tub. Cody nodded yes, and I hurried to his room, where I grabbed some clean clothes from the dresser.

I washed him—all his parts— although not as thoroughly as I should have, not having a clue what I was allowed to touch, and pulled him up out of the tub to dry him. The sleeves of Birdy's robe were so heavy with water they weighed me down, the water dripping on the floor and falling like rain as I carried Cody to the sofa to rest. After covering him with a blanket and kissing him on the forehead, I went to change his sheets and then hurried back to his side.

"Pet me, Mama," Cody pleaded with me, tucked tight in a blanket, his eyes large in his pale face. "Pet me," he softly said.

I settled myself next to him on the sofa, pulling the blanket over the two of us, and stroked his face while the cuckoo clock slowly ticked off each minute.

"Savannah, what happened?"

I must have fallen asleep, because I didn't hear Birdy come home, and he stood before me, his nose wrinkling at the smell of sickness.

"They're all sick, Birdy."

Birdy's eyes grew wide, and a fleeting expression of panic flashed across his face. I got the feeling that for the briefest moment, Birdy thought I'd poisoned them. Poisoned my own children.

He sprinted down the hallway to check on them, finally returning to me. "It must be the stomach flu," he said, walking back. "There were other kids that stayed home from school today because of it." Birdy gazed at me with compassion, shaking his head in apology. "I'm sorry, Savannah. I'm sorry you had to go through that." Birdy squeezed my shoulder and then patted my head as you would a dog, probably unwilling to get any closer to me because of the way I smelled. "Dolly, too?"

Tears of exhaustion stung my eyes, and I pushed the filthy hair back from my face. "How would I know, Birdy?" I snapped, trying to blink away the tears. "Baby crap looks just the same as diarrhea. How would I know?" I swiped my wet sleeve across my face.

"I left Becky Lou's number for you in case of an emergency," Birdy said gently.

I glanced at Cody to make sure he was sleeping. "Yes! *An emergency*. For anyone else, an emergency means a fire, or a broken arm, or maybe your child choking on something stuck in their windpipe. It doesn't mean a kid with the stomach flu. Unless that kid has me for a mother!" I pushed aside the blanket and got up from the sofa, slowly backing away from Birdy, my palms up in surrender. "I can't do this, Birdy. This isn't me. I'm sorry. I can't be their mother." I backed up, step-by-step, away from Birdy and away from the responsibilities of motherhood. "I can't."

My back hit the door with the last step and I twisted around. Gathering the heavy hem of the robe so I could run, I yanked open the door and I ran out of the house and into the cold damp morning.

"Savannah!" Birdy shouted at me. "Savannah, stop!"

But I couldn't. I knew what needed to be done. Those kids didn't deserve a mother who couldn't remember them, a mother who was incompetent to care for them. And Birdy didn't deserve a wife who didn't remember how to be a wife.

I ran down the street, knowing Birdy couldn't follow. Not with all those kids so sick. They needed him. There was no way he'd leave them alone to come chasing after me.

The rocks and the pebble cut my bare feet, and the air was damp and cold, but I didn't care. I needed to get away. Away from that place I didn't belong. I ran. I ran not knowing where I was heading, but knowing what I needed to do. I ran past the rows of the tired old houses and toward the smell of the water, my lungs burning from the effort, the stitches in my head throbbing, while the sounds of the water grew nearer, and the air biting cold, as I imagined the water would be. I didn't know where the creek was or if it was deep enough for what I had planned. But I was determined to try. That family didn't need me, and they certainly didn't deserve the me that I was now, any more than they deserved the sorry depressed one I was before. Bringing down their lives and giving them a world where everything was gray because of me.

I heeded the call of the water, the rushing noise of it, the angry sound, loud and crashing in my ears, magnified by my chaotic thoughts. And I ran some more, the hem of the robe falling from my grasp, the weight of the robe dragging down heavy with the dew and the dirt.

I ran until I could run no more.

I stared at the water, dark as ink in the morning light, unfathomable, and heard it call my name. Whispering to me so loud, I was deafened by the noise of it. I didn't know if the water was deep. It didn't matter. All that mattered was the release from my mind's prison.

Slowly, I crossed the first smooth rock, slick with green moss, the water biting cold at my feet. I closed my eyes, and I let the hem of my robe fall, willing myself to stand still. Like a wick, the filthy robe, covered in vomit and sickness, sucked the water, soaking the length of it. Drawing it higher and higher, so high, the cold of the water hit my chest, freezing the air in my lungs, and I gasped from the shock of it. I dipped my head and gazed down at the water swirling below me, mesmerized by it, watching it churn and crash over the rocks that filled the swollen creek. With purpose, I stepped over to the next rock, toward the center and the deepest part of the creek, untying the sash and letting the weight of the water pull open my robe, where it revealed my breasts, the hem trailing behind me in a sodden shroud …

"Don't do it, Savannah May!" Birdy shouted from the bank, squatting down to unlace his boots, his face wild with fear, his eyes never leaving my face as he struggled to remove his boots with shaking hands. *"Don't you dare do it!"* He untied the first, and then the other, throwing his boots to the side and pulling off his socks, his eyes pleading with me.

I stood perfectly still, tears falling from my eyes.

"I'll come in after you. You know I will!" Birdy shouted over the roar of the water, holding my gaze the entire time, willing me to listen—to hear him, to see him. "If you go, I'm coming in after you!"

He ripped his shirt over his head and flung it in the dirt. "Savannah, you jump, I jump," he said, unbuttoning his pants and kicking them off, standing there in the cold morning in nothing but his drawers. "I can swim good enough for both of us, Savannah. You know I can. Don't you dare do it!"

Birdy tore off his glasses and pitched them to the side. "Savannah, look at me! Look at my face." Anguish paled his skin, and his body shook from emotion, but Birdy's eyes never left mine. He slid down the embankment and into the water with a sudden intake of breath when the cold assaulted him.

"If you go, I go!" he yelled out to me, his expression pleading me to stop. Birdy balanced himself, his arms at his sides, and stepped onto the first rock, briefly slipping but righting himself before he went in past his ankles. He went to the next rock, and still, his eyes never left my face.

"I'll fight to save us, you know I will." Birdy held his hand out to me, beseeching, navigating the rocks that staggered across the creek worn smooth and slick by the force of the water. "If we drown, we drown together, and then who will care for our children?" Birdy opened both his hands to me. "Don't do it, Savannah. *Please,* don't do it."

"*Don't come any closer!*" I put up my palm as if to stop him.

I stared down at the water swirling at my feet, pulling me down, down to a darkness I needed to return to—to remember what I had forgotten.

I raised my head, the wind blowing my damp hair around my face. "You tell me I'm a wife and mother, Birdy? Those are just words!" I screamed at him.

The water dragged at the robe, and it floated out behind me, pulling my shoulders down with the weight of it. My teeth chattered from the cold, and my legs and feet were numb, throbbing with each accelerated beat of my heart.

"Empty words, Birdy! My heart doesn't feel it!" I pounded my naked chest with my fist. "My brain won't tell me it's true." I yelled, slapping my head with my hand. "You tell me I'm twenty-seven-year-old mother? In my mind, I'm a twenty-year-old girl!"

The strength of the water tugged the robe from my body and tried to take me along with it. I struggled to stay on the rock, to say what I needed to say, knowing it wouldn't take much to succumb to the water's force, knowing all I needed to do was let my lungs fill with water to release me from the struggle. Tears coursed down my face, and my voice shook with emotion.

"You don't deserve to be saddled with someone as damaged as I am! Those children deserve a better mother. A mother who can love them and care for them. A mother who knows who they are!"

Birdy held out his arms to me, pleading, begging. "You go, I go, Savannah." Birdy was just a step away from my rock. "I'll catch you." He was nearly at my side, his arms reaching for me. "You jump, I jump."

Birdy lunged for me, his arms seizing me, clutching my waist, the strength of his grasp crushing me, and the force of it so sudden it knocked me off my feet, tumbling us into the water. We splashed down into the muddy darkness, the intense biting cold of the creek sucking the air from our lungs, and we gasped and choked, the water filling our mouths. Birdy struggled to swim for both of us, but the weight of the robe and my sodden sweats tugged and dragged with the current, catching on a jagged rock and forcing us under, while Birdy wrapped his forearm around my neck to keep me afloat, choking me, and the darkness of unconsciousness threatened to overtake me. With his free arm, Birdy struggled to rip the robe from my shoulders. He tugged it loose, releasing it to the current, where it floated downstream, before catching on a tree branch, the water of the creek pouring over it, until it broke loose and disappeared from sight. With his right arm gripped tight around my waist, Birdy swam to the bank, and then crawled up it, dragging me with him, collapsing with me at his side.

We lay there for a time, face down in the mud, struggling to catch our breath, our chests heaving, burning, trying to suck the air into our lungs. I rolled to my side and vomited creek water, my hair covering my face and my shame. When I finished, Birdy picked me up in his arms and climbed up the embankment, nearly throwing me down when we reached the top.

"Don't you *ever* do that to me again! Do you hear me, girl!" Birdy dropped to his knees, in front of me in the wet sand, his neck muscles corded, his lips blue with cold and rage as he shouted at me. He shook me by the shoulders so hard my head bobbed, and I felt my stitches pull tight while his fingers painfully dug into my naked shoulders. "Savannah May, don't you *ever* do that to me again." With an anguished cry, Birdy pulled me to him, crushing me in his embrace, his body heaving with sobs.

CHAPTER TEN

Something happened that day, the day Birdy kept me from heeding the call of the water. I expanded somehow. It was as if his burning love for me filled the frigid empty bottle I had become and poured into it all the warmth of him. The heat capturing inside, starting at the base and filling the bottle, working its way up and allowing it to expand my vacant heart, permitting it to beat again, to live, and continuing upwards past my shoulders and neck until it reached my head, where my mind accepted what my heart now felt. And as a cold bottle will do when suddenly filled with warmth—it cracked—allowing some of that warm tenderness to start trickling out and find its way to our children.

"She'll be fine," Birdy said to Becky Lou, who sat on the sofa with Cody shocked to see him carrying me in his arms through the door, shirtless and wet, and me in his arms, my sweats dripping water, and wearing his shirt. "She went out for a walk and she fell in the creek, that's all," he answered to a question not voiced, trying to believe it was true. "She'll be fine," he repeated, sounding as if he needed to convince himself of it. "Becky, can you run her a bath?"

Becky tucked the blanket tighter around Cody and hurried off to do what Birdy had asked.

Birdy carried me into our room, the sheets now changed, the minis gone, and the scent of pine cleaner filling the air, mixing with the fading smells of the children's sickness. He sat me on the bed and bent down to remove my sweatpants, pulling them off me with a roughness that spoke his anger, but softening his touch as he reached out to push the hair from my face and pick a leaf off my cheek. His fingers lingered, and his hand curled inward to caress my face, staring into my eyes, trying to understand.

I stared back, unblinking. There was nothing to say, and instead, I allowed myself to *feel*. I felt Birdy's love for me, filling me, warming me with it, knowing he would have jumped in to save me.

If I went, he went.

No matter if we both went down together, swept away with the current, no matter if his struggles to save us were unsuccessful and we both drowned. *If I jumped, he jumped.* I bent my head down in shame, the tears of my sin falling.

Birdy began to unbutton my shirt—*his* shirt, the shirt he'd wrapped me in before carrying me home, his fingers trembling so hard he struggled to undo the buttons. Gently, he pushed it off my shoulders, until I was naked before him. He went to the closet to find my robe, a short worn thing, the color of oatmeal and with a stain on the torn right pocket, helping me on with it while he waited for the tub to fill.

"You okay now?" Birdy sat beside me on the bed, now covered in a different blanket, the sheets and my granny's quilt in the washer from the sounds of it. He took my stiff hands and laced his fingers through them, squeezing them tight together. "Talk to me, Savannah. I need to know what you're feeling, what you're thinking. I need to know what we're dealing with." Birdy was shirtless and shoeless, his boots and socks still at the edge of the creek where he'd left them, and his body trembled and shuddered in waves.

I fell back against the bed, my arm covering my eyes, covering the shame of what I'd tried to do. Birdy stretched out beside me, half covering the length of me with him, just the same as a blanket, rising to his elbow and removing my arm from my face so he could see it, watching the emotions change the contours with humility, shame, embarrassment—and *thankfulness*, most of all.

Who was that desperate woman out there in the middle of the creek? Certainly not me. Birdy was my friend, and he was my husband. If he said I could do this—be a wife and a mother to our children—then I must believe him.

I must believe him.

"Savannah May, I need to know what you're thinking."

Becky tapped at the door. "The water's ready," she softly said.

The sounds of clothes thumping in the dryer came through the wall. The washer and dryer must be in the garage, my mind registered.

"Let's get you warm," Birdy said, taking my hand and leading me into the bathroom off the hall. The same one where I'd bathed Cody.

"The children?"

"They're all sleeping. Becky gave them something to help their stomach, and they're all sleeping." Birdy undressed me as if I were a child, untying my sash and pulling the robe from my shoulders and then off each arm, helping me into the warm water scented with bath oils Becky thought I might like. "You did good with them kids, Savannah May. You did real good, baby girl. Hell, you did better than I could have, having them all get sick at once and still getting Dolly fed. There is no way I could have done *that*," he added, smiling kindly at me, referring to my breast-feeding Anna.

I relaxed into the water, slipping down enough to let my hair float into it, knowing I wasn't supposed to get the stitches wet, but realizing it was far too late to care. If there was damage, it was already done.

Birdy kneeled at the side of the tub to bathe me, wetting the rag, then lathering it up, his gentle hands working the soap into my skin. Washing me. Washing away all of my sins. He stroked and caressed all the parts of me: my feet, cut from the rocks and the pebbles, tenderly swabbing the rag over them, the soap a gentle sting; my legs, scratched from the tree limbs that littered the water; my arms: still bearing the bruises of my IV. When Birdy got to my face he stopped, pausing to take me in, to read my thoughts. Or try to read them.

"Please, talk to me. I need to know," he whispered.

I knew what he was asking. Birdy needed to know, did I mean it? Would it happen again? Was it safe for him to work, or leave the house, knowing I'd been driven to the point of despair. He knew I would never harm our children, but he wanted to know if I would harm myself.

"You did good, Savannah. Just as good as any mother could. You took care of our children. Three sick children at once." He squeezed some baby shampoo from the bottle into his hands and worked it in my hair, mindful of my wound, massaging it slowly, gently, and then using the plastic cup to rinse it out, tilting my head back so the water wouldn't get in my eyes. "You did it, Savannah May, all by yourself, and you did a great job. Only, maybe next time, don't use the bleach to clean." He gave me a lopsided smile. "I imagine we'll have to get new carpet."

Birdy put down the toilet lid and he sat, his head tilted toward me at an angle, patiently waiting for me to talk. He wouldn't demand it of me. He'd wait until I was ready. Then he'd listen, as he always did. Listen to the long of it, listen to the short of it, whether it took an hour or a minute. He'd listen.

"It's gone, Birdy," I finally said, and sat up, my long hair covering my breasts. "Whatever was inside of me—it's gone." I gathered my hair to the side and twisted to remove the water. Birdy extended his hand and helped me from the tub, then he dried me with a towel, the same as I did for Cody, only his drying was more thorough, and he got all of my girly parts, making me open my legs wider so he could reach them.

"Powder?" Birdy held up the white plastic bottle of baby powder.

"No, thank you."

Birdy tidied the bathroom and then opened the door. Putting his arm around my shoulders, he led me back to our room, and he found me some clean clothes to wear—more gray sweats—and a sweatshirt with a picture of some bulldog wearing a red hat. The logo was faded, and I didn't much care what it said, too fatigued to read it. He gave me some of his thick white socks for my feet, tugging one on the right, but I told him I could do it, and I tugged on the left.

"You can stop staring at me, Birdy, as if I'm some time bomb waiting to explode," I said, wishing he'd stop watching me as if he needed to prepare to duck and cover. "I'm fine now. I promise."

Maybe I was being a bit over-optimistic so Birdy wouldn't worry so much. Maybe "fine" wasn't quite the right word to describe what I was feeling, but I definitely felt *better*. Almost as if some heavy burden had been lifted from me.

Birdy pulled back the sheets from the bed, indicating I should get in. "You come get into bed and get some rest. I need to shower and get to work." Birdy shook his head and sighed, the muscles on his chest expanding with the effort. "I wish I could stay home with you, but I've got a load to take north. I'll be back before dark. Becky Lou will be staying to help out."

I started to protest I didn't need a babysitter, but who was I kidding? With three sick kids, I needed all the help I could get. And now I felt fevered and had the chills, so I probably was sick, too. Besides, she could do all the laundry.

"I'd rather lie on the sofa with Cody, if that's all right."

I watched Birdy strip off his pants, appreciating the outline of his muscled thighs beneath the contours of his boxer briefs. *I'm wearing a tattered robe, and Birdy is wearing designer drawers?* The thought came, and stayed. Must have been my idea. A link to my past. They were the same kind I'd purchased for Bobby Lee one Christmas, the year after we graduated high school, so it must be a Savannah thing. All the men I sleep with must have to wear CK.

Birdy watched me watch *him*. His thumbs were hitched in the elastic waistband of his shorts, watching my reaction, as he got ready to remove them.

"I promise not to faint," I said, a weak smile playing on my lips.

"Can I remind you, I'm cold?" he drawled.

I laughed and covered my eyes with my hands. "Okay, I owe you. Better to impress me when you're warm." I uncovered my eyes in time to see Birdy's fine backside heading to our shower.

———◆•◆———

Kids can grow on you. Especially sick, sad ones, the kind that remind you of the abused animals on those TV commercials, of the dogs with the missing limbs and the weepy eyes with the flies nesting in the corners, and those tortured expressions as they stare soulfully into the camera while Sarah McLachlan sings, urging you to adopt or send money to help feed them–a one or a five.

By the end of that first day spent with all of us cuddled up together on the sofa, not feeling well, but at least feeling miserable together, reading story books and watching the fake gas fire in the fireplace, I'd have sent in a twenty to help feed those kids. Assuming I had one, (but figuring I didn't).

Becky Lou babysat us, earning her five dollars an hour or whatever we paid her, washing the foulness from the clothes and the sheets, scrubbing the floors, and heating us some soup, and then baking us some cookies when I asked. I didn't have to do a thing but sit there with my children and share in their fever, feeding Anna when she needed, but handing her off to Becky when she needed a diaper change or to be put in her crib to nap.

The day was pleasurable, almost. Of course, the children were as limp as rags and lethargic, but they were sweet and pleasant, nestling up to me like puppies, burrowing, and wanting the lick and the love of their mother. I pet and I stroked for most of the day, not caring who or which, just petting and stroking, reading, or resting, not even watching TV. Spending it as old-fashioned people did, people without running water or cable, holding one child on my lap until he or she slept, and then another, and taking comfort in the feel of Anna in my arms nursing at my breasts, her mouth cool on my skin, drawing the heated milk from me.

At one point, I told Becky to fetch me the guitar, and I played some sweet songs, gospel mostly, the words bringing tears to my eyes as I brushed aside the enormity of what I had set out to do that day. Birdy had saved me, and then washed the sin from my body, and I put it all behind me, where it would stay.

Children are resilient. So are twenty-year-olds going on twenty-seven. By the next day the children were better. Antsy even, not screaming, or shouting the way most normal kids do, who talk and laugh and play rough, unlike my reserved kids, the children of the corn. I sensed an unsettledness about them needing to be released, the way a nervous dog demands a walk or a horse requires to be let from the barn to run free. Maybe it was because of me, feeling trapped inside that small house, restless, staring at the dark fake paneling on the walls and the gas fire in the fireplace sputtering out of the clogged carbon-filled holes of the gas line, the walls closing in around me. It was as if there was some sort of slight turbulence in the air, accelerating our healing and charging the atmosphere with the electricity of it. An undercurrent of energy building up, waiting to be spent or freed. I think some people call it cabin fever, when you're shut in a small space for an extended period, isolated and claustrophobic, out in the wilderness with no one but your thoughts for company. Only this would be more like trailer fever, because the house was no bigger than a new doublewide—or a single, if you counted the canvas awning extension—and it was crammed with children and one teenage babysitter I'd long grown tired of having around.

My parents were seldom home when I was growing up, too busy with their active social lives to bother much with me. There were parties to attend, benefits to organize, or meals to eat with friends. They weren't home fussing after me, baking me cookies or warming my tea, or asking if I wanted the crusts trimmed off my peanut butter and jelly sandwich, the way Becky did. We had our housekeeper, Zula. Sour Zula, whose mouth always puckered as if she'd just eaten a dill pickle, and her brows pulled so low it was a wonder she could see. Zula watched after me some, made sure my clothes were clean and there was food in the kitchen to eat, occasionally baking me pies and such. Although often I wouldn't eat them if she was mad at me, thinking maybe they'd be poisoned and she could finally be done with me.

And she was mad plenty, especially after I started seeing Bobby Lee, her expression staying sour, not just coming and going as before, when at least sometimes she'd smile when I said please and thank you. After Bobby Lee started coming around, she grew meaner, which was hard for me as sometimes Bobby could be mean, too. So I'd have the two of them to deal with, their bad moods and their bitter expressions, wanting things from me but not always telling me what, exactly. Zula always loved Birdy, adored sweet Birdy Johnson, the poor boy from Tennessee, with no mama and the white trash no-good daddy, the quiet boy with those gentle, soulful eyes the color of chocolate cake. Those were Zula's words, but I have to say she was correct. She'd find Birdy in my room, not seeing him enter through the front door, coming in with the wind, she'd say, and yet not be angry he was there. She knew Birdy would keep me safe from harm, that Birdy had the sense God gave him, when I must have left mine at the hospital the day I was delivered, she'd say,

Zula hated Bobby Lee. Not that she ever said anything to me or my parents, at least not that I know of. She didn't need to; her silence was as loud as a bang. Bobby was always respectful to Zula, as Southern boys are taught to be—even to the help—saying his please and his thank yous, and I'll have her home in time for supper. Zula would grow quiet when my parents talked about me and Bobby Lee as a couple, when they remarked they needed to start setting aside money for our wedding, and joking how Bobby and I would need to have sons so there'd never be the necessity to change out the sign of Thomas and Sons at the mill. For a time, the kitchen would grow noisy with the sounds of her clanging the pots and the pans. Until Daddy would yell out, asking what all the noise was about, and the sounds would grow still, until the next time it got brought up, the mention of a wedding, when the racket would start all over again.

"I've got two loads to deliver after I drive the bus," Birdy said, "and I don't know if I'll be home by dark, but I'll try." He shrugged on his jacket and grabbed his thermos from the counter in the kitchen. He had to make his own coffee since I didn't know how to use the machine. Our old one broke years ago, and this was a new one he bought me for my birthday, which I wasn't yet taught how to use.

"Will you kiss me goodbye?" I slapped my hands against my arms to warm my myself, my feet freezing despite my slippers. Was there no insulation on that house?

Birdy set the chipped green thermos on the counter, and he took me in his arms, sharing the heat of him. He kissed me on the mouth, letting his lips linger.

We'd tried French kissing the night before as we lay in the bed together, before going to sleep, and it was even better than the last time. Feeling more familiar, like a fourth date, or a fifth. So much better that he rolled on top of me, and I let him, the hardness of him scaring me just a little, but working my way through it, forcing myself to lie still, and he didn't take it any farther, knowing I was scared. His tongue explored my mouth, probing and urgent, the same way his hands explored my breasts. And even though you'd think I'd be sick to death of having someone tugging or pulling on them after having Anna mess with them all day and night, his touch flushed me with pleasure, and my milk started to run, ruining my moment, but not his, it seemed.

Birdy finally pulled away, but let his fingers linger on my cheek. "You okay? You seem …" he tried to come up with a word, "I don't know, jumpy." He tilted his head to the side, trying to figure it out while I hugged myself to stay warm in the drafty kitchen.

I poured myself a cup of coffee just to heat my hands with the cup. Not to drink, just to heat my hands. Apparently, caffeine was another thing I wasn't supposed to have as a nursing mother. A cosmopolitan and a cigarette, I could see, but a beer or cup of coffee? The things have to filter through me first, it's not as if I'm giving it to Anna straight from the cup. Worse, the information kept coming via the babysitter, the girl who, just months ago, had a locker with colorful stickers and boy band photos pasted inside and needed to raise her hand in math class to get permission to tinkle.

"You're right. I am jumpy. You'd be jumpy too if you had a babysitter watching your every move, making sure you changed a diaper the right way." Birdy raised his eyebrows at me. "Hey! How was I supposed to know you have to wipe from front to back? Come on! Who knows these things? I don't know that I wipe myself from front to back. I just do it, and yet somehow it all works out fine." Birdy remained silent, a smile tugging at the side of his mouth as he grabbed his thermos, tucking it securely under his arm. "Birdy, I don't want a babysitter today," I whined, sounding just the way a child who needs one sounds. Maybe if I stomped my feet or threw myself to the ground in a fit, I'd get my way. "Come on, she's driving me nuts. The kids are all better. I think I can now handle them on my own without her."

"One more day, Savannah. Give it one more day."

The next day, Birdy gave me my reprieve. The kids were well by then, but as the flu was going around, the school felt it best for parents to keep their children home an extra day, just in case. Of course Becky Lou said if they needed help with their homework, she could help them, as she helped all of her brothers and sisters with theirs. I'm sure she fit it in between darning their socks and knitting their sweaters, right after she finished with the blood donation for the Red Cross and working in the soup kitchen for the homeless, not only serving it, but also making it. I had half a mind to call in and recommend her for that "Heroes" segment on CNN I remember watching with Bobby and Birdy one Thanksgiving weekend at my house. Becky Lou was right up there with the man who chewed through a fence to save those abandoned kittens, or the nun who saved all of those young Russian girls from becoming mail-order brides.

The walls were falling down in on me, and not only the ones in my mind. The drywall in the kitchen needed repairing, which might have been one of the reasons it was so dang cold in there. I spotted mold growing on some of the floorboards, a result of the humidity, I'm sure, but not something I remember being a problem in my mama's house. The washer and dryer were so old some of the clothes came out spotted with rust stains. How did people live like this? In a worn-out old house crammed together same way as mice in a cage and so cold you needed to huddle together just to get warm in front of the fire. Which didn't give off much heat to speak of, only some blue flames same way as a stove, and with the smell of gas or butane in the air, where, instead, wood smoke should be.

I had a plan.

The idea started with the phone call from my mama checking in and apologizing why she and my daddy hadn't been by to visit or see the babies. They'd been too busy, she said. Crazy busy, visiting old friends of theirs that they missed since moving down to Florida, with the exception of the short visit to Granny Ellie, who wasn't a friend, but who they were forced to go see, to find out if she was still breathing, I suspect. Mama went on about this or that or the other, finally saying good-bye and adding they'd come to see us before they drove home, because it had been so long since they'd seen the children, she was sure they'd all grown, and to give "James" their best, and for me to try and not wear him out so much.

CHAPTER ELEVEN

I began to implement my plan.

Forty-five minutes later, I'd managed to get Anna fed, and dressed into her best clothes, if that child owned such a thing, as even her cute dresses must have been handed down from her sisters. I'd forgotten to change her diaper first, but one of the minis reminded me it was the correct thing to do, and then she helped me do it, watching all the while as I wiped from front to back, and then wiped again, for good measure.

I fed the kids their breakfast—cereal and milk—adding sugar to sugared cereal, as one of the girls pointed out, but saying it tasted better, just to be kind, I gather. And then I got both the girls dressed, an easy thing to do as they dress themselves, and their clothes are as identical as they are. Cody I dressed in the same clothes he wore the day before, which I found folded on the chair in the corner. They seemed clean enough, and who would care? Not Cody. The child is what? Four? It's not as if he has an opinion one way or the other, or a voice in which to offer it.

I bounced around the kitchen, putting things away wherever I pleased, but trying to make it sensible, full of nervous energy. The sad Savannah was getting a formal burial by cremation, so she could never be exhumed. I was a new person. A better person. And I had a plan.

"You seem happy, Mama," said a mini, catching me in the children's bathroom, searching for the baby lotion to rub on my dry hands.

I tried to do one of the minis' hair in one long braid, and two in the other, so I could tell which was which, but they said they both wore their hair the same way, so I left their red hair straggling down, and I still didn't know who was who. So far, I just called them both darlin'. That way it made me seem nice, and they didn't catch on, but I had half a mind to find a permanent marker and put an X on one. Only then I'd have to ask who she was, and I didn't want to hurt either of their feelings and have them realize what a sorry excuse of a mother I was, asking their names, for heaven's sake.

"I am happy, darlin'. Your mama is happy to be home." I figured if I said it often enough, I might start believing it. "Can you watch Cody and Anna while Mama takes a shower?"

It wouldn't be hard to watch Cody. That little boy hadn't moved an inch since I'd parked him in front of the television set. Watching paint dry might be harder.

"Is that a new television set? Have we not owned a television set before?" The way Cody stared at it, you'd think we'd just got the first one on the block and he was watching the moon landing, or the Super Bowl the year of the Steelers and the Cowboys matchup.

"It was broke for a while. But Daddy bought you a new one because you were mad and wouldn't talk to him for a long time."

I put Anna inside her handed-down playpen, and she smiled her toothy smile, which was more than I could say for the minis. I think Anna had more teeth than they did. She played with some toys, and I'm happy to say they were *real* toys and not some homemade thing from scraps of fabric or a plastic food takeout container. These kids were so well behaved and reserved I never heard them shout or holler once. It was like being around alien pod people, or the children of Stepford, from that old movie that came out before I was born but is on the Sci-Fi Channel, now and again, about humans who get turned into robots. I left the kids watching some cartoons on basic cable, not premium—no doubt we couldn't afford the upgrades—and I went to take a shower.

In less than twenty minutes, I was dressed and wearing some homely gray dress that must have come from the Goodwill and been donated by the Amish, it was so plain. But at least it fit. Under the sink in my bathroom, I found an old curling iron stuffed behind the cheap one-ply rolls of toilet paper, and I used the iron to curl the ends of my hair, trying to give it some bounce. I didn't find a makeup drawer filled with assorted choices, the way I had at home, the drawer with so much makeup it would take a lifetime to use. Instead, all I found was a small black cosmetic case with a broken zipper and inside it some drugstore mascara, a pink lipstick, and some powder that was crushed and too yellow for my skin. At least the lipstick hadn't been eaten and the color wasn't half-bad. With light steps, I swept down the hallway in my Pennsylvania ball gown.

"Mama, you look pretty!" The minis said in unison, something they did quite often, when they weren't whispering to each other in the strange alien children language I'd heard was common in twins, their saucer eyes wide under their colorless lashes.

Cody unglued his eyes from the TV long enough to come over to me. I leaned down, and he put his thin arms around my neck, burying his small head into the curve of it, his glasses pressing up against my skin. "You're pretty, Mama," he whispered. I hugged him back, and then I gently untangled his arms, removing the glasses from his face and cleaning his greasy lenses with the hem of my dress.

"Kids, as your daddy would say, you ain't seen nothin' yet! You just wait to see what your mama has planned for today."

I felt so light I almost skipped into the family room and toward the big window that faced out toward the front yard. Moving the red polyester drapes to the side, I scanned the driveway and the street for signs of the school bus. Not seeing any yellow, I said, "I'm getting something from the garage," and went out the front door, praying our garage was manual and not electric. I needn't have wasted the prayer. I lifted the handle and there it was—my beautiful car. And inside that car was an extra key. Hidden in plain sight and hanging from the rearview mirror, along with a bunch of other keys. Keys Birdy probably thought were some sort of decoration, but were actually keys to every door I ever needed to unlock: my car, my old house, Bobby Lee's car, his house, my granny's house …

With shaking hands, I quickly removed the car cover, and then I removed my car key from the chain and inserted the key into the ignition. That old Mustang, she roared to life. Just as quickly, I turned her off and replaced the cover, hoping the kids wouldn't say anything to Birdy or he'd notice the smell of gasoline. I didn't imagine he would because of the way that bus spewed diesel fumes enough to make you choke. I made it back inside and was sitting on the sofa watching TV with the kids, the picture of normal and domestic, or so I hoped, when Birdy walked through the door.

He looked around the house, his head tilting to the right before tilting to the left, and then he regarded the kids, a smile tugging his lips crooked, and then at me, bouncing Anna on my knee. Without saying a word, he walked back out the door and stood on the porch for a moment or two facing the street, before turning back around to face the front door and reaching out to ring the doorbell.

"Birdy, what on earth?" I pulled open the door, finding him, his eyebrows high with surprise, his smile creasing the corners of his eyes. Anna got all squirmy recognizing her daddy, and she reached for him with an eagerness that tugged my heart. Birdy took her in his arms, kissing her loudly on her drooling lips and hugging her tightly to him before burying himself in her chubby folds, while Anna laughed and used both hands to clutch his hair.

"Excuse me, ma'am," he said, holding Anna against his shoulder, "I think I'm at the wrong house. I'm looking for my wife and my family. The Johnsons?"

"Very funny. What did you expect to find? The children locked in the closet and my head in the oven?"

The way Birdy's smile dropped, that may have been exactly what he expected to find.

"Daddy, it's us!" the minis said, jumping up and down in their blue elastic-waist pants and flowered shirts that I found in their drawer underneath some denim—I swear, I am not

144

making this up, *overalls*—that I threw away in the trash. "It's us! And Mama, too. Isn't she pretty, Daddy?" said mini one.

"Kiss her, Daddy, kiss Mama!" said mini two.

How strange, I thought, before Birdy leaned over and kissed me chastely on the lips in much the same way he'd done to Anna, that our children had to tell their parents to kiss. Did Birdy not show affection to me in front of our children? Or maybe he did, and I was the one who didn't. So far, I noticed Birdy seemed to reach out to touch me more than I did to him. Without thinking, he'd casually place a hand on my arm or my leg, or brush a crumb from the corner of my lips, or the hair from my face. And each time he did it, I felt it with a heaviness. Not in a bad way. But in a new way. The same as when you first meet a person and they accidentally touch you on your bare shoulder, you feel the weight of it, the pressure. The way it leaves an impression almost, an indentation on your skin that lasts long after they have removed their hand.

"You've done great, Savannah. Good job." He strode past me and surveyed the rest of the house, coming back to the front room, and stopped in front of me, holding still in expectation, his face tightening, observing the dress and the makeup. "You goin' somewhere?"

"No," I lied. "But I do have that doctor's appointment tomorrow."

"I know. And that reminds me." Birdy left the room and came back with my discharge papers. He read through them, his eyes squinting at the page, even despite his glasses. "How you feelin'? Any pain? Headaches? Are your stitches bothering you?" He sat down on the sofa, and the girls and Cody crawled in his lap like ants around sugar while Anna scuttled along on the floor stopping to play with some lint. Birdy must have found a troubling line on the page because he seemed embarrassed, and some color came to his cheeks. He cleared his throat. "Savannah … uh …"

"What's it say, Daddy? What's the paper say?" said mini one, or two.

Birdy exhaled while his eyes lifted to mine. "Savannah, when was the last time you did your duty?" he said, sounding formal and serious.

"My duty?" I repeated, confused. I swear, it was less than two hundred and fifty miles from Tennessee to Georgia, and yet sometimes Birdy seemed to be speaking a foreign language. He used more euphemisms than anyone I'd ever met. "Like a military one? One to my country?" I went to Anna and pulled the lint from her mouth. "I think I've voted one or twice, does that count? Honestly, Birdy, if you have something to ask, just spit it out." I dried my fingers by rubbing the slobbery lint on the sides of my dress.

The minis started to giggle, and within seconds they were laughing their little red heads off, falling to the floor in a fit. Even Cody almost laughed. It was the most animated I'd ever seen them.

"Mama," said a mini, trying to catch her breath, "Daddy wants to know the last time you went poo."

I twisted my head toward Birdy, who held up his hands, palms out. "Hey, don't blame me. I'm just reading the notes. The doctor wants to make sure everything is still in working order. According to this paper, when someone has a head injury they need to be supervised. I'm supposed to be in there with you to help. In case you faint or something."

"Daddy has to watch Mama poo, Daddy has to watch Mama poo!" the minis sang, jumping up and down and going around in a circle in the hillbilly rendition of "Ring Around the Rosie."

"It's not happening." I got up and put Anna in her playpen. "I am not having you in the bathroom while I do my 'duty,' as you call it."

I know Birdy was just following orders, but for some reason I felt angry. Controlled, even. As if I had little say in even the simplest things of my life. Things as simple as the freedom to poo without someone hovering over me. Watching. To make sure I did it correctly. Yet another thing I might manage to screw up.

Something started to boil up inside me. It started with a simmer, until it began to roil, the bubbles just breaking the surface.

Birdy's jaw was set, and he seemed willing to match me. He hooked his thumbs in the tops of his pockets. "I'm your husband. I've been in the delivery room for the birth of each of our children. And believe me, in spite of what folks say about the miracle of birth—and it is a miracle, I'll grant you that—there's some parts that ain't so pretty. Most times, you push out something more than just the baby."

"That's disgusting!" I snapped. The minis started to giggle again. "You're still not going in there with me!"

Cody came over to me and put his arms around my legs, his face almost buried. "I'll go in with you, Mama. I'll watch you go poo."

I didn't know whether to laugh or cry. The entire thing was too ridiculous for words.

"Fine! Okay, who wants to go in with me and watch me poo? Birdy? Girls? Maybe we can invite Becky Lou, or some of the other neighbors."

"Don't yell at me, Savannah May. I'm only following the doctor's orders. I don't care if you shit or not," he said, his voice getting softer, his expression hardening.

The girls clasped their hands over their mouths that Daddy said a bad word.

"Girls, you go on inside with her, and make sure your mama does what she's supposed to do."

Birdy was ruining all of my plans. I was on a timeline, and he was interfering. I was going to take my car and go see my Granny Ellie. There had to be some way out of Hooterville for this family. If the family didn't want to come with me, if they'd grown attached to this wreck we called our home, I was getting out of it by myself, now, and would just have to convince them later to join me. Certainly if they saw how the other half lived, they'd want to come along.

The girls led the way, each holding my hand, stopping at the bathroom in the hallway.

"I don't want this one. I'll use the toilet in my bedroom," I insisted. They resisted, pulling back, but I tugged and continued down the hall, dragging them along with me and going inside my room.

"You can't, Mama," said the mini on my right.

"Sure I can."

"No, this one isn't the one Daddy uses. Daddy uses ours," said the one on the left.

This was insane. I didn't give a rat's rear where Birdy wanted to take a crap. It was bad enough I was forced to have an audience, but those girls were not going to tell me where it was, in my own home, I needed to go "poo."

I opened the door to where the toilet sat, but left it open just a bit. In case what Birdy said was true, and I passed out while giving service to my country.

When I was finished, still alive and with a beating heart, I pushed the lever.

Nothing.

I wiggled it. Nothing again. Dammit. What the heck was wrong? I pulled the handle up and down. Hadn't I used this toilet before in the past week since coming home from the hospital? No, come to think of it, I used the kids' because it was next to Anna and Cody's room, and I needed to wash my hands every few hours or so after I changed Anna. I went then. I guess I hadn't used this toilet at all.

"See, Mama? It don't flush," said a mini from behind the door.

I flung open the door. *"Doesn't!* It *doesn't* flush!" I shouted at her.

"That's what Mini May said, Mama. It don't flush. It's broke. It's been broke for a long time," Mini Ray explained, taking the hand of her sister, who now held her head down low because of the sting of my harsh words.

"It *doesn't* flush, and it's been *broken* for a long time!" I said through gritted teeth. "Do you understand me?" My voice was tight, and I was about to break my vow I wouldn't cry ever again.

I glanced up to see Birdy standing in the doorway, mad enough to rip me a new one.

"How long have these girls been attending Montessori?" I demanded. "They *do* go, right? That's what you told me. You said we drive around in that old broken-down school bus so our children can attend Montessori. Where, pray tell? A coalmine town in Kentucky? The Appalachia's of Tennessee?"

Birdy held his chin high, his legs planted wide, and I saw a vein in his neck pulse. I'd crossed the line. I knew it, and it was too late to take it all back. Something had unleashed. I was a hateful person, a horrible person. It seemed mean was spilling out of me from every pore. That instead of memories coming back, something cruel was oozing out of me in its place.

The minis' lips trembled, and their eyes went wider and bright blue, blue as a cloudless sky, the same color mine used to be.

"Girls, go to your room. I need to speak with your *mother*," Birdy said, enunciating the word without a trace of his drawl. His face was flushed and mottled, and his lips were drawn together in a tight line. I'd never seen him so mad in my life. Not even when he saved me in the creek. That was more desperation. Not this. This was seething anger. Anger at harsh words thrown into the faces of innocent children who did nothing to deserve it.

Anna started to cry in the other room, and I tried to brush past him.

"Oh, no you don't!" He grabbed at my arm and stopped me. "You let her cry." His fingers roughly bit into my flesh.

He pulled me to the bed and pushed me down. Not violently, but with enough force I bounced. He turned on me in a fury. "If I *ever* hear you speak to those children like that again, Savannah, I swear—"

"What, Birdy? You'll hit me? Is that what you want to say? You'll hit me?" I stood up less than a foot from him, my body heaving, trying to catch my breath, the heat so hot in my head I felt my stitches throb. "Is that why I'm so sad in all of those pictures on the wall, because I let you hit me?"

Birdy let out a whoosh, as if he'd been kicked in the gut. His face went white, and he breathed loud through his nose. He took a step back, and sweat beaded on his forehead.

"That's what you think? You think I *hit* you? As God is my witness, I have never laid one finger on you, Savannah. Not even when you may have wanted to push me to it."

"I think I remember!"

"You remember no such thing! I have never done anything but love you, Savannah May, the best way I know how. And if those kids don't talk right, or *articulate*, or *enunciate* the way you'd like, then it's my fault, not theirs. And they don't need you holler … *yelling* at them. They've only been going to the Montessori for four months, and we're all trying. We've tiptoed around this house for years because of your depression. But I'm tired now. I'm dead tired. I don't know how much longer I can take it."

Anna wailed from the front room. "Birdy, I—"

"Don't speak! I don't want to hear you speak." Birdy went to the closet and changed into a different pair of boots, jerking hard on the laces. So hard, one of them broke. He tied it anyway and headed for the door. "I'm going to work, and then I have to pick the dog up from the vet. I won't be home until supper. Becky Lou will come and help out."

Birdy stomped out, and moments later I heard the front door slam. Birdy had never actually yelled at me before. At least not the same way I yelled at him. He's raised his voice louder, or it went softer, but he's never really yelled. But he sure did seem to love to slam doors. And I wondered where Moonshine had been.

One of the minis saved Anna from her torture. The way she was crying, you'd have thought someone was stabbing her with a red-hot poker, instead of just wanting to be fed. Mini one or two held her on her lap while Anna sucked on a pacifier. I'd never imagined how much babies like to suck at something. Come to think of it, if I remember correctly, teenage boys weren't too far behind.

I went to the sofa and had one of the minis move over a bit so I could sit next to her, unbuttoning my dress and pushing the tab on that stained bra to do my other "duty."

"Ouch, Anna! Quit biting." I swear, before week's end, that baby was on formula. By my calculations, I'd spent the better part of three years having a child nurse at my breasts. More, if you count two at once, although for the life of me, I could not imagine how you feed two babies at the same time. Cody sat on my other side, and I patted his back over his little black plaid flannel shirt with the missing bottom button. "It's all right, Cody. Mama's sorry to be so mean. Girls, Mama's sorry." I stroked a mini head, noticing yes, it was red, but when the light caught it just right, her hair was woven with strands of gold, almost the same as the beads in my pageant gown.

Dipping my head and brushing my hair over to the one side with my fingers, I exposed the row of stitches in the shaved part of my hair. "You see this?" I pointed to it.

"Yes, Mama. That's where you hurt it when you fell off the ladder reaching for the sewing machine in the attic. Ain't it?"

the mini said, and then caught herself. "Isn't it?" she corrected, proving she was at least part mine and not solely the property of her father.

"Yes, it is," I said, trying to get Anna to take my breast and finish her feeding of me. "And I think that's why I've been so crazy. Because I hurt my head." I fastened the tab on the one side of the bra and then unfastened the other. Anna spent more time pulling away and observing the goings-on than she did nursing, and I'm no expert, but she didn't seem all that into me, so maybe she was just about ready to wean. Or my milk had soured and turned bitter, the same as I had.

"Is that why you're so sad, Mama, because your head always hurts?" Cody murmured, saying more words in that one sentence than I'd heard him speak since I came home.

"Maybe so, Cody. But no more. Mama won't be sad anymore. I promise." I ruffled his hair. Anna burped on her own, making her brother and sisters laugh, and I pulled myself together, both in clothes and mental capacity, and stood gathering diapers, the pacifier, and the diaper bag. "Now, show Mama where we keep the car seat. We're going on an adventure!"

CHAPTER TWELVE

I tooled down the highway in my custom-painted pink Mustang, the windows down, singing country songs with the minis, our hair flying in the wind. It was a bit of a struggle to get us all in my car, because honestly, until Mini May showed me on carseat.org to prove it to me, I had no idea all children under the age of eight have to ride in a safety seat. Eight? *Seriously?* I'd seen Birdy driving a tractor when he wasn't but ten or eleven, and goodness, I don't even want to think about the things my girlfriends said they did with the boys in school when they weren't but four years older than that. One would think if you allowed a boy to get to first or second base, you'd at least be able to sit in a car without the help of a booster.

There was a mini in the front next to me and a mini behind in the back, with Anna in the middle facing toward the trunk, as a mini pointed out was safest, and Cody on the other side. All, except for the baby who was in a bona fide car seat, sat in booster seats that had to be dragged out of that stupid bus. Attaching them was tricky, but I think I got it right after the first few tries.

The minis were a big help getting us ready, and they found my cell phone, some strange white plastic thing with no cover and an open face and filled with all kinds of bright tiny icons that did things I don't ever remember seeing before. Including ways for taking pictures and playing games, and with music, even. They told me where to find my purse and some cash money, which was hidden in the kitchen inside a cookie jar without any cookies. The cookies were in Tupperware, a mini said, to keep them fresher. The tacky jar was in the shape of a bear, next to a monkey that held some sugar and a lion that held flour. Zoo jars, they called them. I called them ridiculous and said we needed to get some new ones. Chrome or bushed nickel ones with airtight lids and not chipped ceramic tops that didn't seal. Then they told me where to go to find some gas. And not the truck stop station, because I didn't want to chance seeing Birdy. A pink Mustang is not exactly incognito. Instead, they pointed the way to a Mini-Mart, (they got a giggle out of the name) where I could fill up, which I did, and then ran inside to buy them some junk food. We were on an adventure. And what's an adventure without junk food?

"Where we going, Mama?" Mini yelled over the radio and the window, trying to keep the hair out of her eyes, using her hand to hold it back. It flew about her, resembling a red banner trailing behind a crop duster.

I told her how to roll up the window, and I turned down the music. "We're going to see my mama and daddy at the hotel. Then we're going to see my Granny Ellie, and after that, the mall, so Mama can get her hair cut and some new clothes."

With the help of the minis, as those girls are smarter than they look, I navigated my way out of the subdivision, and once free of it, I got on the interstate, remembering my way completely, and headed to the Hilton nearest the airport, where my mama and daddy were staying.

Having four kids is harder than it sounds. Not the birthing part, the pushing them out part. I'm sure that's a difficult task, not that I remember, but the getting everyone in and out of a car. There is so much that needs to be done. Buckling, unbuckling, lifting up, putting down, unstrapping, unfolding. By the time I got them all out of the car and Anna into a stroller, I was worn out.

"Y'all hold hands. Let's go find your grandmother and your granddaddy." The Johnson quartet and the crazy mother in the Amish dress strode through the lobby of the Airport Hilton Hotel. "Mini, call my mama and ask her where to meet."

"Which one of us, Mama?"

"Either one."

We found my parents in the hotel restaurant with the wild-patterned carpet and the fake potted palms, having dinner.

"Savannah! What are you doing out driving? Did the doctor say it was safe?" Daddy stood up, wearing khaki slacks, a white collared shirt, and a baby blue sweater, this time, knotted around his shoulders.

"Daddy, I told you this once and I'll tell you again, if I didn't know you, I'd think you were sweet. How many of those silly sweaters do you own, anyhow? Is it cold enough in Florida to need them? Or do you wear them just like you would a necklace?" I winked at him but meant it just the same.

"Savannah May!" Mama puffed, and then she got over it and started kissing and hugging her grandchildren. She stood and came over to me, whispering in my ear, "Why your husband won't let us help pay for that boy's surgery, I just don't know. Seems to me, that eye just keeps getting worse."

"Um … well, Mama, that's the reason I came to see you."

Daddy overheard, and with a nod toward me, took Anna out of her stroller and told the children he'd take them to get ice cream. Mama sat back down in their booth by the window overlooking the parking lot and invited me to sit next to her, patting the red vinyl, her bracelets jingling with the effort, her lacquered fingernails the color of skinned salmon.

"I wondered how long it would take," she whispered to herself.

There was no need to start with preamble. I knew what I'd come to say, and I'd just say it. I put my hand on hers, a vivid contrast, my nails bitten and ragged, hers long and slick. "I want my money, Mama. I want my trust fund."

She moved over a bit, away from me almost, as if distancing herself from the request, nervously fussing with the neckline of her colorful Chico's cruise wear blouse, her large diamond earrings flashing with the movement. "Savannah—"

"I can't live this way," I interrupted her. "I *won't* live this way." I took a sip of water from her glass, my hand shaking, the water spilling over the top. "Look at me, Mama!" I tapped my palm to my chest, tears stinging my eyes. "This isn't me. Why am I poor?"

"Savannah, you're hardly poor—"

I pulled at the bottom of that stupid dress that ended below my knees and stared down at the vinyl sandals on my feet and the toes without polish. "Look at what I'm wearing!" I gathered up the lap of my dress, twisting it in my hand, my fist tight, wanting to rip that ugly thing from me and kick off those awful shoes.

"I always hated that dress," Mama sighed. She turned her body and faced me, taking my hands in her slender ones, now old and wrinkled and covered in liver spots. Mama squeezed my hands and then released them. She began to speak, her tone measured but her eyes darting, and nervously twisting her wedding ring, the diamond the size of a dime, around on her finger. "Your husband is a proud man and a hard worker, Savannah May," she began.

"I know that, Mama, and that's why I want to help him."

Mama held up her hand to stop my interruption. She was on a roll and she had no intention of stopping until she'd had her say. "That rig of his cost him over a hundred thousand dollars, between the truck and the trailer. A hundred thousand dollars! That's a lot of money, and it's almost paid off, and with no help from anyone else. That boy has worked long and hard for what you have, and yes, it's been a trial for me to see you sad and wanting all these years, but we spoiled you as a child, Savannah. A new Mustang every year? And your daddy getting it painted custom. Pink. Because that's the color you wanted. Good Lord, I've never seen so many pink cars come and go in all my life. It was like being at a Mary Kay convention, only with Mustangs instead of Cadillacs."

"I only asked for the first one, Mama. Daddy didn't need to keep getting me a new one every year. The first one would have been enough. Daddy asked me what car I wanted, and that's what I said. I never expected a new one every year since."

It wasn't as if they couldn't afford it. Mama got a new car every year, and so did Daddy. They even bought a car for Zula, although hers was used. They had money. What about the country club memberships, or all the trips to Europe they took without me, saying they'd send me later, when I was old enough to appreciate it and not want to spend all the time on my phone talking to Bobby Lee or my friends? What about the expensive parties for hundreds of people, with the rented tents and the bands, or the jewelry my father kept buying for my mother that she never wore, not having enough fingers to wear the rings on?

My parents had money to burn, if what Allie June's parents said was true the night of her slumber party, their voices coming up through the heating vent in the kitchen and into her bedroom upstairs. It's not as if I ever asked them for things. I was spoiled, yes; I lived a life filled with nice and expensive things. But except for my car, I never asked for much except the normal stuff, some clothes or makeup or to pay for my yearbook.

And I wasn't unappreciative for the things I did have. My best friend came from nothing. Birdy was dirt poor. I knew what money could buy and what it couldn't. It could give you *things*, transient things that fell apart or broke down, or you grew out of. But it couldn't give you a smile of joy as you were pushed on a tire swing in the summer afternoon, so high you thought you could fly, or fill your heart to bursting with gratitude when you found your best friend has littered your bedroom floor with as many of the first flowers of spring he could find. It couldn't give you a tender touch from a girl who held you while you cried after your daddy beat you for just breathing, or the appreciation of finding a rented tuxedo on your front doorstep so you could attend senior prom. As the third wheel, but at least you could say you went.

"You know it's true, Mama. I never asked for all those cars," I insisted.

"Well, your daddy did buy you a new car every year, regardless," Mama said, tightening the back of her earring. "He got you a new car every year, same as the last, until they changed the style, or quit making them, I don't know which. Up until you married Birdy, and Birdy told him that he could take care of you without our help. Daddy thought that was a fine idea as well, so you could see how other people live, and appreciate what you had, and I thought was fine, too." She pushed her dinner plate of meatloaf or pot roast away, wiping her mouth one last time and placed her napkin on top.

I bet Daddy did think it was a *fine* idea as well, since he didn't come from money and married my mama and had all of her millions at his disposal when he married her. Not that my daddy wasn't generous, because he was, but it's easy to be generous when you're spending someone else's money.

"I want my money," I said, my voice tight, nervously playing with the bottom of my hair. "I'm not asking for a trip to Europe, Mama, or a new sports car." This request wasn't only for me. The money was to help better the lives of the people I cared for. I tried hard to hold back my tears, but my voice shook with the effort of it. "I want a better house, Mama, with a toilet that flushes. A better school district for my children. I want surgery for my son. And my husband to have something other than a bus to drive. What do I have to do to get it? Do I ask Daddy? Granny Ellie? I can't wait three more years, Mama. I won't last that long." My eyes welled and finally spilled over, running down my cheeks.

"All right, Savannah," Mama sighed. "I suppose you've gone without for long enough." She reached inside her purse and pulled out her wallet, removing from it a business card and a platinum American Express. Opening my palm, she placed them both in my hand. "Go see your granny. I'm sure she'll be happy to release your trust. It just about killed her to see you become so dowdy. Now go buy yourself some new clothes and some for the children. And burn that dress. Lord, how I hate that dress."

The nursing home was on the other side of town, in the nice expensive part. It was white and pillared, and so cliché with black shutters framing all the windows, and a great expanse of green lawn and flowers that bloomed red and yellow, so bright it was hard to miss them. Plus, the sign on the post showed a woman in a rocker as the logo, so we figured it must be the place. One of the minis called ahead to let my granny know we were coming to see her, and there she was when we drove up, sitting on the front porch in a rocker, just the same as the logo, only my granny was more fashionably dressed. She sat playing a game of cards with an orderly, or a man who just preferred white, and she must have been winning, because she was laughing.

She appeared to be a hundred, between all the wrinkles and the snowy white hair, and rightly so, as she must have been nearly seventy or ninety, but she was as fit and spry as a spring chicken, as they say. "They" being anyone Southern or corny enough to use that expression. She fussed and cried over me and the children. Especially Anna, having never met her, and saying the minis had the same hair color as granny's when she was their age, but they had more freckles than she did back then, and granny's eyes are green and not blue, so their eyes came from me. She wholeheartedly agreed Cody needed the surgery and then she suggested I pay for Birdy to have LASIK, surprising me she even knew the word, or what it was for.

I mentioned this and she said she was old, not stupid, and she knew all about such things and more: cataracts, and glaucoma, angina and bypass. Even starting to explain how it's all done. I stopped her before she went too far, as she was scaring the children with some of the reenactments. Then she about dropped me to my knees when she asked did I want to move back into the house? *Her* house still, come to find out, and not Daddy and Mama's. The house that goes to me when they all die. Granny said I might as well take it now, since she's halfway up that stairway to heaven and Mama and Daddy might as well be dead than to be living in Florida in a condominium.

She walked us all to my car, with only the help of a cane, sharp in her tan slacks and a yellow twin sweater set, her white hair done up perfectly in a tight bun, diamond earrings twinkling in her ears and just as bright as my granny's eyes. She kissed me good-bye, her lips as dry as an onionskin, and then reached inside her bra and pulled out a wad of bills, handing them to me.

"You take this, now, and get yourself some new clothes and a decent haircut. And do something about those children. They're downright raggedy. I'll go call the lawyer and tell the tenants they need to move out of the house. They're getting divorced and won't need it anyway." My granny stood as straight as her age would let her, compassion filling the lines of her face, smoothing the years from it.

I leaned into her with my baby between us, all sharing one heart, and I hugged her tight, not wanting to let go. "Thank you, Granny. Thank you so much," I choked.

"You're welcome, darlin'." She pulled back and stared into my eyes, hers now filling with tears, and she held my face in her gnarled hands. "You're a good girl, Savannah May. A good, sweet girl. And don't you ever let anyone tell you otherwise."

"Okay, Granny."

"And child, please burn that dress. Lord, how I hate that dress."

There is nothing better than a beauty makeover to make a girl feel complete again. I was a new and improved Savannah after spending some of that money. I looked pretty and fashionable, and maybe just the tiniest bit rich, not that it was my intention. I was still fat compared to my pageant weight, but in my new stretch jeans with the tapered pencil legs and my black strappy sandals and silk, *real silk*, blue top, I appeared thinner. And my hair! I had blond hair again. Dyed and cut at an expensive salon in the mall, and not cut at a Fantastic Sam's, where believe me, there is nothing fantastic about him or his fifteen-dollar haircuts. I had on brand-new eye makeup professionally done by the makeup artist, which might have been a bit heavy for daywear, but what the MAC girl told me was the latest trend.

The minis were adorable, too. Even if I would catch hell when Birdy saw them. It made me so nervous to think about it, I was sweating into the silk of my new shirt. And Cody had an appointment for his surgery, and I got one for Birdy, if he wanted it, and they all had new clothes, and we'd gone to that dealership in the city, where I'd bought Birdy that new truck ...

I pushed the sign deeper into our dead grass and wiped my hands on the sides of my jeans. If I'd done so much good, then why was I so nervous? Sick almost. Change is good. Change is a good thing. Birdy would just have to get used to it, is all. I glanced over at Birdy's new truck and hoped he'd like it. What man doesn't want a new truck? It was the most expensive one on the lot. Surely, Birdy would like it. Men love all that expensive macho crap.

"Here he comes, Mama!" Melissa Ray said. "Here he comes!" She jumped up and down, her newly styled and French braided hair with the color highlight bobbing up and down and dressed as a city girl in purple leggings and a graphic T-top and her purple kids Keds. Her sister was dressed the same, only her outfit was pink.

"There's the rig! Look, Mama. There's Daddy!" said Emma May. "And I think Daddy has Moonshine. I see him out the window wearing that cone!"

I folded my hands together and sent up a prayer. "*Amen,*" I whispered.

Birdy was forced to park the rig on the street alongside the house because his new truck was parked next to the bus, and there wasn't enough room for it to fit beside it.

I watched Birdy from behind my sunglasses, thankful for their protection but still growing uncomfortable from him staring at me. The rig rumbled to a stop, and the brakes hissed air, sounding deadly as a snake. He yanked open the door, letting the dog out, who barked and ran around the yard in circles trying to shake off the plastic cone on his head. On fire, Birdy strode with long angry strides stopping in front of me, his head jerking from side to side, his eyes taking in the new truck, the girls and their new clothes and hair, and me and my clothes and my new hairdo. But he mostly fixated on the "For Sale" sign I'd just planted in our dead grass.

"What have you done, Savannah?" he said, his voice so low it sounded unnatural, the warning growl of a bear or a lion before it attacks. Birdy's chest heaved beneath his flannel shirt, and his face was deep red. His neck stretched forward, and he kept clenching and unclenching his fists, dying to hit something. Me, most likely.

"I … uh …"

"I want answers, Savannah. And I want them right now." Birdy's voice was shaking, but not half as much as my legs.

"Daddy!" Emma said. "Mama took us to the mall."

"Look, Daddy," Melissa Ray said. "Mama got our hair done and some new clothes. And our nails, too." She held up her painted fingers. Melissa went to run to Birdy, but he held his hands out to stop her. "Girls, go inside, and take your brother with you. Mini Ray, where's your sister?"

Melissa stepped back, frightened by her father's tone, her lower lip trembling. "She's inside, sleeping, Daddy. Mama fed her and then put her to bed," Melissa said, her voice soft, sticking up for me, trying to prove to her father I was at least attempting to be a good mother.

Melissa took Emma's hand and they walked to the porch, their new shoes dragging. They took Cody, too, who stood waiting, wearing his new jeans and a bright green collared shirt, his hair cut and gelled, looking adorable. The solemn trio slowly walked back inside the house, too frightened even to play with the dog, who barked and howled and followed them inside the house.

I put my hands up to deflect Birdy's anger, not wanting it to sear me and ruin my makeup. "Birdy, I know you're mad. Just let me explain. You see, I went to my parents, and then to my Granny Ellie—"

"Mad doesn't begin to describe it." Birdy's nostrils flared, and perspiration beaded on his forehead and in the crease of his neck. "What the hell have you done? Why is that truck in our driveway, and why is there a "For Sale" sign on our lawn? My son is dressed like a fag, and our daughters have a blue and purple stripe in their hair … and those ridiculous clothes. And your hair is white!" He took a step toward me. "Take off those goddamn sunglasses so I can see what else you've done!"

With trembling hands, I removed my designer sunglasses, sunglasses that cost half the price of that stupid bus, and held my chin up. I wasn't backing down. It was my money. I'd do what I want with it.

"You look ridiculous. Go wash that stuff off your face. You look like a streetwalker."

"Screw you! The girl at the mall said it's the newest style. It's Lady Gaga's, and it's called Viva Glam. I'm sick of being plain and ugly, Birdy. Same as some poor girl. I want to be glamorous again. If this makeup is good enough for the future queen of England, then it's good enough for me!"

Birdy was still hot angry, but I must have said something humorous, because a muscle twitched a bit at the back of his jaw, and he squinted his eyes to keep a smile away.

"Do you even know who Lady Gaga is?" Birdy's legs were planted wide, and he crossed his arms in front of him.

"No. But I assume she's engaged to one of the princes. Either that balding but handsome one, Prince William, I think, or the redheaded one who's always in trouble."

"Newsflash, sleeping beauty. Lady Gaga is a singer who dresses in outlandish costumes and wears ridiculous makeup."

"*Oh.* They didn't tell me that."

"And while you're washing your face, go wash that colored shit out of our daughters' hair and the gel crap out of our son's. Have you lost your damn mind? Did that fall destroy every last brain cell in that white head of yours?"

"It's *blond*, Birdy! My hair is blond. The same way it was ever since you first met me." I touched it, liking the way it bounced up, and the new bangs. The hairstylist referred to it as The Taylor Swift bangs. At least *she* was someone I remembered, even if I don't remember her having bangs.

Birdy reached over and yanked the sign out of the grass. "Your hair was never that color. It's unnatural, same as your eye makeup. I liked you better the other way."

"Too bad."

"Go!" He pointed to the house. Go wash that color out of the minis. I imagine we're stuck with yours." He broke the sign in half over his knee and threw it to the side.

I smoothed the fabric on the sleeves of my blouse for something to do with my hands. I had half a mind to take a piece of that wood from the sign and bash Birdy over the head with it to knock some sense into him. For goodness' sake, I just raised his social standing, not to mention his net worth. And not just a little, but by a whole heck of a lot. You'd think he would thank me for it. I bought him a new truck that every guy dreams of, according to the salesman, who also said I was the kind of woman every man dreams of. And then blathered on how lucky my husband was to have me and slipped me his card with his cell phone number written on the back of it, just in case.

"The color won't wash out. It's semi-permanent."

Birdy jerked his head up so fast I'm surprised he didn't rupture a disc. "What!"

"Birdy, I needed some way to tell them apart. I can't just keep calling them *darlin'* forever, because I'm too stupid to know which is which. This way, I'll know which one is Melissa and which one is Emma, until I get to know them again and can tell one from another."

Birdy swallowed so hard his Adams apple bobbed. His voice was icy. "If you'd bothered to ask, I could have told you Mini Ray has a cluster of freckles on her nose in the shape of a clover and Mini May has a birthmark on the side of her neck."

I put my sunglasses back on and went to pick up the pieces of the sign. Sign or not, we were multiple listed. Birdy could tear down a hundred signs and it wouldn't matter. Tomorrow the realtor would install the lockbox.

"*Now* you tell me," I muttered.

Still, it was worth all the money because the minis got that nice shampoo and cut, and the stylist assured me eventually their red hair would turn a beautiful auburn. That information alone was worth those ridiculous prices.

"That's about two out of the two hundred questions I have for you. Whose truck is that? Is there someone inside the house?" He turned around and headed for the house, suddenly seeming nervous someone was inside.

"It's yours. I bought it for you. Paid for it with my own money. Our money now. Just as I paid for Cody to have his surgery and for you to have LASIK, if you want it. We're going home, Birdy, to my old house. My Granny Ellie gave me my trust. I'm rich, Birdy. *We're* rich. We don't have to live this way anymore."

Birdy stiffened and stopped dead still, slowly turning around to face me, his eyes dark and stony.

I mustered up some courage, buoyed by my wealth and a decent haircut. "You want to hear it straight, Birdy? Let me tell you simply, so you can understand." I removed my sunglasses and held my head up high. "I won't live this way anymore, in this house where the toilet doesn't flush and green mold grows up the walls like moss on a stone. I won't let us drive our family around in an old school bus, or eat peanut butter and jelly because we can't afford the cost of deli meats. I'm moving us out of this town, to a place where there are better schools for our children. And you better get used to it quick, because we're moving in a week."

CHAPTER THIRTEEN

I took my time walking inside the house, my steps slow and unsteady, my feet feeling almost too heavy to lift in my new shoes. Birdy stomped off after I told him we were moving, his boots pounding on the wooden porch, the noise of it still hammering in my head. He went inside, slamming the door so hard the plastic wreath fell off, cracking the "Welcome" sign in two. I stooped to pick it up and held the pieces of it in my hand, noticing the paint was chipped and the colored letters so faded the L now appeared to be an I. Silly me—I thought Birdy would be happy we finally had money and we didn't have to struggle any more.

I stopped a foot shy of the door and stood on the porch, turning my head right to left, viewing my surroundings, trying to find a reason why Birdy might want to stay. Our subdivision seemed as tired and sad as the people who lived there, gray and colorless in the afternoon sun, except for that one god-awful house, third from the corner, the one painted fuchsia, a shock of color in a row of white, an angry shout of independence.

Most of the houses were in need of repair: new vinyl siding, or front door screens to keep out the flies and the fresh air that might bring in a promise of better things to come. A few houses, including Becky Lou's, were littered with forgotten toys, left to rust, neglected and broken, on dirt patches that wouldn't grow grass, never installed with sprinklers by owners too poor or too tired to care.

We had us some trees—junipers I think—natural, or planted as seedlings, to the left of our house where the subdivision ended, or began, depending on where you were standing, and still more at the back of our houses where our small yards stopped, just the same as our dreams of something better. But the front yards where bare and few were landscaped, as if the folks housed inside were happy enough to have a roof over their heads, or peanut butter and jelly, and that indoor plumbing, even if the toilets didn't flush.

It wasn't an urban ghetto with Atlanta's forgotten, where people lived in fear of gangs and guns. I'd never seen Birdy lock our front door, proving our things were safe and our neighbors honest. The houses weren't shacks in backwoods small towns, like where Birdy was born, one of those places time forgot, in a state where less than two hours away crowds of people filled shopping malls and multiplex theaters and the folks had more money than sense. There weren't any rubber tires or old refrigerators in the front yards or piles of trash in need of burning when the wind died down. But there were cars that didn't run perched on cinderblocks in dirt driveways, and fake flowers, faded and threadbare, pushed deep in soil not rich enough to grow real ones. And a constant feeling permeating the air, a heaviness of sorts, pressing down on me with the weight of a humid summer, pushing me closer to the ground.

I didn't need my big house, the one with all those rooms, rooms even Birdy and I and our children couldn't possibly fill.

The thought of living there without my parents, or Zula, scared me, it was so big. Bigger than five of these houses, with my property stretching out far and wide, and extending farther still, out past where all our little houses ended and the trees trailed off. But I didn't need or deserve this either. This tiny house that made me sad, the moments all captured in pictures hanging on our wall.

I took a deep breath and pushed open the door.

Birdy hung up the phone on the wall in the kitchen and turned to face me, his expression unreadable, his body stiff, his arms ramrod straight at his sides. From the corner of my eye, I saw Anna's diaper bag, spilled open on the pine kitchen table, the can of formula discovered and lying on its side on the table, still rocking, as if it were a grenade and Birdy had pulled the pin.

"Becky Lou is coming over to get the kids. We need to talk." Birdy wouldn't look at me and instead picked up the can, turning it over in his hands. "I see you've decided to quit nursing." He placed the can on the table.

I took off my sunglasses and put them in my back pocket, knowing I'd forgotten to remove the price tag attached to the inside frame. "So what if I have?" I asked defiantly. "It's my body, Birdy. I'll do what I want with it. Anna can crawl, sit up, and eat real food. And she bites. I love her, but she's beginning to tear me up."

The front doorbell rang and Birdy went to answer. Becky Lou came into the kitchen, shocked to see the new me.

"Mrs. Johnson, you look beautiful!"

"Thank you, Becky Lou." I turned my head and stuck my tongue out at Birdy, who saw and didn't verbally respond, instead narrowing his eyes at me, his jaw clenched tight.

"I'll get the girls," he said tightly. Birdy left the room, and the air suddenly felt lighter with his absence.

"Did y'all get a new truck? It's hot! Is that the new Ford F-250?" Becky Lou said, knowing far more about trucks than I did. I let the kids pick it out. All I knew was what I'd been told, and that it had a crew cab and enough room for everyone in our family. Then I handed over the credit card and told the salesman the address of where it needed to be delivered.

"It's new, but I don't think my husband likes it."

Birdy came back into the room and handed Anna to Becky Lou. "Dolly drinks formula now. There's mix and some bottles in the bag." He touched our baby's blond hair with his fingers, letting them linger, his hardness softening for a moment.

Becky Lou's face registered surprise at the news of the formula, but she didn't say anything as she gathered the bag, balancing Anna on her hip and unclasping her hair from Anna's fist.

Melissa and Emma came into the kitchen, soundless as mice, and tugged at the back of my shirt. "Mama, we had fun with you today," Emma said, her eyes wide and her toothless grin shy.

"Yeah, Mama, can we play again tomorrow?" Melissa asked, her voice soft, and glancing up at her daddy, feeling the tension in the room.

I squatted and hugged the girls to me. "I think tomorrow is school, but we can play after you come home. You too, Cody." Cody came out from behind his sisters to get in on the group hug, his glasses knocked sideways in the mix.

I kissed Anna good-bye and walked Becky Lou and the kids to the door, trying to calm their fears. "Don't you worry.

Everything is fine. Becky Lou is just taking you out for a walk. You go on now, and have a good time." The dog started to bark, and Birdy told him to hush.

I closed the door and stood with my back to it, taking a deep breath to calm me. This wasn't going to get any easier. I turned and strode purposely into the kitchen.

Birdy sat at the scarred pine table and rolled the saltshaker, the cardboard kind with pictures of cherries on it that come in a pack with the pepper. I went to the refrigerator to remove the chicken for the night's supper, placing it on the counter. I'd defrosted it, but was ignorant on how to cook it. Emma said I could research the directions on the Internet, and be sure and take it out of the plastic before putting it in the oven or frying pan. I sat down next to Birdy at the table and contemplated the dog, struggling to lick his privates while wearing the plastic lampshade.

"What's wrong with the dog?"

"He was neutered."

"Moonshine, huh? Nice name," I said, sarcastically, not surprised Birdy would have some brown-eyed sad hunting dog with patches of missing hair and wearing a head cone.

"You named him," he said tonelessly. Birdy never raised his eyes from the table. "The kids wanted to call him Skippy." He didn't elaborate, but went from rolling the salt to spinning it in a circle, instead.

"Out with it, Birdy. What's your problem?" I put my hand on his, to stop the spinning.

He jerked his hand away as if he couldn't stand my touch and stood up so fast the chair fell over, crashing to the floor and scaring the dog who ran from the room.

Birdy planted his feet, shoulders wide apart, putting his hands in his pockets, then pulling them out again to point his finger at me. "You want to know what my problem is? *You* are my problem, Savannah May! You are the only problem I ever seem to have. Are you completely addled? Have you lost your damn mind?" He took off his glasses and threw them on the kitchen table, where they skidded and fell to the floor.

"Where do I begin?" He took a step toward me, and I took a step back. "For one thing, you're not supposed to drive for another two weeks. Do you know how dangerous that was? And you not yet home from the hospital for a week! That car of yours? It's not equipped with the right type of seat belts, so you also put our children in danger. You dyed your hair. And I don't know how they did it around those stitches, but that's just plain foolishness." He ticked off his list of complaints on his fingers, and if he didn't quit soon, he'd need to remove his shoes and socks and count on his toes. "You also dyed the hair of a six-year-old child. Two of them! And I don't know how I'm going to explain *that* to their school." He continued down his mental list. "You put a 'For Sale' sign in our front yard …"

I held up my hands. "Stop. I get it." I went to get a glass of water. I pulled on the sink handle, and it fell off, clattering into the sink. I handed it to Birdy with a sigh. "You should be thanking me, Birdy, not giving me your crap. So, I got my money. So what? How can that possibly be a bad thing? I bought you a new truck, because you needed one—"

"That truck is red. And I don't need it. Take it back. I don't want it."

I advanced on him in a fury. "And I don't want to drive a yellow school bus! I guess tomorrow I'll be buying myself a brand-new car with better seatbelts." I pushed my way past him, and I bent to retrieve his glasses from the floor before correcting the chair. *"Right after I move back into my old house,"* I whispered under my breath while still down on the floor.

"What did you say?" Birdy's voice deepened. Deeper than I think I'd ever heard it.

I straightened, rubbing my palms on the back pocket of my jeans to dry the sweat from my hands. With my new shoes, I was almost as tall as Birdy and was able to look at him at eye level. "I *said*, tomorrow I'm buying myself a new car with better seatbelts." I held his gaze, refusing to be the first to break away.

"Don't play with me! The other thing. What did you say?" Birdy's posture was dead man stiff, and he seemed angry enough to throttle me right there where I stood.

I put my hand on his forearm, feeling him tense and knowing he wanted to pull away, but I held on tight to the sleeve of his shirt, not letting go. Still holding his gaze, I said, "I'm moving back into my house, Birdy, and I hope you'll move with me. The kids can go to a better school, and maybe Zula will move back in to help us with them and the house. We have money now, Birdy. We don't need to be poor any longer."

Birdy broke free of me and went over to the sink, holding onto the counter for support, taking in deep breaths and trying to control himself. He slowly turned back around, glaring at me, all signs of the sweet man I knew, gone.

"You think we're poor? *You don't know what poor is,*" he sneered. "I don't want your goddamn money, and I won't live in that house." He moved away from the counter and went to the screen door, opening it, and taking in gulps of air. After a moment, he rolled it shut, struggling for a moment to put it on its track. Once fixed, he turned around and stood with his back to the table and stared down at the floor, his hands massaging his forehead.

Tears filled my eyes, and I tried to blink them back, but they struggled free, running down my face and smearing my new mascara.

I didn't want it to come to this. Why couldn't Birdy see things my way? Why did he have to be so stubborn? Could he not see I just wanted the best for him? For our family? He didn't need to struggle so hard, working two and three jobs, just to make those small ends meet. We were both looking old, older than our years. That's what happens with the pain of poverty, with the worry and stress and sleepless nights lying awake, trying to figure how to pay the electric bill or get the dog neutered or where to get the money to fix the stupid toilet.

"Then I want a divorce," I said softly. "I love you, Birdy. Maybe not in the married way as before, because I don't remember that, but I've loved you as my best friend for most of my life, and that means something to me, and I hope it does to you too, but I can't live this way." I put my hands to my face to cover my crying, and when I pulled them away, they were black with makeup. I went to the sink and wet a towel, wiping the eye makeup from my eyes and leaving the dirty towel on the counter.

Birdy's eyes were shiny too, and his voice was husky. "And just like that, you'll walk out the door on me and those children?"

I slowly shook my head. "I'm taking them with me. Those kids deserve a better life, Birdy."

"*Over my dead body.*" Birdy's voice was so low I strained to hear it, and I wondered if he'd really said it, or if I just imagined that he did.

"Then we'll split them. I'll take Anna and one mini and you can have Cody and the other. I'll even let you pick first because you know which is which."

"Split them!" he raged, advancing toward me, his face contorting in fury and the veins bulging in his neck, the strength of his anger almost scaring me sick. It was the first time in my life I'd ever heard Birdy yell that way—loud, angry, and hateful. So mad, the spit collected at the sides of his mouth, and the color in his face went purple. He moved in so close I saw the broken red lines in the whites of his eyes and felt the heat radiating off his body with the shimmer of a blistering road in August. "You want to split our daughters?" he shouted at me. "Twin girls who grew for nine months inside of you, hearing the beating of each other's hearts? Little girls who still sleep in the same bed clutching on to one another because they only feel like half of a whole!"

Birdy's eyes were hard and dark as black diamonds as he stared into mine, reflecting his hatred of me, his jaw clenched, the muscles twitching beneath it. His body blocked mine, and I turned my face away from him, to put some distance between me and his anger. Roughly, he pushed me aside, and in one move, he snatched a butcher knife from the worn wooden block and unsheathed it, the sun catching the blade, glinting and menacing in his hand. An awful sound, a growl almost, rose up from somewhere deep inside him, and he roared. With unbelievable force, he slammed the blade of that knife down into the center of the defrosted chicken for our supper, the sound raising the hairs on my neck, chopping the meat in a neat half, and all the way through the foam packaging, the shocking sound of shattered bone and gristle, harsh, giving me chills. Dragging the blade through the flesh and the muscle, he quickly pulled the knife toward him and out of the meat, the fat greasy and slick on the blade. In one fluid motion, he twisted his body and hurled the knife against the wall, where it landed with a thunk, bull's-eye center on the calendar, on Wednesday of next week, quivering, but holding firm.

Without acknowledging me or saying a word, he walked over to the wall and pulled out the knife, coming back and tossing it noisily into the sink. He stood in front of me breathing heavy, in and out, as if he'd just run a mile, pulling the air in to his lungs and even leaning over, the same way those runners do, before he was finally able to stand up straight and face me, his features hardened with contempt.

"You see that?" He pointed to the chicken halves, limp and mostly colorless except for a bit of blood oozing down the middle and onto the buckled kitchen countertop. "That's what it would be like to split those girls. You want out? Then go! But the kids are staying with me." He strode from the room.

The bedroom door was locked shut against me, and I pounded on it, the hollow sound reverberating, the door so thin I could break it down with my fist if I wanted.

"Birdy Johnson, open this door!" He didn't open it, no matter how much I pounded, and I slumped to the floor, sitting on that dull laminate, leaning my back against the door, figuring I'd sit and talk through it. He'd hear me just the same. "Things need to be said, Birdy, and you need to listen. I'm going back to my house. And I'm bringing Anna with me. You're right. It's not fair to split the girls, and Cody needs a father, but I'm bringing Anna. There's not a judge alive that will give you custody of a baby still nursing at her mother's breast," I said, now reconsidering the formula, "no matter how bad of a mother she may have been."

The door flew open, and I fell into the room flat on my back and staring straight up at Birdy above me, glaring down at me and probably wishing he could stomp on me like a spider.

"Goddamn you! Where are you, Savannah? Are you ever coming back?" He towered above me, his hands clenched in fists at his sides.

"Where? Or *who*, Birdy? Who am I?" I laid there for a second, staring up at him and then rolled over to my side and pushed, standing up, Birdy not offering a hand to help me. "I don't know. I don't know who I am now. But I do know who I'm *not*." I kicked off those new shoes and went to the shopping bags spilling out on the bed, pulling from them some soft designer sweats in pink, in a pink that made me smile when I tried them on, and removing the clothes I wore, so I could change. I stood there proud, in nothing but my new panties and bra, ridiculous things that cost more than half of the awful thrift store wardrobe hanging in my closet.

"Let me tell you who I'm not. I'm not the sad Savannah in those pictures on the wall, the one with the gray eyes and the pain so dark you can see it in a picture. I don't want to be the scary mama to those kids, one they talk to in whispers, the mopey mama who won't laugh or play with them, who takes to her bed for days, so incapacitated with grief the eighteen-year-old babysitter has to care for them. This is a sad family, Birdy. Each and every one of us. Why did you let us all get so sad?"

Birdy's eyes went wide with shock. "You think this is *my* fault? Is that what you're sayin'?" He yanked off his flannel shirt, not bothering with the buttons, and they scattered like pebbles on the carpet. Another flannel, in a closet full of them, all smooth and worn soft, velvety as salve, and each with his smell infused in the warp and the weft of their fabric, even the ones freshly washed. I had buried my face in the middle of the frayed plaids when I discovered them after coming home from the hospital, dozens of them, each as worn as the first, my arms hugging them tightly to me, their scent triggering a wave of emotion and the thread of a memory.

Birdy balled his shirt in his hand and then he threw it to the floor. As he stood shirtless before me, another memory took hold. Birdy's scar. The scar on his back where he'd cut it when he caught me in the creek, all of those years ago. Another day where Birdy jumped into water to save me. Only that day Bobby Lee was there, laughing from the other side, calling us pussies and saying we were made for each other. Birdy held me in his arms in the water, the blood from the cut of the rock coloring the water orange while the minnows swam through his blood, filtering it through their gills.

"You were sad and depressed, and somehow it's *my* fault?" Birdy blinked his eyes and I noticed the lenses of his glasses were badly scratched but felt it best not to mention the LASIK again. He removed his belt, rolling it tightly around his fist. "You knew what you were getting when you asked me to marry you. You knew who I was and what your life would be. And yet you did it just the same." Birdy sat on the edge of the bed, his head bent, his hand smoothing the fabric of my granny's quilt, his fingers tracing the edge of a square of yellow calico. "You knew we would struggle and that your life would start off small, and not be the way it used to be. And yet, you married me just the same."

I sat beside him on the bed, bare arm to bare arm, and felt his heat radiating off his body in waves, the smooth hairs on his arm touching mine and making my heart catch.

"I know you loved him, Savannah, although I can't imagine why," he said, not wanting to say his name. "And you probably still do, still calling out his name in your dreams. Even after all of these years, Savannah. Still calling his name and crying in your sleep. The tears dry and salted on your face come morning. Well, I'm tired of the tears, and the sadness, too. You leave if you want. But I will fight you to keep my children. So help me God, if I have to sell my rig to pay for it, I will fight you to keep my children." Birdy's voice broke, and he got up from the bed.

I followed him. "I'll win this, Birdy. You know I will. I've got more money. Lots of it. More money than you know. You go ahead and fight me all you want. I will win this."

CHAPTER FOURTEEN

Money is good. It's a good thing. And I'd come to find out I had a boatload of it, even more than I'd originally thought.

I found me the best lawyer money can buy. Even according to him, he was the most expensive in all of Atlanta. And maybe the entire state, too. But he was the best. Coincidentally, he was a friend of Daddy's, but that information came out later because Daddy and Mama refused to get in the middle of "my nonsense," as they called it. They said Birdy and I just needed a little vacation, that's all, to have some time alone together. That maybe I needed to use some of my money to take us on a vacation to Europe, same way as they do, and they'd be praying for us, and that we needed to come to our senses soon because all of those kids we chose to have deserved to have parents who weren't so foolish.

"It doesn't have to be like this, Birdy," I said, riding in the bus in the seat behind him, with Anna in her car seat next to me, who was laughing and cooing and playing with her feet, her socks and shoes long discarded. I touched her chubby cheek and wiped the slobber from her lips with my finger.

I'd ridden along with Birdy to take the kids to school, to help explain we'd be separating, and the kids might be changing schools. What a disaster that was, with me insisting they were going to be changing schools and Birdy insisting they weren't. In the end, the director threw us out of her office and said she'd wait to hear what the courts had to say.

I was so angry at Birdy when he first told me he wouldn't move into my house, so angry I was fighting him for custody of *all* the kids. I now could tell the difference between the minis, which meant I was improving as a mother. He was right, there were slight differences in the girls, besides the cluster of freckles on Emma's nose, or the birthmark on Melissa's neck, if one bothered to look. I didn't think it would have helped my case if we went to court and Birdy told the judge I was some addled woman who couldn't tell her children apart. Poor or not, that might have tipped the scales in Birdy's favor.

I bounced along on that stupid bus, watching the cars drive by, wondering if everyone else's lives were as screwed up as ours. "It's not too late to stop this, Birdy. You can come with us. I'll even have the dealership come and pick up the red truck, and you can keep your old piece of crap if it makes you feel better to pretend we're broke and humble."

"Shut up, Savannah." Birdy kept his eyes on the road in front of him, his expression grim, driving so erratically he cut someone off. The guy pulled up next to us to shout obscenities at Birdy and give him the finger.

"*Ma-ma,*" Anna said, and I turned around, surprised to hear her call my name.

"See, Birdy! She called me Mama. You won't win this."

"She calls Becky Lou Mama, too. That don't mean nothin'."

"Thanks for raining on my parade," I mumbled and then turned around again to tug on the toes of my little angel. I adored her. Even if she did wear me out now and again.

I sat up straighter and held onto the back of Birdy's seat, watching his face in the mirror. It was a nice face, madder than hell, but nice. If I could convince him to get LASIK and a better haircut and use some gel ... oh, and some nicer clothes—he'd need some nicer clothes—he'd be downright handsome. I was still mad at him, but my new financial security was making it easier to be objective about his positive attributes.

"Why are you so hardheaded, Birdy Johnson? What is wrong with my house? You've been in my family room more times than my daddy has, watching TV and playing pool with me and Bobby. What about my kitchen? How many hours would you spend down there with that old goat, Zula? Eating those biscuits she always made for you and listening to her old boring stories about her family's struggle with slavery a million years ago. And just how many times have you spent the night in my bedroom? I bet almost as many times as you listened to Zula's stories."

Birdy would sleep over sometimes, the years we were growing up, not with my parent's permission, of course, although I imagine Zula knew he was there. He'd crawl up the rose trellis and climb through my window after my parents were asleep or while they were out with their friends, thinking I was safe and asleep in my bed. When we were young, he'd come to escape, and we'd read stories together, or I'd struggle to play him songs on my guitar, and I'd take care of him. Not with my actions, but just by being me, I guess. As we got older, the roles changed somehow, and he began to take care of me.

He'd come the nights when he thought I had too much to drink after a football game or a party, or the nights Bobby Lee and I got in a fight, or when he sensed I just needed to talk. He'd come in the spring and the summer, and as the leaves started to fall, even during the winter, when the roads were slick and covered in frost, walking the two miles each way, then getting up before the sun rose to go home and get ready for school. His daddy didn't know, or care. Too drunk most days to know anything that went on in his son's life, coming home so piss drunk he'd sometimes pass out on the floor of the garage where they lived, leaving Birdy to make his own supper and put his daddy to bed before coming over to my house.

Birdy would climb up to my room, and he'd sleep on the floor by the side of the bed, tossing and turning mostly, and getting up to check on me from time to time. In the winter, when the floors got so cold it chilled my feet even in my socks, I'd invite him to crawl in beside me on the bed. Birdy would sleep on top of the covers, next to me, with my granny's quilt over him and his body hugging the wall. After Bobby Lee and I started having sex, it didn't seem proper, me coming home from being with Bobby and even after showering still smelling of our time together having Birdy in my bed, even just as a friend. Besides, Bobby Lee would have killed us both if he'd ever caught on that Birdy was in my room, let alone in my bed, so Birdy went back to sleeping on the floor, even in winter.

Sometimes, I'd catch him staring at me sleeping, which of course I wasn't, or I wouldn't have known he was watching. He'd be on his knees, just as the other night, when I woke and caught him praying and staring at me. I'd see him from beneath my eyelashes in the darkness, with just the hint of light coming in through the windows, a ray from the moon or the gaslights on the front porch. I'd see his face, so open it pained me to watch, saying things with it Birdy wouldn't dare say out loud, telling of his troubles and his anguish, bringing the tears and making him cry, running in rivers down his face. Silent tears that cut to my heart and spoke of the grief of a boy. I don't know what it was about seeing me lying there in the dark that made Birdy so troubled. Memories of his mama, maybe, or his silent suffering from that wicked daddy, but he'd sit and watch me and sometimes stroke my blond hair until I fell asleep, dreaming the dreams of a girl.

"I ask you again, why are you so hardheaded? Do you like being poor? Are you testing me? Is this some contest to see how much I love you?" I stood up and held onto the safety pole, my high-heeled feet over the white line on the floor, and stood beside Birdy in my new yellow dress and those cute high-heeled shoes.

"Get back, Savannah, it ain't safe." I narrowed my eyes at him, mindful of his language. "Screw you. The minis *ain't* here," he said, just to tick me off. "I'll talk any way I damn well please."

"I'm sure you will, Mr. Professor," I snapped, still holding onto the chrome rail.

Birdy slammed on the brakes, pitching me forward, so I stumbled against the front console, putting my hands out to break my fall.

"You did that on purpose!" I accused, moving back to my seat.

"I told you. It ain't safe."

Anna was asleep in her car seat, her long lashes fluttering with dreams. There was no way I was going to let Birdy have that baby. She was the prettiest baby I'd ever seen, and she was sweet. Everybody who saw her said how beautiful she was and that she was her mama's mirror image. She didn't nurse nearly so much now that she was on real food. Only once in the morning, once at night, and before her afternoon nap. And maybe once again, if she was fussy. I'd grown to like it just fine—the nursing. The feeling it gave me of fulfilling her needs, of satisfying both our desires. Hers, of filling her belly, and mine, the need to be needed, to feel wanted and useful. I know Birdy was the better parent, better by a country mile. And probably not just now, but always. He was so gentle, so quiet, the opposite of the new me, anxious and ready to blow, the same as champagne when you shake the bottle before you open the cork.

I went to my doctor appointments, and I even dragged Birdy with me, so they could tell him I wasn't crazy, tell him it wasn't my fault. That it was something they called psychogenic amnesia, and dissociative disorder, and it might get better and I'd remember someday. But most of all, I wanted them to tell him it didn't make me any less capable of caring for my children, assuming I'd ever physically cared for them at all.

I asked the minis if I was a good mama to them, as I put them to bed last night. If I cooked and cleaned and did all of the mama things. Before, when I could still remember. They told me, yes, and I think it was just to be kind, but daddy mostly took care of us all, including me, and he'd learned to play the guitar and sing, so that he might make me smile.

They told me I learned to sew their clothes, and I read them the Bible when I'd tuck them in at night. And I'd sleep in the bed with Cody when he had his bad dreams, and even if he wet the bed. I'd get up and change his sheets, Emma said, and then change his clothes, holding him tight in my arms while I rocked him to sleep in the rocking chair in the corner of the room. Then Melissa said sometimes I'd cry when I was melancholy, and daddy would rock me like a baby. Take me by the hand and rock me to sleep, just as I did with Cody. He'd hold me and rock me in the rocking chair in the corner of the room.

My eyes stung at the memories, real or imagined, and I leaned forward, putting my arms around Birdy's neck. His body stiffened, and his foot slipped off the accelerator, but he didn't tell me to stop.

"I love you, Birdy, and I don't want to have to live without you …"

"Then don't. Don't leave me, Savannah." In the reflection in the mirror, I saw Birdy swallow and his eyes grow moist beneath his glasses. Birdy used his right hand to steer, and with his left removed his glasses, rubbing his eyes with the back of his hand.

"Do you love me?" I whispered, resting my head against his, feeling the softness of his hair against mine. "Don't you want to see me happy?"

Birdy turned the bus down the corner of our street.

"You know I do."

He pulled into our driveway.

"Then please say you'll go with me," I whispered in his ear, before sitting back in my seat and gathering the diaper bag. "Say that you'll move into my house. It's only a house, Birdy. A big, old, expensive house. And it's mine, and I want to go home," I said, growing weary of the arguing.

The bus pulled into our driveway behind the new red Ford truck that hadn't been touched, and Moonshine came from around the back of it, barking, and wagging his tail.

"You *are* home, Savannah! This is your home." Birdy stood across that white line on the rubber floor of the bus, in front of me in some black graphics trucker tee, his lean muscles tight in his arms at his sides, hollering at me in frustration. "Our house! The house you've never complained about once in seven years. The house I worked three jobs to save up the down payment for. *This* is our house."

I stood face-to-face with my husband, the father of my children, my best friend, and took my first step into the future.

"This may be your house, Birdy Johnson, but it sure as hell *ain't* mine!" I grabbed my baby and headed off that ugly bus.

———◆•◆———

My new black Mercedes-Benz R350 4MATIC with leather interior and seating for six roared down the road to our subdivision, and I pulled it next to the curb, shaking my head at the eyesore the house was becoming. Not the house itself, but the driveway and the curb in front of it. The Johnson lot was half new car dealer, half salvage junkyard. Birdy's old dented truck was back from the repair shop and parked behind the yellow bus, which was parked behind the new red Ford, and behind Birdy's eighteen-wheeler. My pink Mustang was in the garage. And now, here was this new car. A car never seen before in this part of town, I'm sure, from the way all of the neighbors started coming out of their houses to stare at it.

I waved to them and slipped out of the car, pressing the key ring twice to lock it, as instructed, where it beeped a silly sound, before rushing inside the house. I don't know why I was rushing, with the way I knew Birdy would lay into me. It's a wonder I wasn't crawling inside from the curb on my hands and knees just to slow the pace.

"Come see Mama's new car!" I yelled, once inside. Melissa and Emma ran out of their rooms and Cody followed. Birdy came out next from the bedroom and Becky Lou after him. Odd, I thought, that Becky Lou was coming out of our bedroom with Birdy. It was strange, and I didn't care for it a bit. It didn't seem proper that she was in our bedroom with him. Something burned inside me.

I gave the kids a quick hug, my eyes over their heads, never leaving Birdy's face. "I want to talk to you!" I said to Birdy, and then quickly kissed the kids on their heads, telling them I'd take them for a ride in just a little while, and encouraging them to settle down some, that they were riling up the dog, who barked in the backyard wanting some attention.

Birdy looked guilty for a second, until he peered out of the front room window and saw the car, his face draining of color. "Not half as much as I want to talk to you," he said through clenched teeth.

Becky Lou started to fidget, and she pulled her lip gloss out of her jeans pocket to reapply it, smearing it on, her face coloring under my scrutiny. "I … I think I'll go get Dolly and take the kids over to my house to bake some cookies." She glanced over at Birdy, who nodded. "Come on, let's go make some snickerdoodles," she said to the minis, taking Cody's hand

191

after ruffling his hair. Birdy got Anna, still groggy with sleep, from the bedroom, and he handed her to Becky Lou.

Birdy shut the door, his head down, shaking it the entire time.

"What was that girl doing in our bedroom with you?" I advanced on Birdy.

Birdy's head snapped up. "Oh, so now it's *our* bedroom? Three hours ago this wasn't your house, and now suddenly it's *our* bedroom?"

"Don't be a jackass!"

"I'll stop being a jackass when you stop being a bitch."

I gasped, my mouth dropping and my eyes wide. Birdy had never called me a bitch before. Not that I hadn't been one to him, because I had, lots of times before, especially when we were younger, and I'd certainly been one the last few days. Yet it didn't seem proper for him to call me one.

"What? You don't deserve it? Well, sorry there, Miss High and Mighty *deb-u-tante*," he drawled out, sounding more Southern than ever. "But you can't say it ain't so."

Birdy was deflecting, and I didn't like it. He knew I was mad about Becky, and he was trying to come at me first. I jiggled my new keys in my hand with half a mind to gouge him with them. Not that it would hurt much, the keys weren't keys at all, and instead were some black plastic thing not much bigger than a pendant on a necklace.

"I'll ask you again. What was that girl doing alone with you in our bedroom?" The cuckoo clock chimed the hour, and I searched for something to throw at it, those keys, maybe, to knock that annoying bird right off its dusty perch.

"Why? You jealous? You don't give me the time of day for months, and barely tolerate my touch, and now suddenly you're *jealous*?" he taunted, crossing his arms so tight across his chest his muscles jumped.

"It's not right for that girl to be alone with you in our bedroom!" I took a deep breath, trying to regulate my breathing and slow the accelerated beating of my heart. My mind was going to some crazy places. "She's barely eighteen, and it's not right. Now, I don't know what you were doing in there …"

"Give it a rest, Savannah. What kind of a father do you think I am? You honestly think I'd do something with that girl while my children were in the next room?"

"Would you do something with her if they weren't?" But Birdy didn't take the bait.

"I needed privacy, to tell her that you and me are breaking up and you're moving out of the house. The bedroom was the only place to go where the kids wouldn't hear. When we tell them, it will be together, to reassure them none of this is their fault."

I glared at Birdy. "And just whose fault will you say this is? You tell me, Birdy. Whose fault is it? It sure as hell isn't mine, and I won't take the blame. This family is splitting up because of *you*! Because of you and your stupid pride. You remember that when you destroy those children. This was your fault, Birdy. This was all your fault."

●●●

Pride is evil. Not all pride, some kinds of pride are good. The pride that makes you hold your head up high, straighter maybe than it's ever been, even in your pageant days, because someone told you your baby is the prettiest they'd ever seen, with those big blue eyes and that golden blond hair. Or the pride of hearing the director of the Montessori say your daughters are the best behaved in all of the school and have never once been told to shush by the teacher, and they're mighty quiet, but they're smarter than most. And the pride of your little boy, when you take him to the doctor to fix that lazy eye, and he doesn't cry when you tell him he needs to have surgery to have the eye corrected. Not even when you explain exactly what surgery means.

I'm talking about the other pride. The one of resolution and distance. Unyielding. The pride that allows you to destroy a family. The pride that comes up from pain, rising like sweat from your pores, so tiny it's impossible to see, and bathing you in the salt and the toxins of your grief.

Birdy held the guitar in front of him, holding it like a shield, originally intending to play for the children, to ease into what needed to be said. It didn't matter. Music wouldn't save him. No song was going to ease the pain of what was coming.

We gathered the minis and Cody on the bunk beds, and I held Anna in my arms. She was my shield, and I was holding onto her as if my life depended on her. I glanced at Birdy, his body pulled sharp and tight as the strings on his guitar, his movements jerky, starting and stopping, while he worked out in his mind what to say.

"It won't get any easier," I whispered. "Either you say it, or I will." And I prayed it was Birdy, because I didn't have the words.

Birdy gently placed the guitar against the wall, his hand lingering on the neck, his thumb running up the strings on the fingerboard. He heaved a deep sigh, and then he released the air, and it was as if I were watching all the air being let out from a circus balloon. Not a pop, but slowly, the way it is when you untie the knot and hold the rubber tight at the ends with your fingers, controlling the airflow, letting it go a little at a time, watching the balloon shrink, until finally the air is all gone and the balloon is empty and shriveled.

Birdy turned to face us. "Your mama and me ..." he started, staring into the worried eyes of our children, so quiet and solemn, knowing things weren't good. More sorrow was coming into their lives. Birdy pulled in hard, trying to form the words, but couldn't seem to find them. He tipped his head down so low it almost touched the top of his open collar, and then he removed his glasses and rubbed his eyes with his fingers. He slowly raised his head toward me and shook it, meaning he couldn't go on.

Closing my eyes, I said a silent prayer for strength, and then I handed Anna to Emma, where she set her in the middle of her lap, her arms instinctively coming around her for protection, Emma's hair a cloak covering the two of them.

I extended my hand toward Birdy, and he let me take it, my heart breaking for what I was about to do to my family. I gave Birdy's hand a tight squeeze and forged ahead.

"Do y'all know what love is?" Except for Anna, they all shook their heads yes. "Can you tell Mama?"

"Is it like happiness?" asked Melissa, nervously twisting the ends of her hair around her finger. "Playing with Moonshine and letting him lick my face?" She smiled shyly, and I could see the bottoms of her new top teeth coming through the pink of her gums.

"Yes, I suppose so."

"Or eating snickerdoodles with Becky Lou?" Emma chirped.

Birdy coughed, and I yanked hard on his hand. "Well, maybe not that."

"Mini May, that's not love, silly. That's gluttony," Melissa said, making me think my mama may have been preaching to them because I'd heard that sermon once or twice myself, which was ironic, as the woman owned more diamond rings than anyone I'd ever met. But that's not gluttony, that's avarice, I think.

Cody climbed out of the bed, his old clothes rumpled, his glasses askew, and came to me, pulling on the bottom of my new shirt with the sparkly rhinestone front. "I know what love is, Mama," he whispered, so softly I had to bend my head to hear.

"And what is that, darlin'?" I let go of Birdy's hand and squatted down to face Cody.

The wind blew in the open window, ruffling the curtains, and I smelled the scent of the trees, triggering a memory. I closed my eyes, and for a moment I saw myself running through them. Running through trees and away from something. Or toward it.

Cody stared at me through his black crooked glasses, his eyes wide and solemn. "Love is when you rock me in the chair and kiss me, Mama." His dark eyes held mine. "Same way as it's love when Daddy rocks and kisses you, too."

Birdy and I both audibly gasped, choking on pain, strangled with the power of Cody's words. Or maybe it was just Birdy I heard. Or just me, struggling with the effort to breathe again. To reflate our lungs, to ease the punch to our solar plexus, hitting us so hard it almost brought us to our knees.

I put my arms around Cody and pulled him tight to me, absorbing him, not wanting to let go. He relaxed in my arms, and I held him for a moment longer before releasing.

"That's right, Cody. That is exactly what love is. Now you go get back on the bed with your sisters."

I tipped my head at Birdy, silently asking if he wanted to go next. He wiped his eyes with the back of his hand, and I knew it was all up to me.

My children—*our* children—stared at me, patiently, expectantly. So still, it was as if they were in a tableau, or playing a game where you needed to be perfectly still and not move. Even Anna stilled for a moment, her forehead puckered, her head tipped to the side, waiting.

I willed myself not to cry. Because if I did, I might never quit.

"Me and your daddy have loved each other for most of our lives," I began. "And we love each other in the way mamas and daddies do." I turned to face Birdy, who refused to look at me and instead stared down at the floor, his fist jammed deep in his pockets, never raising his face. "And I know we always will love one another, just the same way we will always love you." My eyes touched on each of the children. Anna played with her toes and chewed on the bottom of her sister's hair, but the others sat quiet, too afraid to move.

"But sometimes a mama and a daddy start to fuss and argue, and it has nothing to do with how much they love their children, or how much they love each other." My gaze went to Birdy, who still wouldn't lift his head. "They argue about grown-up things. Things maybe even they don't understand. And sometimes, one of them needs to move into a different house, so they won't fight so much …"

Emma broke down in tears, and Melissa followed, holding onto each other for support. Cody's brown eyes filled, and a lone tear rolled down his face. Anna had crawled to the side and was asleep on the pillow.

"Daddy's moving out?" Melissa cried, stricken. "Same as Becky Lou's daddy?" she hiccupped, trying to catch a breath, her freckles bright on her flushed face.

Birdy unplanted his rooted feet and went to hold Melissa. "No, sugar. Daddy's staying right here. Right here with you and your sisters. Your brother, too." He raised his head at me in defiance.

"Birdy …" I warned. "Don't do this, Birdy. You promised me. You promised me we weren't going there right now."

"Mama," Cody said, finding a strong voice I'd never heard him use. A desperate voice. "You're going away?"

"*We're* going away, Cody. We're going to Mama's big house that she told you about. Remember?" If Birdy wanted to fight dirty, then I'd fight dirty back. "Mama's big house with the pool and the ponies, with the big pond for fishing, and the trampoline in the backyard …" I could have gone on for a while yet, but the heat coming off Birdy was about ready to incinerate me, and I didn't know how far I could go.

The kids still seemed stricken, but at least I had their attention. I could outspend Birdy a hundred to one. Hell, I could outspend him a million to one.

"Damn you, Savannah May!"

"*Stop.* Birdy, just stop," I hissed at him. And he did. He stood there glaring at me, clenching and unclenching his fist, itching to hit something, trying to calm down, his shoulders heaving.

Birdy cleared his throat, and he went to the kids, ruffling all of their hair, one child at a time, trying to smile. "Daddy's sorry. Don't you be scared now. Daddy's sorry for hollerin' at Mama and sayin' bad words. Don't you worry. Now you'll have two houses to visit, that's all. You'll have one house with Daddy and one house for when you *visit* Mama." Birdy was moving to shaky ground with his last remark, and he knew it.

I went over to the wall and picked up Birdy's guitar, pulling the chair from the corner.

"No more tears." I tried to lighten my voice. "We're going to be all right. We can get through this. Hear me? We will all be fine." I gave the children a smile that was too bright, the force of it hurting my cheeks with the effort. "This is a good thing. I promise. We will all be fine," I said, trying to believe it myself. "How about I sing to you?" I looked at the minis. "Or do you want to?" I turned and held out the guitar to Birdy, who shook his head no. I positioned myself on the chair, plucking at a string. Satisfied, I positioned my fingers.

In hindsight, I should have picked a more upbeat song. "Nine to Five," or maybe one of her duets, or even that butterfly song, the uplifting one, about daffodils, laughter, and sunshine. But I didn't. I should have, but I suffered a lapse of reason, and I didn't. Instead, I sang a song that had everyone crying. Except for Anna, who was still blissfully unaware. I sang them the Dolly Parton song, "I Will Always Love You." A song about leaving, about being in the way if I stayed, a song about bittersweet memories and taking them with me, and saying good-bye, and not to cry. A song that told Birdy I'm not what he needed. But that I wished him joy and happiness, and I hoped he had all he ever dreamed of. That I loved him. I would always love him.

Birdy ran out of the room and out of the house, the sounds of the tires on that old truck pealing down the road, a memory I don't suppose I'll ever forget. He left me to pick up the pieces that night. To hold those children for what seemed like hours, until they all cried themselves to sleep, tired from all the weeping.

He didn't come home the next morning, or the next afternoon, either. When he finally did come in through the door in the evening after I made the kids a pancake supper, he reeked of booze, and his eyes were red and swollen, and he wouldn't talk to me. Birdy gathered the kids in his arms, and that noisy dog too, still wearing his plastic cone, and reassured them Daddy had been working, but was home now for a spell. And as Monday turned to Tuesday, Birdy still wouldn't talk to me. Or Wednesday either, when I wanted to scream at the silence.

I spent the days making plans, making calls on the phone. Packing my things: a toothbrush and my new clothes. And the picture of our wedding in front of that lighthouse in Savannah.

I cleaned the house, and I dusted that silly clock, Birdy's only link to his mama, smiling at the little bird that poked his head out at the hour, and suddenly wanting to take the clock with me to my big house, the house of my childhood. I brushed the dog and took him to the vet, all of us fitting in my new car, Moonshine in the far back, probably scratching the crap out of my new leather.

I talked to the children, trying to explain what divorce means, saying it wasn't their fault and it's just something that happens when daddies and mamas can no longer get along.

Come Friday, a day when the sun shined brighter than most, but a day when my eyes saw nothing but shadows and raindrops on the faces of the people I loved, and on Birdy most of all, I gathered my baby and said good-bye to my other children, and I promised I'd be back to get them just as soon as I could, to take them home with me, to the home I remembered.

CHAPTER FIFTEEN

Memories are a fickle thing, like a falling star flashing across the midnight sky. A blink and it's gone, and you never quite know if you saw it, or if it was never really there, only something in your mind's imagination. The same as the fireflies Birdy and I used to catch in the summer nights in the darkness, capturing their magic in the palms of our hands. They started out a real living thing, caught and put in a bottle, so many that we could read by them at night for a time, curled up together on my bed, reading of kings and queens and knights in metal armor, until slowly their light faded, growing softer as they lay dying, until eventually their light flickered still. Leaving us to wonder, did we ever really see it? And Birdy opening the bottle in the morning to toss the dead carcasses in the grass for the warblers and the crows to feed on.

I walked along the polished wood floors of my home holding Anna tight to me to ward off the chill and the loneliness. Mama and Daddy were gone, and Zula, too. Not dead, of course. Right about now, Mama and Daddy were at the golf course turning as pink as those flamingoes in the hot Florida sun, or playing bridge with their new friends, the Cohens and the Rosenbergs. And Zula, our old housekeeper, was in her apartment over on Haven Road, just as mean and ornery as ever. But they were absent. The same way as Birdy and Bobby Lee.

Bobby Lee ... so many unanswered questions ...

What happened between us? Why had I married Birdy and not him? Birdy, my best friend and the keeper of my secrets. The secrets of me and Bobby Lee.

Anna started to fuss at my breasts, and I sat on the top step of the second floor opening the buttons of my new red blouse, a color too harsh—the color of blood—bright and brassy against my light hair. She went at me hungrily, mindless of the turmoil in our lives, safe and comfortable in the hold of my arms. I bent to kiss her forehead. My Anna, my little dolly.

Yes, memories are a fickle thing, and love, even more. What does a girl know about love, but what she's been told, or read in books: fairy tales, of handsome princes and magic castles, of horses with wings in which to fly away?

The doorbell rang once before the door pushed open, scaring us both. Anna raised her head, her face beginning to pucker, and I buttoned my blouse and started down the winding staircase.

"Zula! You scared me half to death." I reached the bottom step and went to hug Zula hello.

"Don't bother with that nonsense for now, Savannah May. I'm here to finally get a chance to see this beautiful baby. Now hand over that precious thing." Zula snatched Anna from my arms. "Your mama says her name is Anna Sue. I thought you promised me you'd name one of your children after me." Zula brought Anna to the sofa in the parlor and started undressing my daughter, unwrapping her to get a better look, the same way you'd rip the paper off a present.

I followed behind. "Sorry," I apologized. "Zula Sue was a bit of a tongue twister," I lied. Not about it being a tongue twister, because it is. *Zula Sue Zula Sue Zula Sue.* I lied because I couldn't very well tell her I didn't even remember having my child, let alone naming her. Or the three that came before her.

It mattered little, because someone beat me to the punch.

"And what is this nonsense about you losing your memory, Savannah May? Is this some sort of trickery? Haven't you put that poor boy through enough heartache yet?"

"Apparently not."

"Don't sass me, girl."

Forget the stupid stereotypes of sweet motherly black nannies with the ample bosoms on which to pour out your childhood heartaches like the ones you see in the movies, the ones who soothe your bloodied knees with a kiss and a cookie, before tightening the strings of your corset. Zula was to Mammy what acid is to milk, or whatever those logic tests say, and you'd think I'd remember them because I went through an entire battery of them recently.

We inherited Zula from Granny Ellie, who gave her to Mama along with the house. If I could get Mama to confess, I think she's part of the family. Safe to say, it's far back enough everyone can pretend she isn't. Zula's skin is the color of a Starbuck's mocha after the whipped cream melts, and she's as thin as the stick to stir it. A calorie wouldn't dare attach itself to Zula, she's so mean. I'd forgotten just how mean she was.

After Zula was satisfied my child had all her toes and fingers, Zula redressed Anna and took her upstairs, coming back down with Anna swaddled tight as a papoose and flushed red with overheating.

"Uh … Zula, I think Anna's too old to be swaddled."

Zula's sharp eyes stung me, blue and cold as icicles. "Are you telling me how to care for a child, Savannah May? I helped raise your granny …" An impossibility, of course, unless she was a hundred and fifty. More likely, she was her playmate, being they seemed about the same age. "And your mama, too, and I raised you …"

Zula didn't raise me, exactly. By the time my mama had me, I think Zula was retired, she just didn't inform my parents. I remember Mama serving Zula more times than Zula served us. My daddy was so afraid of her he'd bring in some local German girls to do most of the work, the cooking and the cleaning. Zula would come out of her rooms on occasion (she had several) if the weather was nice or to say hello to Birdy. She always had that soft spot for Birdy. The sun rose and set on him, as far as Zula was concerned. Zula got to oversee the running of our home, a role she reveled in, I'm sure, as bossy as she was.

Zula placed Anna on the sofa, reverently. The way Mary placed Jesus in the manger. Only Jesus was a newborn and not crawling like Anna, who managed to twist and turn and wiggle her way off the sofa and was hightailing as fast as she could to get away from Zula. My baby crawled her way to me and stood up using my legs to support her, raising her arms for me to save her.

See, that's the thing about memories. You can't trust them. In my mind, I *thought* I remembered it differently. And maybe I did. Surely, there were times Zula held me gently, or dressed me, brushed my long blond hair, and tucked me in at night saying kind things such as, "God bless you, honey child," or "Sweet dreams, darlin'." If she did, I don't remember.

My eyes scanned the front room, filled with most of the same furniture, some of it now worn and faded. Or damaged by the renters who didn't care if they trashed a house that wasn't theirs. It was a stately house filled with antiques made from dark heavy wood covered in carvings done by hand centuries ago, and the paneled walls were the color of tobacco, rich and burnished. Ancestral paintings hung in their garish gold frames on the wall leading up the grand staircase to the floor above, including one of a man who looked suspiciously like Zula, with those same blue eyes as hers, cold as icicles. Heavy green drapes hung at the front window, although Mama had remodeled some of the house, so not all of the rooms were so dark and dreary, and my bedroom she draped in white fabric and lace, to offset the parts the color of Pepto-Bismol.

Zula came and plucked my daughter from me, Anna's cries forcing a tightening in my chest. "Quit your fussin'. I'll give you back to your mama, I just wanted to kiss you good-bye."

Zula must have seen the relief on my face. "You thought I was coming to stay to help you and the children?" she said, shaking her head. Zula picked up her purse and removed a patterned scarf, tying it around her wavy white hair. "You'll do fine, Savannah May. You don't need me or anyone else but your husband. You'll do just fine." She reached for the door.

I put my hand on hers to stop her, not to beg her to stay and help me. God no. I'd rather muddle on my own with eight kids than to tolerate Zula. I stopped her because I needed to know. Needed to remember the seven years, my years with Birdy.

"Tell me, Zula." My eyes searched hers, my stare trying to draw the answers to the questions she didn't want to hear. "You know, don't you? You know why I married Birdy Johnson."

Zula's eyes softened, and it was as if I was watching icicles melt on the eaves, the spring sun finally arriving, and the crocuses starting to bloom.

"You married him because you love him, Savannah May. And because he loves you. More than you will ever know. Lord, how that boy loves you."

———◆●●◆———

Birdy called me Sleeping Beauty, the day of my reawakening. I don't recall how long Ms. Beauty was asleep, but losing seven years of one's life can be a shock. Things didn't progress so quickly back in the days of antiquity when dwarfs mined for gold below the earth, but now technology changes in an instant.

Take that new car. Sure, it still has a steering wheel and four tires, but the thing has so many buttons, I don't know what to push. *And it talks!* Whoever heard of a talking car? Emma said it's my new phone that is doing the talking and my car is just connected to her. Melissa said the woman speaking is named Siri, and I can't say I like her much. Siri can sometimes have an attitude. But she did make the kids laugh when I asked her how much wood could a woodchuck chuck if a woodchuck could chuck wood, and she answered, "*A woodchuck would chuck as much as a woodchuck would chuck if a woodchuck could chuck wood.*"

Emma told me there is this thing called Facebook. Although, of course the kids don't have it. Birdy's not much of a reader, but I have seen him read the Bible on occasion.

I took the kids to the mall, I feel guilty to say, to spoil them rotten with so many toys and gifts that when the judge gives the children to me instead of Birdy they won't feel nearly so bad about living with me and not their daddy. I got myself a new camera too, to take pictures of all of us, although Emma told me my phone could do that if only I press the right button. (That girl is so smart.) But the camera is so darn tricky, I can hardly use it. It's digital and has a memory card that stores the pictures. Lord, how I wished my brain had one of those. A memory card, so I could plug it in and retrieve all of the pictures of the last seven years of my life.

"Emma, Melissa, wake up, sugar, we're home. You too, Cody."

I unbuckled Anna first, removing the car seat from the back, and then I undid Cody's seatbelt for him, ruffling his hair. In less than two weeks, my son would have his eye surgery, and his eyes would focus straight ahead. The doctor said someday he may no longer need those glasses, and then maybe the kids at school would stop making fun of him. Maybe my boy would finally emerge from his quiet world and raise his dark head high. And maybe even yell. Wouldn't that be nice to hear?

Our feet crunched beneath us on the gravel of the circular driveway, a driveway so long it curved back around on itself, with a fountain in the middle, and grass and flowers growing around it—so many pretty flowers, the children thought I'd brought them to the park the first time I took them to my house. There were trees leading all the way up that long road, which twisted for miles, the road where their daddy would walk up most days, from two miles or more, away from the house he lived in—a garage not any larger than the size of my kitchen. A garage converted into a house he shared with that no-good daddy, who seldom worked, but when he did, he was a handyman of sorts, fixing or hammering things on the property in exchange for free rent and a small amount of money. But mostly took to his bed, sick of the whiskey and his poisonous ways.

All those things I thought, but didn't tell the children, just saying instead their daddy walked two miles to come visit their mama, and their granddaddy died in a car wreck when daddy was still in school.

Emma and Melissa held hands, their red hair softer in the evening light, the colored hair dye long since faded. They shuffled their feet and kicked at the stones, watching them scatter. I kicked at some too, and Cody followed, but not in fun. I think we kicked them to get rid of some of the anger, of the hollowness we felt without their daddy around, his gentle ways softening all the sharp corners of our lives and balancing us somehow. That's it, I thought, Birdy balanced me, the same way your dog can balance you just by lying next to you at your feet, or in your lap, if they're small. You pet them and all the tension flows right out of you.

Some folks said Birdy reminded them of a Labrador. Not just because he was the catch-and-fetch-it guy, no matter what Bobby Lee said, but because he was known for being sound and athletic, well balanced, and hard working. He had a gentle temperament and was good with children, same way as the dog, making him an excellent family companion. He was resistant and had a clean-cut head and a broad back and a powerful jaw, but a soft and gentle mouth, unless of course he was mad at me, then it could set tight. He could be enthusiastic, but not hyperactive, and required only moderate amounts of attention, and relative to other dogs, or men, seemed to acclimate well to his environment, except for now and this mess with my house. With his gentle ways, his above average intelligence, and obedient, calm nature, he was the ideal family companion.

"We could go on the trampoline," I suggested, not really in the mood, but wanting to change the air of stillness. To charge the ions in the atmosphere and fill it with some level of excitement. We went up the steps and inside those big oak double doors with the leaded glass panes and past the doorknocker in the shape of a lion.

"That doorknocker is scary, Mama," Emma said, sticking her tongue out at it while we filed on inside.

"I'm too tired to jump, Mama," Melissa said. "And Cody is, too. Isn't that right, Cody?"

Cody came up to my side, hugging my thighs, desperate for my touch. "I'll jump with you if you want, Mama," he said, eager to please, his voice muffled by the hem of my sweater.

I placed Anna, asleep in her car seat, on the floor and bent down. "That's okay, darlin', I know you're tired, we'll jump tomorrow. And maybe I can call the groom and have him ready us the ponies. Would you like that?"

Tomorrow.

Another day in that old big house where I grew up and learned to play the guitar. A house Birdy knew better than I: the creaky step fourth down from the top, the one Birdy told me to skip when I'd come home past curfew, so nobody would know

I'd snuck in the house; the loose tile in the kitchen with the crack in the middle we made the day Zula was gone, when we dropped the cast-iron skillet while frying us up some eggs. And the rose trellis that crisscrossed up the side of the house to my second-story window, that Birdy would climb into at night, and sometimes in day, appearing in my room as a vision.

I thought my house would heal the brokenness inside of me, put an end to the bitterness and the hurt, and finally trigger the memories of the past that were lost to me. Problem is, a house is not a home without the ones you love. It's nothing more than a container, an empty vessel, not much different than that old grocery sack Birdy brought to the hospital, the brown paper one with the lettuce stuck to the bottom of it. Yes, my house was filled with memories, more memories than the dishes in Mama's cupboard or the panes of glass in the leaded windows of the front room, the huge window that went up to the second story, the one that brought in the light, and the dark. But most of my memories, the good ones, at least, were the days spent with my best friend. And a house is not a home, without the ones you love.

I settled Anna into the porta-crib I'd placed in my old bedroom, next to my bed. I had all of those extra rooms and didn't want to sleep in one. We'd all sleep together in my double bed on the nights the children came to stay, cuddled close and near as kittens in that bedroom where I learned to play the guitar, the one where their daddy would sleep next to me on the floor in the night.

But not after tomorrow. Tomorrow I was going back to Birdy. Not to live in that drab little house, but to take him with me to find us a new one, one we could all live in together with our children and a dog I named Moonshine.

I didn't want to live my life apart from Birdy, and I didn't want my children to suffer another day. I'd put them through enough, me with all my silly distress over who knows what. I'd put Birdy through enough, too. Not just in our marriage, but in all the days prior, going on about my troubles with Bobby Lee when there was little he could do to fix it, because I wouldn't move my own two feet to step aside, always going back for more. We could find a way to resolve this. There must be a way. Birdy was stubborn, but he wasn't stupid. Surely we could find a way to make this work out between us.

"What's in your hand, Mama?" Emma asked, sitting on my bed, reading *Oh The Places You'll Go!* by Dr. Seuss, a book from my childhood we'd found on the floor in the closet.

Melissa saw what I'd hid behind my back. "Mama, what are you doing with that toilet tissue? Is your plumbing bad, too?"

Cody rubbed his sleepy eyes with his fist. "What you doin', Mama? Are you leaving?" Poor Cody's face appeared stricken. Goodness' sake! My poor child suffered from separation anxiety in addition to that lazy eye. I'd need to love on him even more, so eventually he'd see he could depend on me and I wasn't going to abandon him.

I threw the roll of toilet tissue at Emma, who was too clueless to catch it, and it gently hit her on the arm.

"Sugar, Mama was throwing that at you so you'd catch it," I said, thinking soon was not soon enough to enroll these children in soccer or T-ball. Do poor children not play organized sports? "Quick now!" I clapped my hands together twice. "Come on, gooses. We're going to the teepee!"

"Pee pee, Mama? We're going to pee pee?" Melissa said, sitting at my vanity going through all the little drawers filled with the useless treasures of my youth, her voice rising with confusion. "Is that why we need the tissue? Because we're going to pee pee?"

I went to my closet to grab a coat and shrugged it on before covering Anna with another blanket. I palmed the portable receiver to the baby monitor sitting on my dresser, slipping it into my coat pocket. "Not pee pee. *Teepee*. It's where you get toilet paper and throw it up high in the trees, letting it trail down so it looks like the trees are covered in fresh snow. Then you take the little pieces, the squares, and you rip them up, and toss them about the yard, so it seems the yard is covered in snow, too. Snow, or toilet tissue ripped to bits," I added.

"But why, Mama?" Cody whispered, confusion apparent on his face.

I paused for a moment to think. "Why? Hmmm. For fun, I guess. And it is fun. You'll see. Your daddy and I teepeed lots of houses when we were growing up. Until *his* daddy found out, and whipped him," I said, but wished I didn't. There were some things children didn't need to know.

The children felt my energy, saw it in my eyes, and started to get excited, trembling with the newness of it, catching it like a fever. They ran around that big house finding all the toilet tissue they could. Rolls and rolls of it in all the bathrooms and the storage cupboards, even venturing into the four-car garage, the one attached to the house, not the one out back with room for four more. And my tissue was the expensive double-roll two-ply, thick and downy as a towel, not the scratchy cheap stuff their daddy buys.

I went out in the coolness of the night, my body warm with excitement and restlessness, and I taught my solemn children to finally have some fun. To let loose and go crazy, flinging and throwing, and shredding that tissue, so it flowed down from the trees, white as an ermine cape, trailing and sprawling from the branches and littering the ground with white petals. We played and laughed for hours, laughing so hard sometimes we'd fall to the grass with tears in our eyes, trying to catch our breath. We threw the rolls until the tissue ran out, until we'd thrown all that paper in the trees and the bushes, and the flowers too, until my house was draped in white tissue, a snowy palace in the dark of the moon.

"Now what, Mama?" Emma said, her face flushed and breathing heavy with her efforts as we stood staring at the house. Melissa and Cody held hands, taking in all they had done, awed by the sight of our fun. And our destruction. The beautiful destruction.

I threw the last empty cardboard roll into the topiary boxwood by the front door.

"Now we sell the damn thing and go home to your daddy."

CHAPTER SIXTEEN

I watched my children's faces in the rearview mirror of my car: open faces, freckled faces, faces Birdy and I created. They were wonderful children, full of love and compassion, humble and sweet. They were still shy and somewhat awkward, and maybe more of their father than me, but laughter returned to their lives, or maybe entered in for the very first time, knocking at the door and sayin' how do you do?

I didn't need to recall those seven years past. The sorrowful ones, the ones of more frowns than smiles, giving me that crease in the middle of my brow, furrowed as a line in the soil. I'd created some new memories to hold onto, taken new pictures to hang on those walls.

"Tell us again, Mama, about the surprise for Daddy!" Emma said.

"Well, now, let me think." I changed lanes, heading past the truck stop station off our interstate exit. "I'm going to tell Daddy I'm selling that spooky old house. That we'll buy a different one, wherever Daddy wants. As long as it's not by the airport, and the schools are better, and where the yards are bigger so we can have a pool. Oh yes, and it has to have at least four bedrooms, so Cody doesn't have to share." I smiled at them in the rearview mirror and then fluffed my hair.

"I don't mind sharing," Cody said, handing Anna her pacifier to stop her fussing.

"Ma-ma," Anna said to him in thanks. So far, it was her favorite word, but Da-da was coming in close.

"Oh course you don't, sugar. But big boys don't need to be sharing a room with their baby sisters." It entered my mind—and then went out the back door just as quickly, Cody could use a brother.

I drove my new car down Rocky Road and past the dead-end sign and pulled into the driveway behind Birdy's old truck. The new one was gone. I had it picked up the day I moved out, taken back to the dealership in the city, to that salesman who called me once or twice saying it was a courtesy call and did I want to get together for coffee sometime? I never called him back and deleted the message, hoping he'd not call again.

The kids helped me get all their things out of the car, and Anna's things too, and we walked into the house, greeted by Moonshine's bark. The dog licked Anna's face, all smiles and dimpled cheeks, when I set her on the floor still strapped in her car seat.

"Daddy! We're home," Melissa said, and was ready to run to the master bedroom where Birdy must have been hiding.

I smelled perfume.

Cheap dime-store perfume, the kind that smells like sticky candy or spun sugar at the fair, and it stilled me, prickling the hairs on my arms and at the back of my neck.

"No, Melissa!" I caught her by the arm before she'd hit the hallway.

"I think Becky Lou is here, Mama," Cody whispered.

"Yeah, Mama. This is her sweater," Emma said, coming out of the kitchen, holding it in her hands.

The door to our bedroom squeaked open, and Birdy came out, his eyes going wide when he saw us standing there, his jaw moving, but not speaking, the words caught tight in his throat.

"Daddy, where is your shirt?" Emma asked.

My breath left me and my stomach start to coil. I covered my mouth with my hand to stop the sounds of my horror.

Becky Lou trailed out behind him, her head down, her dress rumpled and the buttons undone, her shoeless feet silent on the vinyl floor.

Birdy's eyes took all of us in, the tortured, panicked faces, and he struggled to find the right words to say.

"Savannah, you didn't call," was the best he could do.

I didn't know whether to stay or run. I wanted to run—far and fast—and never come back to that house, but I couldn't do that to my children. I'd brought them into the light, and I didn't want to send them back into the darkness.

I glanced from Birdy to Becky, who was now gathering her shoes and accepting her sweater from Emma, her face flushed with passion, or fear, her lips pink and swollen from kissing. I felt sick, the sour bitterness of the taste filling my mouth. I swallowed it down and then went and kissed the children on their foreheads, brushing the hair back from their knowing eyes. Birdy and I needed to talk without the children, and there was no other choice than to send them off with Becky.

"You go now with Becky Lou. Emma, take Anna. You go now. Mama needs to talk with your daddy."

"About coming home and the new house you want to buy for Daddy?" Melissa asked, her voice breaking, trying to hold back the tears.

Goddamn, Birdy. Goddamn him!

"You go now, and Mama will come get you in a bit. Go on."

Becky Lou gathered the kids, and in a single file they went through the door, stopping once to peer back over their shoulders for reassurance. I forced a wave and a tight smile and then locked the door behind them, leaning against it for support.

"Savannah …"

Something inside me broke wide-open right then as the cuckoo clock chimed the hour in that lighthouse room. Not the lost memories of those years, they were still locked somewhere deep inside, somewhere safe and dark, but an unleashing of a pain that comes from love. A tidal wave of it. I flew at Birdy in a fury, my hands hitting and scratching, wanting to hurt him as he'd hurt me, the tears rolling down my face along with the sweat of the afternoon heat.

"Savannah, no! It ain't what you think! I swear. I didn't sleep with her."

I kicked and scratched, hands flying, while Birdy tired hard to restrain me, his arms tight and gripped around my middle and his body shaking with the fight while the smell of fear rose in the air mingling with the scent of sticky candy.

Birdy grabbed my wrists and pulled me out of the room and down the hallway, trying to stay out of the sight of the picture window, to keep our dirty lives to ourselves and away from the neighbors' prying eyes, picking me up when I dropped to the floor, crying in noisy breaths. He brought me inside the bedroom, tossing me easily onto the bed, but breathing hard from the effort of it all.

I pushed off the bed and stood, my hands curled in claws at my sides, heaving and breathless. "*What have you done?*" I screamed at Birdy, not caring the bedroom window was open wide, my voice carrying out through the dusty screen. "That girl is practically a child, Birdy! She is our children's babysitter. *The babysitter!*"

Birdy rubbed the back of his neck with his right hand, his neck and face flushed red with shame or the effort of our fighting, his chest heaving. "I know it don't look right. I know that. We was kissin', is all. Only kissin', nothing more. You left me. Savannah, *you* left *me*," Birdy accused and then winced when his left hand touched his chest and the scratches that now covered it. He pulled his breath in, still trying to fill his lungs, the movement stretching the muscles that corded his bare stomach, smooth with rounded angles. A stomach Becky Lou was lying on less than twenty minutes ago.

"Did you really come back to me?" he said.

I stood in front of Birdy, my own chest rising and falling, my breath so shallow dots of lights danced before me. My body shook with rage, and I desperately wanted to hurt Birdy. Hurt him badly. And there was only one way I knew how.

I forced myself to still, gently tilting my head to the side, my eyes tempering, softening my mouth, and parting my lips, moistening them with the tip of my tongue. Regarding Birdy, watching him … the way the fox watches the rabbit— calculating and keen. Wanting Birdy to desire me. Willing him to.

I gentled my voice and traced the outline of my neck, unhurried, deliberate, letting my fingers travel to touch the outline of my breast, one and then the other—Birdy's eyes following my every movement.

"You said I was a good wife, Birdy. I wonder … how is that so?" I purred, coming closer to him, spanning the space between us, my hands reaching out to trace his stomach with my fingers, caressing, savoring, feeling the warmth of his skin and the pang of his desire at my touch, as his breath caught and he softly moaned. "When I couldn't cook or clean or take care of our children … tell me, what made me a good wife?" I whispered, as my hands outlined the contours of his muscles, making them tremble … touching and stroking, feeling the heat rise off him and filling my hands with it, where I caught it, rubbing it like ointment, slick and velvety, into the planes and the trenches of him. His yearning grew stronger, and I leaned in, closer, knowing he craved and ached with the need for me, longing for me. I forced his legs open wider, moving my body inside the space, wedging my legs tight in between his, our bodies joining, sparking a fire underneath the fabric of our clothes.

And all the while … touching, stroking, running my palms leisurely up the smooth contours of his chest, fondling and brushing, feeling his heart quicken and hearing the deep hitch in his breath. Gently, I pushed him back on the bed, where he lay in the harsh afternoon light, fragile and defenseless, as powerless as a moth with wings singed by a fire. And all the while … my hands, courting his body, strumming and pressing, absorbing the control of him.

"I imagine, Birdy," I said, my voice as soft as a morning breeze, a whisper, really, "that what made me such a good wife to you—is the same thing that kept Bobby Lee from beating me more than he did—all of those years ago," I confessed, as his body undulated beneath my touch, powerless to stop. Ever so slowly, with practiced fingers, I began to work at the fabric and threads of his pants, while Birdy moaned low again and arched his hips, rising up, demanding, silently, begging for release, as I gently peeled his clothes from him, my hands exploring and stroking, lazy as a summer afternoon. Slowly, I drifted to my knees, bending my head, my hair falling like velvet drapes, covering his nakedness in the harsh afternoon light, my lips following the path of my fingers, my tongue tracing a pattern on his skin, moist and salted.

"Savannah, no!" But we'd gone too far to have me stop. Too far for me not to finish what I'd started.

"*I know what Bobby Lee liked ...*" I murmured, my head dipping down to his warmth and drawing him in, slow and gentle, trying to torment him, as he had tormented me. And all the while my hair covering his nakedness like velvet drapes, my left hand holding, stroking, my mouth tasting, while my right hand rested on his chest, caressing, kneading, feeling the accelerated beating of his heart—and doing what Bobby had trained me to do.

Birdy shuddered and groaned. He rolled over on his side and zipped up his pants, lying still, his face hidden under the cover of his arms, his chest rising and falling with the effort to inhale.

I wiped my mouth with the sleeve of my shirt, staring at Birdy, cutting him with my eyes. Walking into the bathroom, I dipped my head to the faucet and rinsed out my mouth, wiping my face with a towel, before returning to the bed and throwing it at Birdy where he lay.

"Go to hell, Birdy Johnson! You go to hell!"

"I love you, Cody Earl. You know that, right? That your mama loves you, and she'll be right here for you just as long as the nurses let her. Mama will be right here by your side. Don't you be afraid."

Cody rested against the pillow on the gurney, his tiny body draped in a warming blanket, his dark eyes wide with fear and glassy from the drops they'd given him to prepare for the surgery. I glanced up at the clock on the wall and wondered where Birdy was. Our son was about to have surgery, and you'd think he could stop diddling with the babysitter long enough to come by.

"I'm not afraid, Mama. I want my eye to be better. I'm not afraid."

I bit my lip to keep it from trembling, trying to keep myself together. I would not cry, I promised myself. I would stay strong for my son. I gathered my coat tighter against the chill of the room and peered again at the clock on the wall. Ten more minutes, and Cody would go into surgery. Where was Birdy?

I listed my house for sale that afternoon I caught Birdy with Becky. I called my mama first, and then my granny, to see did they want it back, or if I could sell it. Both told me it was mine to do with as I wished and that they never cared for it much anyway. Granny Ellie said ghosts walked those hallways late at night, especially the one with the icy blue eyes that looked like Zula's. Mama said she never wanted it anyway. That it was too big, and she only took it because her mama insisted, and it never felt right without lots of children to fill all the bedrooms. Only me, in the one with the white lace, and walls painted the color of Pepto-Bismol.

I stroked Cody's hair, hair the same color as his father's, pulling it through my fingers and seeing the coppery brightness of some of the strands when the light hit it just right. My fingers gently traced the outlines of his face, starting at the top of his forehead, around the edges of his cheeks, and down to the point at the end of his chin.

My boy. My sweet, sweet boy, who lived in a quiet world of his own, and only coming out to visit on occasion. Watching the world and making sense of it, I hoped. I smiled at him, the tug of it releasing a tear in the corner of my eye, the tear traveling down the side of my face, where Cody caught it with the tip of his finger. I gently tweaked his nose, remembering I'd done the same thing to Birdy when we were young, and that he never cared for it, but he let me do it just the same.

I couldn't remember the last time I'd prayed, but I got down on my knees on that cold floor next to Cody's bed, all the while holding his tiny hands in mine, and I did something my mama did, that I always promised myself I wouldn't. I prayed aloud, not caring who would hear. I prayed for my little boy, to a God I seemed to have forgotten, to a God who, at times, I thought had forgotten me.

"Dear Jesus, please protect my baby boy and bring healing to his eye. Please guide with certainty the hands of his surgeon. Please keep him in your grace, dear Lord, and calm his fears—and mine. In your name, I pray. Amen."

I got up and dusted off the knees of my tan pants, blinking away my tears.

"Mama?"

"Yes, darlin'?"

"Why don't you ever go to church with us on Sundays?" Cody asked, in his small sweet voice.

I heard the rustle of a sound, and I glanced up to see Birdy standing in the doorway, wearing his faded jeans and one of his plaid shirts with the smell of the outdoors, his face curious, and his hands tucked tight in his armpits. I had no idea if he'd just arrived or had been there for a time.

"I wasn't aware I didn't." I turned and glancing at Birdy, who said nothing, just watching and waiting, a vein throbbing in his neck with each beat of his heart.

"You don't go, Mama. You say you can't."

"Well, Cody, I don't know how that makes much sense. I always went to church on Sundays with my parents, before I married your daddy. But your mama's been a little crazy, and I expect now that I'm better, I'd be happy to go to church with you if you want."

Birdy came into the room and bent over our son, kissing him on the forehead, before whispering something in his ear.

The nurse came into the room and told us it was time. I gathered Cody in my arms and kissed him good-bye, saying we'd be right there waiting. Mama and Daddy would be right there when he came out of surgery.

The surgery wasn't extraordinary. The doctor told us there were over a million of them done a year and that it was the third most common eye surgery in the United States, behind cataract and LASIK. He explained things we didn't quite understand, about cutting the muscles and ocular alignment and using adjustable sutures. He said there was a chance Cody might someday not need to wear glasses, that children under six had a strong chance of it, and I was encouraged by his information, as my son was only four.

Birdy sat in the chair by the window, and I sat in one by the bed, reading the words in a magazine, yet not seeing a thing on the page.

"Is it true what Cody said, Birdy? About me not going to church?"

"It is." Birdy got up and stood at the window, watching the wind blow through the leaves on the trees at the sidewalk's edge.

"Why is that? Why don't I go to church?"

"I reckon you have your reasons." He tugged his ear. Birdy held my gaze, and I felt his love and his apology. But most of all I felt his suffering pressing down on me so troubled I needed to leave the room to go find some air, taking deep breaths of it in the hallway, sharp with disinfectant.

I returned to the room and handed Birdy a coffee from the machine downstairs. He thanked me but didn't drink it, setting it on the small table on wheels in the corner of the room.

"I got served our divorce papers," Birdy said. "A man handed them to me at the Montessori while I waited to pick up the kids from school." His voice was quiet, but not accusing.

"My lawyer said they would. But I'm sorry it happened there."

I didn't want to fight. All of the fight had been drained out of me, and some of the sorrow, too. I don't know why I lost those seven years. Maybe they were years that needed to be lost, like extra weight you carry around the middle that drags you down and weakens your heart, and needs to be lost so you can become healthier and stronger. And so you can finally buy that size six bathing suit over at Saks Fifth Avenue on Peachtree.

"We've got to stop putting the kids through this tug-o-war. You won't win this, Birdy. Did you know the judge is a member of my daddy's country club? I have a lawyer who is a good friend of my daddy's and a judge whose daughter attended cotillion classes with me. Do you honestly think you can win?"

"Probably not. But I've got to try."

I threw my hands up in frustration. "But that's it, Birdy! You don't. You don't have to try. Why waste all of your money on something you cannot possibly win? You worked hard for that truck and your house. Why throw all that money away? What will it get you? In the end, you'll have children who visit you every other weekend in some rundown trailer park on the bad side of town." I took a sip of my coffee and tried to still my shaking hand, watching him over the top of the paper cup.

Birdy knew I was right. He wasn't educated; neither was I, but he was a smart man. He knew he would never win custody of our children. I'd proved to everyone I would be fine as a mother, memory or not, that I had money and gumption and the willingness to learn.

"Who's watching the kids, Birdy?" Not that I needed to ask. His silence told it all.

"Cody said Becky Lou is staying with you at the house. Is that true?" I set the coffee cup down on the table.

"She's sleeping on the sofa, when she does. And we're not having sex, Savannah, no matter what your twisted mind is telling you. She's only there to help with the kids, so I can drive my rig at night, for some extra shifts."

"You might want to consider how that looks, Birdy. If my lawyer gets wind you're letting your eighteen-year-old girlfriend stay at the house with my children, you'll be lucky if you get them for Christmas."

I've never played poker. But I do believe, I just showed Birdy my hand.

Birdy got up and threw the coffee cup in the trash, where it splashed up and splattered all over the wall of that room, the spots of it running down in dirty streams.

"You win, Savannah. I'm sick of all this fightin'. I'll sign your damn papers."

CHAPTER SEVENTEEN

Houses such as mine on the National Registry don't get "For Sale" signs in the flowerbeds or have open houses on the weekends, with cookies and sweet tea, but my house was for sale just the same. It was listed with Christie's or Sotheby's, not that names matter, (as long as it isn't Help-U-Sell, as I didn't have the time or the inclination).

I'd signed up for college almost nine years later than I intended, needing to relearn things from the past seven years of my life, if I'd ever known such things at all. Which is why, in secret, I was tutored at night, so I wouldn't seem a fool when folks talked of games called Wii, or reconnected with old friends on Facebook. Not that I had many friends to remember. Birdy was my only real friend.

I got myself a new computer, a laptop no bigger than a clutch purse, and one for all my children, too, so we could do something called Skype and see each other's faces on the front of those computers when we talked, and so they'd be able to see their mama and their daddy on those days when we'd be apart. All except for Anna, who was too young for such nonsense. I enrolled her in Mommy and Me classes so we could have quality time together. Although with all those new English books littering my kitchen table, I wondered if it was supposed to be *Mommy and I*.

I stood in that long driveway, the one that wrapped around itself, and picked up a piece of tissue the gardener must have missed, smiling at the memory of the night when my children got to break loose and play the games of my past.

I held my hands to my eyes, watching the truck come up the road, past the acres of trees, and the white picket fence that continued out far into the green of the grass, until the truck came up to the front of the house, stopping at my side, tossing wide the pebbles at my feet.

"Birdy. Is everything all right with the kids?" I wanted to hug him hello, but was afraid to touch him. We had an uneasy truce, neither of us waving the white flag, more of a brief interruption of the fighting, the same way as in war when they stop the shooting and the firing of rifles at Christmas, just for a few days, to observe the significance of the holiday.

"They're fine."

"Let me guess. They're at home baking cookies with Susie Homemaker."

Birdy chose to ignore me. Or maybe he just hadn't made the acquaintance of Susie, so he didn't know how to respond.

"Do you want to come in?"

"No."

"You sure? I'll give you some sweet tea and some stale store-bought cookies I have in the cupboard," I teased. It's easy to be nice when you've won.

I took his hand, the one not clutching tight to the yellow manila envelope, in mine, pulling him along with me.

Birdy's eyes touched on my hair and they lingered. "I like your hair. It's not so white. It's almost the same color as when you were a girl." He shuffled his feet on the gravel, heavy and slow, as if every step closer to the house was one step closer to trouble.

"Come on, Birdy, the house isn't haunted. We had some good memories here."

Birdy stayed silent, and I tried hard to recall some. There were many memories bundled up tight like dirty wash in that house. Many that included Bobby Lee and times I'd rather forget.

"We had fun, Birdy. Maybe not so much here at the house, but remember? Remember swimming in the creek and climbing the trees, and the time we teepeed the neighbors?"

I finally managed to get a smile out of Birdy. His lip tugged up at the corner, and his eyes went lighter. "I heard the kids sure enjoyed messin' up this one."

"That was fun. And so expensive! Next time I decide to deface a property, I need to make sure it isn't mine. The price to clean it was ridiculous."

We stepped over the threshold, and Birdy's eyes lifted to the second floor. "Does your room still have that awful pink?"

I clasped my fingers together in nervousness, holding them in front of my stomach and took a deep breath, trying to calm my nerves. "Yes."

Birdy's eyes never left the second story. He continued to watch and stare, almost in a trance, as if he could see the ghosts of our past wandering down the paneled hallways over the smooth worn wood of the floors. His head tilted to the side, as if listening to the sounds of people talking, or the strumming of my guitar that I'd play for him in my room, or the harsh voices and the violent sounds, and the crying of my pain. Or his.

"It wasn't my pride," Birdy said, his voice weary. "It wasn't pride that kept me from moving with you into this house, Savannah. It was the memories," he said, finally admitting to me what he hadn't during all our recent fights. "All those bad memories of you and Bobby Lee in your room while I waited downstairs for you to finish, not knowing if you were crying out in pleasure or pain. Not knowing if he was doing something you wanted, or if he was hurting you again."

And Birdy *had* waited. He waited downstairs, alone, while we finished with our foolishness, while my parents were out at the country club or at supper with friends. Waited to save me, if need be. To come break down the door and save me from Bobby and the fire that would burn me, sometimes leaving me with purple bruises that faded to green and yellow. Bruises I hid from everyone, even Birdy, at times. Birdy was never Bobby Lee's friend at all; he was mine.

Birdy handed me the envelope, letting his fingers linger when ours met, the touch sending a current that jolted through us.

But the spark wouldn't catch. Too much had happened now, too many harsh words were spoken, and I'd sell my house and start a new life with my children.

I took the envelope and slowly opened it.

"The kid's birth certificates?" I slid the thick documents out of the envelope, walking to the table to have a better look.

"And our marriage certificate. I thought you might need copies. Soon enough, you'll be able to add our divorce papers to the mix." Birdy's voice was soft, without reproach.

I stared at the papers in my hand, foreign and official, touching the flat writing, and seeing our names, and the date of our wedding on the marriage certificate. Next, I read Anna's birth certificate, the most recent, and then Cody's, and finally, the birth certificates of the twins, our minis, Melissa Ray Johnson and Emma May Johnson, listing the hospital and ... I stared hard at the papers before me. My hands began to tremble and my heart quickened. I set the papers down on the table and leaned in, my finger following across the lines, touching the black type, reading and rereading one line, my mind trying to accept what it said. The date of their birth.

The realization hit me, and my stomach lurched. I bent over from the ache that tore through me, not wanting to believe what I'd read. "*Noo!* Oh, my God! No!" I cried, wrapping my arms around me, rocking and swaying, my mind scrambling, doing the numbers. Bile tasting rancid as poison seeped into my mouth and to the rest of my body, and a darkness clouded my eyes, threatening to blind me.

"*I was pregnant!*" I screamed at Birdy, horrified by the truth. "That's why you married me, wasn't it? I was pregnant with Bobby Lee's babies!" I grabbed the birth certificate, clenching it hard in my fist. "That's why I never made it to the festival, wasn't it? That's why I made you marry me that weekend! I was pregnant!"

Tears coursed down my face, and Birdy reached for me, to comfort me.

"Don't!" I pushed Birdy away from me. "That's why I was so sad and depressed for all our marriage, wasn't it? Because I made you marry me! Forcing you to raise children that weren't yours? Forcing you to be stuck with me and those girls!"

I threw the minis' birth certificates at Birdy and ran to the kitchen to get my purse, my knees so weak I thought I'd fall. I needed to know what happened. I wouldn't wait another minute. I needed to know. To finally put the past behind me.

"Savannah, wait!" Birdy ran to the kitchen to stop me.

I wasn't going to wait. I needed to find the answers. Why didn't Bobby Lee marry me? Why did he let our friend become the father to his children?

Before Birdy could stop me, I ran out the door to the carport and got in my car, fumbling to get the key into the ignition, despite my shaking hands. Birdy's palms pounded on the glass of my car, and he yelled at me to stop. I needed to see Bobby Lee, to ask him why he'd abandoned his children, twin girls with the sweet open faces and the blue eyes of their mother.

I clutched at the top of my stomach, holding in the pain, and yet it poured out in my sweat and the tears on my face, dripping so that I could hardly see the road ahead of me.

Bobby Lee ... Memories of Bobby Lee ...

Secrets long since buried unearthed, struggling to rise up from the dirt and the soil of my past. Bobby Lee Thomas with the vicious mean temper. A temper I had to do terrible things to calm. Awful, nasty things. Things that later left me crying at night in my pink and white room with the lace curtains, with Birdy on the floor by my side at night while I sobbed, wanting to kill Bobby, to save me from any more suffering. Save me from things that hurt, things I didn't understand, things that blurred the lines of love and hate. And me, sick and confused, as any teenager could be, giving excuses for Bobby. Saying Bobby didn't mean it. He was sorry. That he loved me. That it was the whiskey that made him do those dirty things. That Bobby promised he'd stop, this time. Promised he wouldn't make me do it again.

And Birdy holding me in his arms and saying he'd catch me. To say the word and he'd catch me.

I drove fast through the streets to the mill, on the other side of town, a place I'd been many times, a place that might have become mine. I knew Birdy followed somewhere far behind, as my car streaked down the asphalt highway, across the bridges and streets we'd all traveled down together. Bobby Lee Thomas, with the violent temper. And the father of my twin girls.

I parked the car and went inside.

He wasn't the same as I'd remembered. His hair had thinned, and his waist had widened, thick with the whiskey and beer. His eyes were still green beneath his heavy lids, but they were reddened with unrest and indifference.

"Hey, Bobby Lee." I stood in the doorway of his office above the mill he'd inherited and never much wanted, a tired thing now, with empty shelves and deserted aisles, with most of the saws quiet, in an era when people shopped at Home Depot or Lowe's.

"Savannah May!" Bobby exclaimed, shocked to find me standing at his office door, the door second to the left down the hallway. "Come in. Wow, it's been a long time. How long has it been? Seven years, I think. Come in and sit down. I have some whiskey in my drawer, if you want a drink. I can probably find some soda to go with it." Bobby Lee slicked his greasy hair back from his face, his fingers chopping through, leaving pink gashes of scalp. "Sit, girl." He brushed off the chair with his hand, the dust from the mill covering the seat like cake flour in a pan.

"No thanks, I'll stand."

Bobby Lee seemed nervous and maybe a little drunk, and he licked his lips, opening and closing his mouth, same as a carp, the words getting stuck inside. "I … I don't understand why you're here," he stammered, tucking his sweat-stained shirt inside his waistband along with the fat. "You look good, though, Savannah May. Damn! You always looked good."

I stood quietly in that dusty office of Thomas and Son Lumber, taking in Bobby Lee, and then my eyes traveled to the dirty trashcans overflowing with coffee cups, and the cigarette butts, and the cobwebs hanging from the ceiling, stained with nicotine and tobacco. My eyes scanned the walls with the dated girly calendar from years ago, and I saw windows too dirty to let in the light.

"Did you ever get married, Bobby Lee?" I watched him twitch and jerk with nervousness.

Bobby Lee sat down in his torn, green vinyl chair with the rusted metal, opening the desk drawer to take a quick pull on his whiskey, before getting up and fretfully pacing the floor of that tired office.

"Yeah, twice. And twice divorced." He laughed an uneasy laugh, plucking at the raw skin on his fingers, the nails bitten down to the quick.

"Have any kids?" I closed and opened my hands down at my sides to disperse the tingling, my eyes never leaving his face, taking in the stubble of his beard and the puffed shadows under his eyes.

"No. But I heard you and Birdy have a shitload of them. Twins, too. I hear they're girls and have red hair and freckles. Too bad. And you have a boy, too. Don't he have a lazy eye? At least you got one good one, from what I hear. My cousin told me your new baby was pretty, just like you."

"Screw you, Bobby Lee."

"Hey! Hey!" He held up his hands, palms open wide. "I'm just passing on what I hear, that's all. Can't say I've seen them myself. Do you have a picture?"

"*Those girls are yours, Bobby Lee!* Twin girls. Those are your children, and yet you let Birdy Johnson raise them as his own, never paying a cent, while we struggled. Didn't you care? Didn't you want to know them?" I shouted at him, my voice carrying over the sounds of the saws, as sharp as the serrated blades of the steel. "You turned your back on your own children, you bastard!"

Bobby Lee's eyes turned mean and dark, changing colors, same way as they did all of those years we were together. I learned to notice the signs of his changing long before it hit— the subtle differences, the edginess of him, the sharpness. Reading the signs, so I could try to deflect them, or bend them. Knowing if I didn't, there were worse things in store for me.

"Are you here for money, Savannah May? Because I'm not giving you a dime! Do you and that country hick need money? Is that it? And now you've come for it because you think those freckled redheaded girls are mine? Lord, not that we didn't have a go of it, *practicing*, as you called it, with as many times as we did it." Bobby Lee advanced on me, slow and sinister as a snake in the field, sidling up to me. "You remember, don't you,

Savannah?" he said, his voice low and raw. And you liked it, didn't you? The way I'd tie you up—"

I took a step back, tripping on a tear in the carpet but righting myself before I fell. "Stop it, Bobby Lee!" I put my hands over my ears to block his voice and the harsh memories.

And closer he came, the snake coiled in the grass, until his body was next to mine, so close I smelled the fear and the stink coming off him like rotting cabbages in the garden. "You remember, don't you, my hands in your hair ..."

He reached out and grabbed my hair, wrapping it around his fist, tight as a belt, pulling so hard it brought me to my knees, making me cry out.

I fought to free myself, leaning my body and striking out with my hands, my struggles only serving to ignite the destructive fire that burned within Bobby Lee's black and damaged heart—forgetting struggling was what Bobby Lee liked best. I twisted and turned, my arms striking out, missing anything of consequence, and only finding the dusty air.

"And I bet you remember how I tasted, don't you?" he said, curling his left fist inward and bringing my head to his thighs, so close I felt the sharp edges of the zipper, cold on my cheek. Farther he pushed, so hard I struggled to breathe, and feeling him harden, while he drew his hand back to hit me, another one of the many things that fueled Bobby Lee.

The sound of the saw silenced the blow, and the bitterness of the blood filled my mouth. He raised his arm to hit me again.

"That wasn't my baby, you little slut," he hissed, "though I didn't know it at the time when I gave you the money to get rid of it. I can't have children, Savannah. I've known that for five years now. I'm sterile. I can't have children," he snarled, his hand still wrapped in my hair while the blood trickled out the corners of my mouth. "Those brats of yours belong to Birdy Johnson, or whoever else you were spreading your legs for besides me."

He pulled his hand back to hit me, and I closed my eyes to pray.

"*I'll kill you, Bobby Lee.* Something I should have done a long time ago," Birdy whispered, the tire iron tight around Bobby's neck, pulling and choking the air from his lungs, making his face turn purple as harsh raspy sounds gurgled at the back of his throat. "So help me God, you touch her again and I will kill you."

Bobby Lee unclenched his hand, and I fell forward, sobbing into the wood-dusted carpet, the memories flooding through me, unleashing in torrents, like sheets of rain lashing against our picture window in a fierce winter storm. Memories, sharp and stinging, of bandages and bruises, of Bobby doing terrible things that hurt me and tore me open, leaving blood on my sheets, dotted speckles as dark as the spots on a robin's egg, and Birdy's face above me, crying in the night as I slept, helpless to save me from myself. Memories of Bobby handing me the money, and the clinic, and Birdy beside me holding my hand, and hearing those awful noises of the air and the sucking of machines. And finding out there were two hearts, not one, beating inside my body.

I remembered.

I remembered it all. The befores and the afters. A vile night, when things went too far, and I cried out for Bobby to stop, but he wouldn't. Of crying out for Birdy.

And Birdy coming to save me, pounding hard up the stairs of my house from where he waited down below, busting through my door to save me. Save me from Bobby Lee. Birdy struggling with Bobby and beating him bloody, and then carefully dressing me, gently as you would a child, carrying me to his car and driving me away from Bobby Lee, away from the cruelty. All those many years of his cruelty.

Birdy had me leave a note for my parents, telling them not to worry. That I'd gone with some friends for the weekend, something I'd occasionally do. And he drove me far, to a cabin in the woods, of which I can't recall, only the smell of the trees and the wet leaves under our feet, and the fire he made in the hearth. But most of all, I remembered Birdy's arms still around me in the early morning hours of the next day, how he'd held me through the long night, driving away my burdens, stroking my long blond hair and telling me to shush when I cried. That he was there for me. That he'd always be there to catch me.

And I remember asking Birdy to love me, as the night slipped away and the dawn blushed purple and the rain fell gently on the roof, singing me its gentle song to calm my anguish. I asked him to love me, by the light of the fire, to erase all the hatred that filled me for so many years, to fill me, instead, with his goodness and the tender gentleness of him. I asked Birdy to love me that day, in that cabin in the woods, of which I can't recall.

CHAPTER EIGHTEEN

"Thank you, Birdy," I said, simply, feeling more drained than I'd ever felt in my life. My bones were weary, and I was so tired. I leaned my head against the passenger window of my car while Birdy drove, closing my eyes with fatigue, fighting off all the memories now flooding my mind. Too many to comprehend.

Birdy said nothing, still too shaken from what had just happened. He didn't kill Bobby Lee, though Lord knows he wanted. Instead, he beat him with the tire iron, asking how did *he* like to feel pain? Then saying words about the shoe being on the other foot, or something similar, before sticking the iron down the back of his pants and carrying me in his arms to the car, leaving Bobby bloodied and barely conscious, lying in his vomit on the dusty floor.

I massaged my temples, trying to block out the noise of the iron as it came down on Bobby Lee and the sickening sound of breaking bones.

"Did you know the minis were yours?" I asked, not imagining he could. Birdy used protection that morning, at least the first time, for what that was worth.

"Not for certain, but I'd always prayed they were. It didn't make no difference one way or the other. They were a part of you, Savannah May, and that's all that mattered. They were a part of you. But my mama's mama was a twin, so I figured there might be a chance."

There were still so many unanswered questions swirling around in my mind, punctured by fragmented pictures in pieces sharp as a broken mirror. Some large enough to give me a clear reflection of them and others little more than silvered particles, small as grains of sand.

"Your new car drives nice," Birdy said, turning his head to glance at me, the slightest smile on his lips.

"Yeah, but the gas mileage sucks. That stupid bus probably gets better MPG than this thing. At least it holds all the kids, and the dog I gave that ridiculous name to," I said, struggling to lighten the mood to make the thuds of the tire iron hitting Bobby Lee's flesh recede by my effort to talk.

Birdy tilted his head at me. "Would it make you feel any better if I told you that you named him Moonshine because the first night we brought him home it was dark and the moon was out and you said you liked the way the moon shined on his coat?"

"Really? Well, that does make me feel better."

"Naw. I'm just messin' with you. You named him Moonshine because you were mad at me that I kept sayin' *ain't*. You told me if I was going to talk hillbilly you'd give the dog a hillbilly name. At least I quit sayin' *pert near*. That one really got you riled up." Birdy quieted and concentrated on driving.

"So, you were just testing me to see how much I remembered." I stared out the darkened window. "I don't think that's how it works, Birdy. This isn't the movies. I don't know that suddenly every piece of my life is going to come back to me crystal clear. I'm going to need some time to heal from all of this. There are still so many questions I have."

"I imagine so." Lights from an oncoming car illuminated his face, revealing his tiredness.

"Birdy, you never told me how your mama died."

Not that I can recall ever asking. Birdy suffered enough, between his own abuse with his father and trying to save me from mine. The time never seemed right to bring it up. I always felt when he was ready, he would tell me.

"My daddy killed her."

"*What?* Oh, my God! Birdy!"

"He didn't murder her. But he killed her just the same. He came home drunk one night, and they got in a fight. He pushed her off the front porch, and she fell and hit her head on a rock. We took her to the hospital in town, but she never woke up. She died the next morning. Accident, my daddy said." Birdy removed his glasses and used the back of his hand to wipe his eyes before putting them on again.

I slumped against the back of my seat. No wonder Birdy cried in the night by the side of my bed, trying to save me from Bobby Lee. And then again when I was in the hospital. No wonder.

"And the minis … You knew I was pregnant before I did, didn't you?"

"I did," he sighed.

"Oh? And how is that, Mr. Fortune Teller?" I said, with an airiness I didn't feel.

"Because I was the one holding your hair back for you most times when you were puking."

"How'd you know it wasn't from nerves about the pageant or from me drinking too much?"

The rain started to fall, and Birdy tried to turn on the windshield wipers, but turned on the high beams instead. Eventually he got it right.

"Because we all knew you'd win that silly pageant, as long as you didn't burn the place down or catch your hair on fire, but mostly I knew because you quit drinkin' and didn't realize it. Even animals quit doin' harmful things when they're pregnant. Your granny, I suspect she knew. Zula, too. I don't think your parents did. They seemed too busy to care what was going on right under their noses." Birdy's voice was harsh. "All that money, and it couldn't help their daughter," he said more to himself than to me.

I wrapped my arms around me for warmth, and Birdy tried to turn up the heater but switched radio stations instead. Eventually, he got it right.

Another memory. Of seeing the lines on that little plastic stick I'd bought from the drugstore, and of breaking down in despair. All of my dreams of pageants and crowns, of my parents being proud and taking the time out of their busy lives, their social lives, to see their daughter with the long blond hair and the cornflower blue eyes, to finally *see* her, were silenced on that day of my affliction.

I drove my Mustang down the long driveway that day, and two miles plus, to that garage where Birdy lived, and he came out, his face knowing and concerned. I showed him the stick, and he held me as I cried and asked me what I wanted to do.

Then he waited outside the bedroom door—Bobby Lee's, that time. Waited while I told Bobby I was pregnant.

Bobby Lee wasn't as mad as I expected him to be. He said he was surprised it hadn't happened before, busy as we were. He simply asked how much money, although I didn't know. Then he unlocked a drawer and handed me some bills. Did I want him to drive me? Or could Birdy do him the favor?

Birdy drove me that afternoon, on a pretty spring day, a day not meant for evil. A day when all the flowers bloomed, their faces wide to catch the sun. A day I should have been happy for my winning the week before, when I'd tossed those batons up high without setting my hair on fire. When I saw the face of my parents, proud, and Bobby Lee, too, and Birdy, missing from the crowd because he didn't have a suit to wear.

Birdy, holding my hand, his eyes mournful with despair, in that room with the white sheets and the metal pan, the sharp instruments beside it, shining deadly in the light. The hissing and the sucking sound of the machines, so loud I covered my ears to block it, and shut my eyes, too.

And finding out there were two hearts, not one, beating inside my body.

Birdy took me away in that old truck. It was not a day meant for harm. Too much had already been done.

"Did you want to say no, Birdy? Did I give you a choice, or did I make you marry me?" I placed my hand on his arm, feeling the strength of it through the worn fabric of his shirt.

The rain fell hard on the road in front of us, so hard even my new windshield wipers couldn't keep up, and Birdy pulled the car over to the side of the road to wait for the rain to stop.

Birdy laughed, a hollow sound in the darkness of the car. "Savannah May, I'd be lying if I said it didn't come as a shock when you said it."

"But were you happy, Birdy, or did it make you sad? Knowing you'd probably be raising children that weren't yours?"

Birdy turned in his seat and faced me, his expression soft in the darkness. "It made me happy. Savannah, you have always made me happy."

"Not lately, I bet."

"You're right. Not lately. But it does warm my heart to see the spark back in you again. You got so quiet, the years after we married, always as if your mind was somewhere else. I couldn't stop thinking it was my fault. That you wished you hadn't married me, after all."

The rain continued to fall on the windshield of my new car, beating a pattern in the darkness of the night.

Birdy and I sat, each lost in our own reflections. Birdy wouldn't tell me his mind—he seldom did without my asking—but as the years of our life passed by, sometimes I knew his mind better than he did.

"Birdy?"

"Yes, Savannah?"

"We told people the minis were premature, didn't we?"

"We did."

"So we lied."

"There are some lies worth telling."

"Did people believe us?"

"Most did."

"My parents?"

"They did, most of all. Some people believe what they hear, and yet turn their heads away from things right in front of their faces," Birdy said, his voice rough. Then he sighed, taking in a breath and releasing it. "But the minis were small, because you wouldn't eat. So small, they each fit in the palm of my hands. Each barely five pounds. That's why you called them the minis. So most people believed us when we said they were early."

And I remembered. I remembered feeling the movement and the stirring of those two little bodies inside of me, children of Bobby Lee, and the violence and the nastiness of the things he made me do that resulted in their making. And a gentle memory of Birdy, but knowing there was no sense in hoping. Years of my torment made those babies—it was a wonder it never happened sooner.

I remembered that Sunday morning, me waving to Birdy from the front porch just as Birdy got in the car to go to church, asking me once more, please come, but me staying behind, refusing to ever go again, feeling so heavy with the burden of those babies I couldn't catch my breath, and waving to him from the porch.

I remembered gasping with pain, and folding over, and Birdy coming back, and the warm water running down my legs and staining my slippers. Of getting in the car and going to the hospital. The pain of them, even as small as they were, the pain of bringing their tiny bodies into my world of regret. And of Birdy always by my side, holding my hand and smoothing the sweat from my brow as I labored, and saying he loved me.

"Birdy?"

"Yes, Savannah?"

"I don't think I was sad all those years. I was angry. And somehow the anger just got caught inside me, until it festered like a cancer and made me sick. Not *twisted* sick, the way I was so screwed up when I was with Bobby Lee …" I couldn't go on for a moment, too lost in my thoughts.

What does a child know of love? Of pain? What happens when you can't tell the difference? When you're so desperate to find love that you believe the words of someone stained, someone damaged. What happens when two children come together, one rich, and one poor, one nearly abandoned, and one ignored, and tightly braid their pain together like the plaited tails of the horses in the circus, the threads of their mane and the ribbons, interweaving—the gold and the brown. Where does one end and the other begin?

"I think, in the beginning I was angry at Bobby Lee for not coming after me, terrible as that sounds. Didn't he care about me or the babies?" I heard the sharp intake of Birdy's breath and a soft moan of his discomfort. "Mostly, though, I was angry with myself. For forcing you to marry me."

"You didn't force me, Savannah. You just asked me, would I, is all. Don't you remember?" Birdy reached across the console to take my hand.

I did remember. I remembered driving back from the clinic, desperate with worry, knowing I'd made the right choice, but regretting there was a choice to be made. The knowing my life would never be the life I'd imagined. That the days of pageants were behind me, of my childhood dreams, of big houses and fancy cars, at least until I was thirty, when I would get my money, but too old to have any fun.

And I remember Birdy driving us to the side of the creek, of walking along the water's edge, and Birdy placing his hand on my stomach and asking if I wanted girls or boys, or one of each. Of Birdy saying he loved me, and asking what could he do to help. And there by the side of the creek, Birdy taking me in his arms and kissing me deeply. Telling me he'd always loved me. Then, suddenly, me asking him, would he marry me—on the weekend of my festival—when everyone we knew would be there, along with the rides and the peaches and all the girls in my court in their rhinestone tiaras. All having fun. Everyone but me, who'd gone to Savannah, to marry poor, sweet Birdy Johnson.

"Birdy?"

"Yes?"

"Are we very far from that cabin?"

Without answering, Birdy started the car and pulled onto the dark road, the rain softening to a mist, the sound of the tires splashing through the water as we traveled. Silently, we drove for about twenty minutes or so, the heavy thumping of my heart pounding a beat in time to the windshield wipers. It was too dark to see Birdy's face, but I imagine it was firm with intention.

Birdy slowed the car and pulled to the left at a fork in the road, driving my car through a clearing, past the rusted gate hanging off its hinges and the trees that stood sentry. Driving over the bumps and the ruts knowing just where to go, until we arrived at last and he stopped the car, pulling the key from the ignition. The two of us stared at the cabin, a small quaint thing made from cedar, the smell of it wet with the rain reaching out to us even from where we sat, each of us locked inside a memory—good or bad, I cannot say. We sat for a moment more, waiting for the rain to stop. Once it did, we opened our doors, quietly walking the short distance along the path of the soggy leaves, Birdy's hand in mine. We walked where we had walked before, on another rainy night such as this, years ago, a night when things finally went too far, and Birdy needed to catch me. To break down the door of the castle and save me from the dragon.

The creak of the door broke the silence as we opened it, the vision before us stirring a memory of the sound of a match being lit, a fire crackling in the hearth, and our joining that followed.

Wordlessly, Birdy moved about the room, finding the matches and wood and striking a fire, stoking it until it glowed hot, putting his hands in front of it and rubbing them together to take the chill from them. Pulling up an old chair from the corner, he urged me to sit, placing it in front of the fire so I could warm myself, too.

Birdy's fingers brushed the side of my cheek, and he stood, mindful, as the emotions played across my face, the conflict and the pain, as I sorted the memories of that first night we were together, the bittersweet memories of it, and the memory prior, that was not. He saw something else, something burning within me as I stared back at him, watching his eyes reflect the flames of the fire, the flicker of the reds and the oranges. He saw my desire for him. A desire born from the knowledge we created those precious lives together. Four precious lives. Lives made from our love of one another.

He found an old blanket on a shelf in the corner and placed in on the floor in front of the fire, the light illuminating his face, tranquil and serene. Moving ever so slowly, so as not to frighten me, he began to take off his shirt, unbuttoning it, button by button, holding my gaze and willing me to return it. Until finally, I stayed his hand, and I finished the rest, my palms caressing the bare smoothness of his chest beneath the soft fabric of it, running up and down his skin, absorbing the fever of him. I pushed the shirt from his shoulders, where it fell to the floor, and my hands traveled to his waist, coming to rest on the fabric of his jeans, the metal buttons cold as snow. My fingers deliberately worked their way inside, and I lowered my body to kneel …

Roughly, Birdy pulled me up, stopping me, catching my wrists, and turning them over to kiss the palms with the softness of his lips, warm and tender. He stepped out of his pants and stood there in his nakedness, his body lit crimson by the fire, all the hard planes and the furrows of him glistening with sweat and the heat of our passion.

Birdy's callused hands sought my skin, brushing and stroking, and he pushed the shirt from my shoulders where it fell next to his, removing my bra to expose my breasts, now aching, full from the need of our child. He bent his head to taste the sweetness of them, and they released, the moisture wet on his lips and in his hands, massaging it like syrup into the fullness of me. He bent his head again, hungry with the need of my body, and I arched my head back and used my hands, pulling him closer to me, holding him, feeling the sear of his mouth on my skin. The pull and the draw of him. Wanting him to drink his fill of me, to nourish him with the goodness of me, as I wanted to be filled with his.

"Love me, James Russell," I whispered.

With one hand, he pushed down the fabric of my pants, slow and leisurely, unhurried and easy, and all the while his hands on me, massaging, kneading, stirring memories of another time. He smoothed out his shirt for us to lie on, worn soft and smelling of the earth and the sky, and placed me on top, the coolness of the floor seeping thorough. All the while, his hands never leaving my body, stroking the softness of me, building my desire, my body wet and slick. His hand traveled to oil my thighs with the moistness of me, massaging it in, until I begged for its release.

There were no shadows here. No ghosts that walked the smooth wood floors of a dark house filled with nasty memories of pain and violence. Only the sounds of the night and our love, as we lay by the fire.

CHAPTER NINETEEN

S ome people are like the leaves on the trees—fresh and new when they unfurl. Green. So supple that when taken into your hand to gather their texture before releasing, they extend back into shape, as if you'd never touched them at all. Springing back, unfolding. And as the seasons progress and spring becomes summer, and just before summer turns to fall, the leaves go from green to yellow, before turning gold. Not as pliable as before, but bigger. Growing much larger than before. Not as malleable as the green, but a broader leaf, a leaf lined with texture and character.

I had gone from green to gold.

The air from the window blew my hair around my face, and I chatted with Siri while I drove to pick up the kids. Honestly, Siri is such a kick, and she says the darndest things. I asked her where to hide a body, and she responded with, *"What kind of place are you looking for?"* Then she gave me my choice of reservoirs, metal foundries, dumps, and swamps. Deep Creek wasn't one of them, but I was near one, if I wanted to add it to the list of choices.

I put my signal on and turned onto Rocky Road, past the dead-end sign, pulling up in front of Birdy's house.

Actually, Birdy's and Becky's Lou's, according to Birdy.

The minis and Cody ran out of the house to meet me, and I wrapped my arms around them tight as a blanket, hugging and loving on them. They were resilient kids and had emerged from their pods, their cocoons of silence, where they were trapped for all those years, in a household where laughter was seldom heard and suffering blocked out the sun. Now they giggled and chatted, as only children can do, excited to see me. Even Cody, with eyes as straight as my old batons, smiled and laughed and fought to be heard over the voices of his sisters.

I hadn't signed my divorce papers, and I'd postponed our court date. There was healing still to be done, things best not rushed in haste. Although the driving across town and the daily pumping of milk was beginning to grow burdensome.

Birdy and Becky Lou came out of the house, Becky holding Anna in her arms. Becky Lou shyly said hi, embarrassed, as she should be, and then handed me my baby to feed. Anna could now hold a sippy cup, but I didn't want to give up her nursing. Partly for Anna, because it was good for her, partly for me, because I had so grown to love our bonding, and partly for spite—so there would be something I could give my child Becky Lou could not.

Becky Lou was nineteen now and still far too young for Birdy, as far as I was concerned. I knew she still slept on the sofa when the children were there, but I knew she slept in the bed with Birdy when the children were with me at my new house—a temporary house, until I found me a new one—as the house of my youth had been sold.

"Melissa, Emma, I do believe you're going to have the prettiest white teeth I have ever seen! Where did you get such pretty teeth?" I stroked one head and then the other, smiling at those eager faces.

"From you, Mama!" they said in unison.

"Certainly not me. It must be from your daddy. If he'd smile more, we could see your daddy's pretty teeth." I followed the children into the house and then sat on the sofa, unbuttoning my blouse to feed Anna, who had some new white teeth of her own. "Ouch, darlin'! Don't bite your mama." I sighed, knowing my child was getting older and more independent, as she kept pulling away to be in on the action. I finished her feeding and set her down on the floor, where she struggled to walk on her chubby legs, standing and falling and then doing the same.

Birdy and Becky Lou stood side by side with an easiness about them, a familiarity born of intimacy, Becky Lou leaning into him from time to time, their bodies touching, as if to say he belonged to her now.

Things did not suddenly change for us that day with Bobby Lee, the day Birdy saved me from Bobby and we drove to the cabin to join our past with our present. Too much had happened, there was healing yet to be done. Scars needing to fade with time.

"Cody, come sit on your mama's lap so I can love you up!"

Cody sat on my lap, his worn flannel shirt soft and warm as a kitten in the sun, and I put my arms around him and rocked him for a spell.

"Mama, I'm a big boy now," he said shyly, but with a voice I clearly heard.

"I know, Cody, but let Mama have her way for just a minute more." I bent my head and buried my face in his neck, while the minis sat at my feet and stared at me with adoring eyes. Probably because of the packages I'd given them filled with glitter polish and lip gloss, and not because I was so wonderful.

"Savannah May ..." Birdy said, his voice warning, but not angry.

"For goodness sakes, Birdy, it's made for kids. All girls their age are wearing it. I swear, I won't buy them a push-up bra for at least another year or two."

The minis giggled, and Birdy said all right, he expected it was fine.

I bit my lip, glancing at Birdy and Becky Lou, thinking soon it would take more than words to pry them apart, when they crossed over from casual lovers to something much more.

"Becky, will you watch the kids while I speak with my husband?" Birdy's eyes widened at my word choice.

I was being mean, I know, but I spent so many years with mean poured on me, sometimes a person just wants to pour some back.

Becky Lou asked the children if they wanted to make some fresh cookies, and they went to the kitchen to bake.

"Sheesh, Birdy, with all those cookie she bakes, it's a wonder y'all aren't three hundred pounds. Just how many cookies can one family eat?" I headed out the front door with Birdy following behind me.

I noticed Birdy had seeded the grass, although the new grass came in sparse and spotted, refusing to take root, and that Becky Lou, most likely, had placed a new wreath on the front door that said *God Bless Our Home.*

"How was Becky Lou's nineteenth birthday party? Did you have fun at Chuck E. Cheese? Did she get to wear a paper crown and have white cake with pink icing?"

I took one guess what her wish was.

"Don't be mean, Savannah. We took the kids to the movies to celebrate." Birdy's arm accidentally bumped against me, and it sent a warm current to my parts below.

"And what did you see, may I ask?"

He coughed just a bit before sheepishly saying, *How to Train Your Dragon 2*, the tips of his ears turning pink, because obviously it was Becky's choice, and not the kids', to see the cartoon.

"Oh, how nice. And what did you buy her for a present? A new dolly to play with?" Immediately I regretted my remark because she got my dolly, to dress and feed and play with, more often than I'd like.

"Stop it, Savannah! Just stop." Birdy stood in front of me and took me by the shoulders firmly to gently shake me, same way you do to a child who's acting naughty, the color rising in his cheeks, his eyes dark behind the black frames of his glasses. "It was your idea to split up. Not mine. Becky Lou is a nice girl, and she's great with the kids. And our house suits her just fine," he said as an afterthought.

"Birdy, the toilet didn't flush!" I snapped at him, breaking free from his grasp and folding my arms tight around my waist to hold myself together.

"The chain inside the tank was broken, Savannah. It's not as if I needed to dig you a new hole for our outhouse." Birdy shoved his hands inside his pant pockets. "Between the time at the hospital with you, and the running back and forth to get the milk to Dolly and taking care of the kids and working, I didn't have the time to fix it."

I suppose Birdy was right.

"She's a nice girl—"

"So you've said," I cut him off.

He narrowed his eyes at me and continued, "Yes, she's young, but she's been caring for kids most her life. Including ours, when you couldn't," he finished softly, knowing he'd hurt me with that.

Tears stung at the back of my eyes, and I dabbed at them, trying not to smear my makeup. I'd ditched the MAC and gone for Clinique, which had a more natural look to it.

"I'm sorry," he said, taking me into his arms and holding me tight, laying his head on mine. Birdy spent so many years with mean poured on him too, I guess he just wanted to pour some back.

I put my arms around him, smelling the scent of him, a slightly different scent now. A smell of Birdy and candied perfume. My heart clenched, and tears gently rolled down my face.

"I just can't go back to being *small*, Birdy. I want a bigger life," I cried, the sound muffled against the fabric of his shirt. "And I'm sick inside knowing you lie with her at night. I don't know how you did it, Birdy, all those years. With me and Bobby in my room, and you downstairs. Waiting. Waiting for us to finish our foolishness."

I felt his body stiffen and the acceleration of his heart. Neither of us moved for a moment until finally Birdy broke free and released me, taking my hand and leading me down the lane of our street and to the woods beyond.

"You're not thinking of killing me, are you? Because if you are, Siri has a few ideas where you can hide my body."

Birdy gave me a curious look. His phone wasn't 5G.

I held his hand, callused from work and toil, as we walked to the edge of the woods, the sounds of the birds and the drone of the bees filling the air with their noises.

Birdy found us a clearing in the woods and sat down, pulling me down beside him to sit.

"I reckon you have a need to talk," he said, giving me my space in his sweet Birdy way. "I'm ready to listen."

"Can I ask you a question?" I said, having already asked him the first.

Birdy nodded his head yes.

"Obviously, you're having sex with Becky Lou."

"That's not a question."

"I know, I know." I waved my hands in front of me to dispel the statement. "That wasn't the question. That would be an *observation*." Not that I'd observed them having sex, but I observed the tension of it in the air between them, strong as the current in the telephone lines buzzing overhead on our street. *Their* street.

"Were you a virgin the first time we made love? That weekend in the cabin, when you saved me from Bobby Lee?"

Birdy's face flushed, and he picked up a rock, bringing his arm back and hurling it at a distant tree, where it knocked down a wasp nest, long abandoned.

"Was I that bad?"

"*No!* No," I said, embarrassed. "You were that *good*, is all. I just wondered where you got the practice." I picked up a rock and threw it two feet.

Birdy smiled at the compliment, his white teeth bright in his tanned face, and there was the hint of a dimple on his jaw, but he said nothing.

"Come on, Birdy. Don't make me drag it out of you as you always do. I'm trying to have a conversation with you, not a monologue of all the years of my discontent. Lord knows there's been enough of that for a lifetime. I'm asking because you seemed to know what you were doing. As if you'd been doing it for a long time. And I can rightly say I never remember seeing you with any girl besides me, and most folks said the same. I was wondering if you found girls in another town."

Birdy found a small stick and unconsciously traced my name in the dirt, before realizing what he'd done and erased it. "There weren't many, but I did all right, I suspect."

I waited. And then I waited some more.

A troubling thought filled my mind. "They weren't prostitutes, were they?" I don't know where Birdy would find someone like that in our town, but I have to believe they existed. And that might explain the condom.

"Of course not. Don't let your mind go to dirty places, Savannah. I saw Jamie Lynn for a time, but it didn't last. She said it was as if we were having a ménage à trois, that's a fancy way of saying a three-way, I think. That she always knew the thought of you was lingering somewhere in the room."

"Jamie Lynn Harris? The short blond girl with the big breasts and the brown eyes? Between Jamie, Becky, and me, I have to say, blonds are your type, Birdy Johnson."

"Jamie Lynn wasn't a real blond. Her hair was black."

"Oh *my*." I felt the color rising to my face at the visual, and I tipped my head, my fingers picking at the dirt. "Can I be honest?" I lifted my head and searched Birdy's face.

"Are you ever not?"

"Not the time I told you I liked that wooden dog you carved for me. I thought it resembled a hog. But I kept it just the same."

Birdy reached for my hand, turning it over and placing inside it a small pebble he'd just discovered in the shape of a heart. It wasn't perfect, in the same way as our lives, our love, was not perfect. One side was bigger, same as our love, with Birdy giving me so much of his, and mine a smaller portion, but a portion big enough to sustain him through those troublesome years together.

"This is my confession, Birdy, and it's a selfish one. I always wanted you for myself. I thought that, in my mind, you would always belong to me."

"Same as those pink cars, Savannah May?"

"No, this is different. More as in, I might not be able to have you, but I don't want anyone else to have you, either."

"You know how to change that."

I stood up, brushing the dirt and the leaves from my new jeans. "I can't! Birdy, I cannot go back to our old life. I want more for us! I want a big house for our family," I cried out, brushing the bangs out of my eyes with my hand. I had let them grow out, and now they were just in the way, not long, or short, just annoying. "It doesn't need to be crazy big, like my old one. But bigger than we've got, so the kids can have friends over and we can have a party."

Which was silly, as we had no one to invite. No longtime friends, or even casual acquaintances in which to spend some time with. We only had each other, and that had always been enough.

Birdy said nothing. Just scratched some more in the dirt. He wrote the names of our children, and then the name of our dog, both of ours absent from the list.

"Why are you being so prideful, Birdy? It's all about sharing. Same way as I came to tell you I'll agree to equal joint custody of the kids if you want it. Fifty-fifty. They can have one week at my house and one week at yours. It's not a perfect solution, but it's the best I've got." I crouched beside him in the dirt. "It's called *sharing*, Birdy. Why won't you let me share?" A lone tear ran down my face, and Birdy dropped the stick and extended his hand to reach out and catch it, where it trembled on the edge of his finger. Then he caught another.

Birdy put the wet finger to his lips, almost as if to kiss it.

"You say you can't be small, Savannah May? Well, I don't know that I can be large. The life you lived, of a big house, and fancy cars, of cotillions and beauty pageants? That's not the life for me." Birdy sighed deep and stared off into the distance. "Your parents had all that money, and yet they let you suffer for all those years. Never once seeing the pain in your eyes or the purple stains on your body you tried so hard to hide with your long-sleeved shirts and your makeup. You lived in a house so large, nasty evil went on right underneath the roof of that house, and yet the cries of your suffering weren't nothing more than a whisper in the night." Birdy took me in his arms and laid his head on top of mine, his voice low and deep, reverberating through me. "You say you can't be small—well if that's what money brings, I don't ever want to be large."

CHAPTER TWENTY

Love is never a choice. The same as breathing is never a choice. Or sickness. Or death. Love is like the blood running through us, warm and salted as the water in the ocean. Pumping, filling our hearts with the strength of it, and then coming back up, all over again and keeping us alive.

But friendship is a choice. And I made my choice, so many years ago, on that lazy summer afternoon by the water's edge, when I met a lonely poor boy from Tennessee who had lost his mama. A boy with the slightest shadow of a faded black eye, and the colors of green and yellow marking his thin body.

That boy became my friend, long before the winds of autumn swept in and brought with it the unwelcoming burden of my teenage years. Years when that boy knew me better than I knew myself, and long before I ever learned how love and hate can sometimes be confused, and how people succumb to fear that festers in them, creating monsters that come out in the night to harm the ones closest to them.

"Mama!" Cody yelled from the window of the bus, his voice projecting loud enough for me to hear him while still seated in my car.

The minis waved from their seats, fourth row back, from my count, and I saw Anna's car seat buckled in tight in the row with Becky Lou, while Birdy drove the yellow bus into the parking space beside me at the mall on Ashford Dunwoody.

The bus groaned to a stop, spewing diesel or oil, or some other noxious odor, and I watched as my children filed off, with Birdy coming out last, behind Becky Lou and my baby.

I hugged the children tightly to me and kissed them, one by one, and then I hugged Becky Lou as well, before giving Birdy a quick kiss on the cheek.

"Please let me buy you a new car, Birdy, so you don't have to keep hauling our kids around in that old bus. They won't tell you, but they're embarrassed by it. I'll buy you a used Suburban. I'll try to find you one with really high miles, if it will make you feel better about it. Maybe even one with a dent, or missing a hubcap," I teased.

"Please, Daddy, please?" the minis said, jumping up and down as if I'd just offered to buy them a new Ferrari.

Birdy shot me a look I couldn't quite read—either annoyance or acceptance would be a guess, or two.

"Maybe so. I imagine it's time. The rig is paid off. But your daddy will be the one to buy it," he told the children.

"Killjoy." I stuck my tongue out at him, making the minis giggle.

I went to the back of my car and removed Anna's stroller, unfolding it with one hand. It was some super-lightweight model that simply needed a touch to open. Much different from the old heavy clunker Birdy used. Mine, I could even jog with, if I had the inclination, which I do not. Although I was going to the gym now and had a personal trainer who was awfully handsome.

I gathered Anna from Becky Lou, burying my face in her neck to breathe in the smell of her. Anna was weaned now, and I cried at night sometimes with the longing of our bonding, sad because I knew there would never be another time when I would hold a child to nurse at my breast.

Of course, then the reality hit me I had four kids to put through college, and this made me mourn somewhat less.

A sparkle caught my eye. Becky Lou, wearing a ring on her finger. Not her engagement finger, but a small ring on the other hand, and one that had not been there before. I felt my heart skip a beat, and I raised my eyes to Birdy, who noticed my concern and ever so slightly shook his head no. We were not divorced, had not even filed the final papers, and my heart resumed its beating. A promise, perhaps. A promise of something that might be. Or might not.

"Birdy, let me cut to the chase. And if we're going to fight, let's do it now, out here in the parking lot so we have witnesses on my intentions and I don't have to haul all the clothes back to the store." I handed Anna back to Becky to load in the stroller. "I plan on buying the kids an entire wardrobe of new clothes, and I suggest y'all have a big bonfire and burn the old ones. What were you thinking letting me sew? No wonder the sewing machine was up in the attic when I fell off that ladder. I must have had the good sense to put it there in the first place. I'm a terrible seamstress. Just look at the hem on Emma's pants. Why, one leg is at least an inch shorter than the other. And good

Lord, what idiot even sews these days when you can purchase clothes for less money than you can make them?" I glanced over at Becky and she blushed pink, as her blouse appeared homemade. A real nice job, but still homemade.

The minis held hands and bounced with nervous excitement. "*We get new clothes … we get new clothes …*" they sang.

"And I am not buying our son one more plaid shirt. Hunting season is over, or not yet started, I don't know which, and I don't care. He is going to have some stylish new clothes. I'll buy then at Old Navy if you want, so they won't be too fancy."

The children were so excited, he couldn't say no. And why would he? His wife had more money than she could possibly ever need, there was no reason for their children to go without.

Birdy held up his hands in surrender. "All right, all right. You win. And you're correct, you never were much of a seamstress," he said, smiling.

Nor much of anything else. If my memory serves me.

My memory was coming back, but still not fully recovered. There remained some missing pieces. All of the borders were there, and most of the center parts, too. Only a few left to be found, the pieces of a puzzle snapped back into place to finish the picture of our life together.

I was a good wife, Birdy had said that night at the end of our street, when I returned from the place my mind escaped to. Escaped to forget the horror of my past. He didn't mean I was a good wife in the way I originally supposed. That I was a good wife because I served him, the way I'd been taught. Taught in the darkness or the light of the day in my time with Bobby Lee.

He meant I was a good wife because I had loved him—the best way I knew how. That I tried to mother our children—the best way I knew how. And yes, that I tried to please him—the best way I knew how, despite struggling to put the violent memories of sex behind me. That I was willing to learn things I was never taught to do, from parents much too busy with their social lives to worry about such trivial things as the cooking and the cleaning. Rich people had servants and nannies to do what they would not.

"You're right. I don't know what was worse. My sewing or my cooking. It's a wonder any of you ever survived."

"Mama, Daddy did most of the cooking," Melissa reminded me.

I touched my daughter's freckled cheek. "I guess that's why you're still breathing, darlin'. You ate your daddy's cooking instead of mine."

Both Birdy and Becky Lou laughed, and the kids smiled.

"Hey, just so y'all know. I'm taking cordon bleu classes down the road from here. I might be able to still kill you with my cooking, only now the food will be French."

The kids were getting fidgety, and I knew it was time to go. "Umm, Becky Lou, may I speak to Bir ... I mean ... Mister ..."

Oh hell, what to call him? I was the only one of the group who called him Birdy, and I doubt Becky Lou was still calling him *Mister* Johnson if she was sharing his bed, so I went with the only other option. "May I speak to my husband, alone?"

Becky Lou flinched, as if stung by a picnic ant, nodding her head in acceptance, knowing I wasn't asking for her permission, as I had every intention of doing so one way or the other.

"Come along, now. Let's go to the food court, and I'll buy y'all an ice cream cone."

The kids kissed their daddy good-bye, and Birdy's eyes followed them until they disappeared inside.

My eyes traveled down to Birdy's left hand, his simple gold wedding band dulled with the passing of our nearly eight years together, but still firmly placed on his finger.

"Is that a promise ring on Becky Lou's finger, Birdy? Are you unofficially engaged?" I clutched my purse tighter to me.

"How can I be engaged, Savannah? I'm still married. Least I thought. It's just a ring, costing less than a hundred dollars, and it makes her feel better to wear it. So people don't talk," he said, stuffing his hands deep inside his pants pockets, making his shoulders slump forward.

"You will kill me, Birdy, if you get her pregnant, after all we've been through." My voice shook, and I tried to keep it together. "It will kill me, same way as if you put a bullet through me. It will break my heart. Please promise me you'll be careful. At least wait until we're divorced." My eyes pleaded with him, and I know they went bluer with my pain. "Birdy, it will *kill* me."

"I ain't gettin' her pregnant, Savannah. Becky Lou's on birth control pills. I know better than that. I don't want the minis having anything else to work against. Someday they'll be able to do the numbers and know you were pregnant when we married. They don't need to have a daddy who got another woman pregnant while still married to their mama."

"Thank you, Birdy." I leaned toward him and kissed his cheek. I didn't like knowing there was so much action going on that Becky Lou needed birth control pills so she could constantly be at the ready, but knowing Birdy cared enough about his family to be proactive made me at least feel a little bit better.

I stared at Birdy a moment more, contemplating what to say.

"There's more," Birdy said. It was a statement, not a question, because Birdy knew me so well.

"There is."

"Well, go on then."

"You know I'm in therapy, right?" I fussed at the neckline of my blouse. "So I can deal with all my issues."

"I do."

"Can I tell you something the therapist said?"

"I don't reckon I'll be able to stop you."

"You're right. You can't." I put my purse under my arm and took a step toward him, almost touching, feeling the heat coming up off him and going dizzy with it. "All right, here goes." I placed my hand on his forearm, holding him in place. "My therapist thinks Becky Lou is drawn to you because you represent a father figure." I smiled at him, "Not that there aren't a million other reasons, too," I added, and thinking of one in particular and the reason Becky needed those birth control pills.

Birdy cocked his head to the side, neither amazed nor annoyed at my statement. I got the sense he was weighing my statement, turning it over in his mind, to see if it were true. I was safe with Birdy, safe to say the most outlandish things sometimes, and he would be still and silent after I said them, turning them over in his quiet mind, a keen mind, a mind that would rather whisper than shout, when a whisper will suffice.

"Feedback?"

Birdy was silent, his eyes never leaving mine.

"Hellooo … Earth to Birdy." I waved my hand in front of his face.

But Birdy stayed silent. That was always the Birdy way.

After a moment or two. Or twenty. Birdy always won the staring game when we played. Birdy simply said, "I won't get her pregnant." Then he walked back inside the yellow bus.

CHAPTER TWENTY-ONE

There comes a time in all our lives when we need to leave behind our childhood dreams. When the dawning of the day brings with it new discoveries, new adventures to encounter. When we expand our lives out beyond the borders of the small worlds we have created and find new soil on which to tread or fresh waters to sail upon. Our feet will take us to the places we are meant to go, and they will follow our imagination, if we let them.

I took my first step.

Dating. Ugh! Who would ever think it would be so hard to find a decent man in a city the size of Atlanta? So far I'd been out with a tinker, a tailor, and a candlestick maker. The candlestick maker gave me some nice expensive candles at the end of our date, a parting gift of sorts, even though he didn't actually make the candles himself. He owned the company that made them, and they were distributed all over the world, not that I took an interest. I didn't care for him much anyway, with his arrogance and talk of money, but those candles sure did smell nice.

The tailor dressed nicely, always in quality suits: wool, and silk blends. He was from England, he told me, and soon enough I tired of his accent, although he said he enjoyed mine. He owned the company who made suits; he did not make them himself. Said he wasn't too handy with a needle and thread, and neither am I, so at least we shared that in common. But little else, because he was not so fond of children, it appeared, and he choked on his food at supper when I told him how many I had.

The tinker only wanted to tinker with me, with his suggestion of finding a hotel, soon as we finished our supper. I have no idea what he did, nor did I care, so I made him take me home, and then I sent him on his way after untangling myself from his unwanted embrace. I stood on my front porch and gave him a feeble wave good-bye, not knowing Birdy watched me from the front seat of his old truck, parked in front of the next house down.

"Hey, Savannah," Birdy acknowledged as I walked down the path to meet him, surprised to see him parked on my street. We embraced, as we always did, and Birdy held me close, but only partly, almost as if he were afraid to let us touch from our midsection down.

"Your new boyfriend?" Birdy said, shaking his head at the man who drove off. Probably because the man wore the silliest outfit. He wore a yellow shirt with a pink sweater around his shoulders, same as my daddy wore, and some plaid pants he said were golf, and he drove a fancy car the color of a pumpkin.

"Oh, God, no. And if you were watching, I want it noted, I tried to get him off me. I swear, it was like being on a date with an octopus. How one person can have so many hands in so many different places is beyond me."

Birdy smiled, and I felt his relief. Or maybe relief was something I wanted him to feel.

"This is a surprise, Birdy. A nice one, but still a surprise. Do you want to come inside?"

I had been waiting to give Birdy a surprise of my own, too afraid to do it before, and now certain it was the right time for it. There are times we need to let the past be the past and raise our thoughts to the future and where it will take us.

Birdy assessed my clothes, I think. He stared at me up and down, a lazy smile on his face. They weren't fancy clothes, a white tee and some jeans, though goodness, they were expensive!

"You look nice, Savannah May. Simple like."

"Thank you, Birdy. And just so you know, having money doesn't mean a woman needs to wear a bustier and a feather boa." I paused for a moment. "Well, not unless you're Lady Gaga."

Birdy laughed, and I saw the dimple in his chin and noticed the lines around his eyes had softened in the past few months, and there was a new fullness to him, a rounding that had not been there before. Not of his body; he seemed more fit than ever, but maybe a rounding *out*, an expansion of himself, a growing into the man he was meant to be, now that the sorrow of our lives were behind us.

I took his hand and pulled him up the porch to the rocking chairs placed there by the owners of the home. I was only renting, and the house was fine for the time, over twice the size of Birdy's, but not something I'd wish to buy. Still, it was fine for a time, until I found a house to make a home for my children.

"Sit," I commanded. And he did. "Would you care for a beer or some sweet tea? I might have a cola, but it's probably diet." Birdy sat without saying a word, just letting me talk, all nervousness and jittery limbs. "I've lost twelve pounds. Twelve pounds! Why did you let me get so fat, Birdy? Honestly, I look at all those pictures and I have to think that was another reason I looked so sad. Brown hair, and fat, too? Yuk."

"I like you just fine any way you are, Savannah May. In most of those pictures, you'd just had a child. There was a reason for it."

"Awww… You're a doll. That's why I love you, because you always know just the right thing to say." I smiled and patted his knee.

We sat for a spell, each rocking in our thoughts, Birdy glancing over at me from time to time. There was something he wanted to say, he just didn't know how to say it.

"You're obviously here to tell me something, Birdy, and I don't know if I want to hear it. Can it wait for just a bit? There's something I want to show you. Do you have some time?" I twisted my wedding ring with nervousness.

"I have some time."

"A little time, or a lot of time? Any chance I can borrow you for a few hours?" Birdy's eyes widened a bit in surprise, and he sensed the edginess that jumped off me. "I promise this isn't some mad plan to seduce you."

Birdy smiled. "I have some time."

"I'm driving. Let me get my purse."

And I drove us far that afternoon, when the leaves had turned to gold with the coolness of fall advancing and the promise of things to come on the hint of the breeze, and away from that rented house in the suburbs, a house that was not a home. It was a silent drive; neither of us spoke. There was no need for idle chatter, each lost in our own thoughts and comforted by the mere presence of the other.

I drove us far, to the cabin in the woods. The cabin where memories started. And babies, too.

"We're here." I put the car in park, but neither of us moved. I heard Birdy's breath grow quick and ragged. He tilted his head back against the headrest and he closed his eyes. Either to remember, or to forget.

I shut my eyes for a moment as well, trying to calm the beating of my heart, pulling the air deep into my lungs, and then I spoke the words that needed to be said, so I could put the past behind me and find my way to the future.

"I bought the cabin for you, Birdy. And the land that goes with it. It's my good-bye gift to you." The tears pricked at my eyes, and I tried to blink them away, but it did little good. They trailed slowly down my face.

Birdy did not speak. He pulled his glasses off, placing them in the center console, and covered his eyes with his right hand, going somewhere I could not follow. I watched his chest rise and fall, breathing in the smell of the trees and the wet leaves and the memory of a fire in the hearth.

"My need for you is still alive, Birdy. It always will be, I suspect. Not for you to save me, because I should have been strong enough to save myself, but because you are a part of me. Maybe the best part. As much as the children we made together out of our love and need for each other are a part of me."

Birdy dropped his hand from his face, and he stared straight ahead, saying nothing. I took him in, trying to memorize him, knowing the time had come for me to give him up. Slowly he got out of the car, going around to my side and opening my door, extending his hand to help me. Silently, we stood together at the side of my car staring at the cabin, where good memories lived.

"I hope you'll take it, Birdy. It didn't cost much. And if you don't want it, I'll give it to Cody someday. It's only money. And what good is money if you can't share it with the ones you love?"

I turned my body to face Birdy, my back to the cabin, where our destiny fused together on that morning years ago. "Money didn't make my parents look the other way when I was being abused by Bobby Lee. Just as the lack of it didn't make your daddy abuse you. Or your mother. Plenty of people, rich or poor, suffer from demons that make them do terrible things."

Birdy looked down at me, his eyes dark with emotion.

"Money doesn't bring pain, Birdy, unless we choose to let it, just the same way money won't bring happiness. I think happiness is a choice. Do you want to know what I discovered in the past few months? I discovered money can give us peace of mind when we lie in our bed to sleep at night. It brings the comfort and the knowledge our children will never have to go without the surgery they need to fix their weak eyes, or new clothes to wear to school, not made by a mama who can't sew worth a darn—or a new car, so they won't be embarrassed when arriving at a friend's house."

A tear spilled down Birdy's cheek, and I caught it midway down his cheek, bringing it to my lips in a kiss.

"Money can give our children an education and the chance to explore a world far beyond the borders of our small lives. Our children deserve that, just as much as they deserve parents who will cherish them, protect them, and save them from harm."

Birdy still was silent as the tears rolled down the side of his face, shadowed with sadness, and I said what I needed to say.

"Is there nowhere to meet in the middle? No place we can start over and pick up the pieces of our unraveled lives to stitch it back together?"

Birdy broke his silence, his voice thick with emotion. "You'll outgrow me, Savannah May, now that you have your money—"

My breath caught, and I put my hands to my heart. "*Is that what this is all about?* You think now that I have money I'll outgrow you? How can that be so? That's like saying I can outgrow my own skin." I reached for his hand and put it to my cheek, leaning into it and placing my other hand on top, to keep it there to comfort me. "You are a part of me forever, Birdy Johnson, like it or not. I cannot outgrow you any more than I can outgrow my arms or my legs or the heart that beats within my chest."

I took Birdy's hand from my cheek and placed it over my heart, his hand warm and strong, and his touch accelerating its beating. Leaning in, I cupped Birdy's face, staring deep into his dark sad eyes.

"You are a good man, James Russell. A tender man with a sweetness not found in most people. You are a part of me forever, and I will carry you with me until the day I die."

We never went inside the cabin of our first desire, but rather, walked around the fields and streams, holding hands in the afternoon sun, hearing the bees hum and the birds call to one another.

"I'll accept your gift, Savannah. As long as you let me give one to you," Birdy said, as he drove my car away from the cabin. I was much too emotional to drive.

We drove for a mile or two, never saying a thing, Birdy still holding my hand with his right, while he steered with his left, dropping it for a moment to turn off the navigation, as he said the woman's voice was annoying, and besides, he knew his way around.

"Are we going to my old house?" I asked, noticing the direction we were headed.

"No, we're going to mine." Birdy glanced down at my shoes, a tennis shoe of sorts, but fancy. "Can you walk far in those shoes?"

"Far enough. If you'd asked me that four months ago, I would have said I couldn't make it around the corner, regardless of what shoes I was wearing. But I have a trainer, so now I'm in better shape."

"I've heard."

"That I have a personal trainer, or that I'm in better shape?"

"Both. The first I heard from the kids, the second I just heard from you."

Birdy drove up the lane to the house where he lived less than a decade ago, the converted garage made of unpainted wood and a roof covered in tin, far removed from the big white house with the black shutters in the front. So far from the goings on of the big house for anyone to know a small boy was left alone each night while his daddy went off to drink. And too far for anyone to hear the noise of the violence, or the cries of pain from the child, when his daddy would come home, drunk, and beat him.

"Wow. Gosh, Birdy. I'm sorry," I said, after we got out of the car, walking around, looking at the rundown house of his youth and the tires and the rusted tin drums that leaned against it, the weeds struggling to survive. "This place is a dump." The difference from the big house to this piece of crap was remarkable. How terrible, the homeowners wouldn't give the handyman a better place to live. Even if that handyman was a murdering no-good piece of white trash. The man had a child. "No wonder you were always at my house. Did y'all even have running water?"

"Yes, we had running water. And a toilet that flushed, too. Although I can't say it was clean. My daddy missed more than he made it in the bowl."

"*Ick.*" I wrinkled my nose.

Birdy turned away from the house and gazed across the long driveway to the road where hedges screened the lives of the folks inside. He turned away from the tiny shack where he learned to hide his pain, away from the big house where rich folks pretended not to know, too wrapped up in parties and themselves to notice the plight of a child.

"I have something to show you, Savannah," he said, his voice low. "No, that's now quite right." He shook his head, reaching out to take my hand. "I have *many* things to show you."

There was a light to Birdy's eyes that was not there before. A spark almost. An excitement had started to build. Though it was a level only I could detect. For most people, excitement means loudness and laughter. For Birdy, excitement meant his eyes went a softer color, and the creases at the corners deepened, and you saw the white of his smile and the hint of the dimple in his chin.

Birdy was very excited.

He held my hand, and we walked down the driveway, scattering stones at our feet, and away from his house, until he stopped under a sugar maple tree by the mailbox, where the two roads met. The tree stood tall, seventy feet, at least. How old, I cannot say, with a trunk that broke near the ground and bark peeling red in narrow plates along vertical grooves beneath a dark green canopy overhead, the rays of the sun through the leaves scattering a lacy pattern on our faces.

"This is the very first one," Birdy said, his voice tender. He reached out a hand to touch the tree. "I carved it the first day I met you, twenty-one years ago, when the bark was still soft because of the rain. I carved it after I'd first come home. After you asked me, did I want to be your friend?"

Birdy's hands lovingly stroked the carved markings in the bark of the tree, still easy to read despite the passing of time. Encased in a heart etched deep inside of that tree were our initials, written in the penknife scrawl of a six-year-old boy, with the date written down below it.

JRJ + SMH, it read. And smaller still, *'94*.

And further we walked, although not too far, until we came to the next. A grand Southern magnolia, its creamy white blossoms now gone, replaced by bright-red seeds nestled in green leathery leaves, its trunk gray and pebbled as elephant skin, marred by the tattooed carvings.

JRJ + SMH, it read. And smaller still, *'95*.

On we walked, down the road that led to my house, until we came to the next, a white ash, the carvings engraved in the gray furrows separated by ridges in the bark.

JRJ + SMH '96.

We walked down that road toward the home of my childhood, to the flowering dogwood, and the box elder, the flowering quince, and the red maples, all showing the outpouring of a little boy's love for a girl. Past the '97 and the '98, the red hickory, and the loblolly pine, and the decade that would end it. To the '03 and beyond. Gradually, as the years progressed, the writing changed, and the initials changed, too. It was the year we married, and I took Birdy's last name.

JRJ + SMJ, it read. And smaller still, *'08*.

We traveled that road together that day, following the path of our love—and our life.

Birdy had written me a song every year, from the year he first met me. A silent song, a song that scarred the trees and left them weeping, the tears of sap running down the bark, brown and amber, crying out the love of a boy for a girl.

We reached the end of the road and gazed at the big dark house in front of us, a house that held all our secrets. Twenty-one trees Birdy showed me that day. Twenty-one expressions of an undying love of a boy for a girl. Over two miles of his expression of what I'd meant to him for most of his life.

My tears ran unchecked down my face. I cried so hard it brought me to my knees, and I sat sobbing in the dirt at the end of my driveway. Two miles of Birdy's love for me. Two miles of scarred trees, the tears of sap running down the bark, amber drops preserved in time.

"*Twenty-one trees*, Birdy," I cried. "Twenty-one." I wept into the circle of my arms.

Birdy got down in the dirt beside me, and he put his arms around me, holding me so close I could feel each breath, each beat of his heart. Just the same way I felt the trees breathing the fullness of the air, and the life that beat inside them, the blood of them filling the leaves and the limbs, the smooth planes and the gnarled knots. Proud to bear the scars that showed they had survived.

"Don't cry, now. Hush. There's one more," he said, rocking me in his arms until I quieted.

Birdy rose and he pulled me to my feet, holding my hand and leading me to one more tree, a tree that stood sentry at the base of my old driveway, a towering sycamore, I believe, nearly ninety feet tall, with a trunk nearly five feet across. Although by then my eyes were so full of tears and my mind so dizzy with emotion, I could not tell you exactly if that was so.

There it was, freshly carved. So new I could smell the sharpness of the wood as it cried its tears of sap. A heart. A perfectly carved heart. Much larger than all the rest. So large the tree wore that heart on its chest like a shield of armor. Proud.

With trembling fingers, I traced the initials of our names and the outlines of the date. The date of that very same day.

"I can't live without you, Savannah. I'll meet you in the middle, or anywhere you want. Come back to me, Savannah. Please come back to me, Savannah May."

EPILOGUE

Birdy and I got back together that day, as we wept in each other's arms at the base of that tree, that twenty second tree, where he carved out his love for me in his silent song. We could never be torn apart; it takes two sides to complete one heart. Two arches that blend together and make one, holding within in it all the love and the memories that made us.

There have been many more trees since that happy day, the day of our rediscovery. One more song for each year that Birdy and I have been together. One more tree that wept with the joy at the love of a boy for a girl. And there have been many years now. So many, we have to take a car to show our children, and our grandchildren. Driving along dirt roads, now since paved, past empty lots where old houses used to stand, and new ones have been built. Down the country roads lined with the red cedars, the sugar maples, the sweet gums, and the hickories. The trees that only Birdy could find, although he's been my sweet James Russell since then. Sweet James Russell, the poor boy from Tennessee, who fell in love with a rich little girl when they were six.

We met in the middle, that day of our rediscovery. We bought a new house, a medium-sized house, although that is a relative term. A house not too far from the ones of our dark years, but far enough away the ghosts and the shadows could not find us.

That old yellow school bus became a playhouse for our children. Although we parked it far at the back of our property and surrounded it by trees, so the neighbors wouldn't think we were hillbillies, and now the laughter and sounds of our grandchildren shout out from inside of it.

Our son's eyes grew straight and strong, and he gave up his glasses, and Birdy, too, who allowed me to pay for his LASIK. Remarking when he opened his eyes for the first time without his glasses that I was even prettier than he imagined, and he missed seeing just how pretty I was, spending all of those years behind glasses that were never quite right.

Our children never went to cotillion classes. There were no debutante balls. But there were friends and parties and laughter. There was education and a world they got to travel. And always their father and me to watch over them, to keep them safe from the dragons of the world.

We kept them safe from evil.

Our daughters are beautiful, our son, too, although he'd want me to use the word handsome. Our minis are mini no more, but, rather, tall and slender with only a hint of freckles on their faces that spring up when they've spent too much time in the sun at our lake house in the summer. And they have the most beautiful hair. Deep auburn hair, the color of fall and the harvest, with copper highlights that catch the light.

Melissa married a teacher, after becoming a teacher herself, and they are expecting their third child. A boy she'll name after her father.

Emma is a family psychologist and deals with women's issues. A calling she found when I finally had the strength to share with her the horrors of my past. She has helped so many women find their way out of the dark.

Cody works for our family business, and his sweet wife, Amy Jo, who is from Tennessee, it so happens, is expecting twins. Girls, from what I've been told.

Our baby, Anna, still lives at home and is trying to decide what she wants to be when she grows up. She teases her daddy and says she wants to join the Peace Corps, but she'd never give up her makeup and her stylish clothes, and it would break her daddy's heart if she ever went far from home.

Birdy finally let me let me buy him a new truck—many, in fact. And we started a business together—Johnson Trucking—although I wanted to name it Johnson *Logistics*. Birdy said no, that he didn't even know what that meant. Of course he was teasing, and Johnson Trucking it became.

And every now and then, when the family is all together, and our grandchildren sit at our feet by the fire in our home, the home we created from the ashes of our childhood, we pull out those old guitars and Birdy and I sing together. Songs of family, of life, of memories, and the love of a boy for a girl.

Healing happened over the long years since we'd suffered the pain of our youth. Healing that allowed our love to go to a better place, a healthier place. A place where love came from desire, and not the coming together of two sad, neglected children who found solace in the presence of the other. Birdy may not have been able to save his mother all of those years ago, but he saved my life. That shy sweet boy from Tennessee, Birdy Johnson—he saved my life.

ACKNOWLEDGMENTS

Special thanks to my Southern gals, Jennifer Weiss and Karen Cagle, for their invaluable words of wisdom (that Southern women go "poo," not poop, and that they have "breasts," not boobs). If I'm off base with anything else, the fault is solely mine.

Well-deserved praise and gratitude goes to my wonderful copy editor, Valerie Brooks of TheWriteEdit.com, whose belief in my talent keeps me writing.

In ending, although *Twenty-Ones Trees* is fictitious, dissociative amnesia is unfortunately all too real. My paternal grandmother, much like Savannah, lost all memory of her husband and their four children shortly after the birth of their last child. Unlike Savannah, my grandmother's memory never returned, and she stayed locked in her adolescent world—and mental institutions—until the day she died, almost sixty years later. My heartfelt wish is that her memories were of happier times.

ABOUT THE AUTHOR

Like her character in *Twenty-One Trees*, Linda is a former teen beauty queen. Unlike her character, her reign was back in the days of the horse and buggy and the 8-track music tape. When she isn't busy polishing her old tiaras, Linda can be found at her computer writing about lives far more exciting than her own (or more often than not, just typing random sentences so that she can appear far too busy to cook dinner for her husband). For more information and to see her other book titles for both adults and younger readers, go to www.LindaCousine.com.

Made in United States
North Haven, CT
06 September 2024

57051808R10174